the launch
STARDUST BEACH BOOK ONE

STEPHANIE TAYLOR

prologue
MARCH 1956

THE ROOM WAS BRIGHT; *there was a glare on the linoleum floor that stared up at Bill Booker as he tried to blink his dry eyes. The lights overhead gave off a faint buzzing sound, cut only by the screams of Bill's wife as she gripped his hand tightly. The pressure of her hand was his only anchor in that moment.*

"Billllll," Josephine wailed, sweat beading on her smooth forehead. She squeezed her eyes shut as she held onto him with all her might. "I can't do this. The pain," she panted, finally opening her blue eyes and looking up into his with an animalistic ferocity that he'd never seen from her. Even the birth of their first two children had not elicited this level of fear or pain, and it terrified him.

Bill stared back at Jo, willing himself not to look away. This was his responsibility, to be here with her, to push aside any of his own fears, to not conflate this day—March 17, 1956—with any other day in his past. He owed Jo this, at least: to bear witness as she went through the physical trauma of giving life to another human being. He would not falter, he would not let her down. He had to stay strong—for Jo.

"I can't...I need..." Jo continued to pant. She looked increasingly panicked as her skin morphed into a shade of clammy white right before

Bill's eyes. Bill reached out and touched her, afraid for a moment that she was turning into melting wax.

This is not before. This is not that. This is not war. There are no casualties. This is not danger. No one will be hurt here. Bill repeated these sentences to himself in his head as he held Jo's hand in his, letting her squeeze so tightly that her nails dug into his skin. He needed these mantras in his head to keep him present, to force him not to slip into other moments in his life that were laced with fear.

"I'm going to need the father to leave the room," a very round, very old nurse said brusquely as she pushed her way past Bill and yanked the edge of the curtain that wrapped around Jo's bed. "OUT," she said harshly, pointing at the door. It was obvious that this nurse had seen battle herself—perhaps of a different kind than Bill had seen, but battle nonetheless—and that she was firmly and inexorably in charge of the hospital room.

"No!" Jo cried out desperately as she reached for Bill with her other hand. Before the nurse could stop her, Jo had the collar of his shirt balled in both of her fists. She clung to him like a drowning woman hanging onto the side of a boat. "I need Bill here."

The nurse shook her head patiently, trying to disentangle Jo's hands from Bill's shirt. "No, ma'am," the nurse said. "This will go faster and easier with him waiting outside."

Bill was torn. He wanted nothing more than to be there for his wife. To support her. To ensure her safety and that of his unborn child. He couldn't stand the idea of her calling out for him as he sat on a chair in another room, head in his hands, waiting. But being in there was proving immensely difficult for him as well. The buzzing sound from the lights seemed to have infiltrated his brain, and everything was becoming so bright that his peripheral vision was fading to a blinding white. He had the overwhelming urge to sink to the floor, to sit on the cold tile, to rest.

"Goddammit," the nurse swore, her tone turning angry. "Pearl!" she shouted, still trying to free Bill from Jo's grasp. "Can you get in here with the smelling salts, please? Husband is on his way down."

The words filtered into Bill's ear as if they were coming through a tunnel: "Husband is on his way down..."

Was this him? Was she talking about Bill? Because he was fine. He felt steady, he felt—

As he slipped from Jo's fingers, Bill's consciousness left the hospital room there in Minneapolis, and suddenly he was somewhere else entirely. First, he was in Phoenix: It was November 1949, in a hospital room so nondescript that it could have been this very same one, save for the fact that he was in a different state and with a different woman. In fact, he was with a different wife—his first. His young love, his emotionally volatile, beautiful, redheaded Margaret. In his mind's eye, Margaret was in the bed before him, curled around her own white-hot pain in a way that was at once the same and entirely different than Jo's present agony. This memory gripped Bill and he stood there, watching an image of Margaret, wishing he could help her somehow. All he'd wanted to do was to take away the thing—whatever it was—that had made her go into labor far too soon. He wanted to unwrap the cord around the baby's neck, to breathe life into that tiny baby girl, and to make everything better. He wanted to put a baby in Margaret's arms so that she'd be whole.

But he couldn't. He couldn't fix it then, and he certainly couldn't fix what happened in 1949 now.

Bill's eyes closed and Jo's hospital room spun around him as he left both Phoenix and Minneapolis behind. He was no longer in a world of mothers and babies, but in a land of stalemates and unnecessary death. As he hit the cold tile with one shoulder and then with the side of his head, Bill parachuted into North Korea in his mind. It was 1951, and he had just ejected from a flight near the border. The terrain was not familiar to this American boy, and falling from a plane into enemy territory was frightening. Bill opened his eyes on that frigid, bitterly cold winter day, and found himself on the peninsula, which was covered in mountains, hills, and hollows. He shivered, grossly unprepared for both the weather and the possibility of attack. Instead of getting up, disengaging from his parachute, and running for cover, Bill rolled up into a ball and shivered in the cold air.

"Sir? Mr. Booker?" a woman's voice was saying from a distance. He felt a hand on his shoulder and he jerked, fearing for his life. "Sir, let me help you up," the woman said kindly, her voice still an echo that reached him from far away.

Bill opened his eyes, surprised to find himself not wedged into the cold bushes and tangled in a parachute on a hillside in Korea, but instead stretched out on the hard floor of the hospital with his teeth chattering. "What happened?" he asked, willing his body to stop its shaking. He was safe; he was not in enemy territory. He was on the floor of the hospital on March 17, 1956, staring at the white shoes of a nurse who looked down at him with professional concern.

"You passed out, darling," she said, crouching down next to him with a cold, wet washcloth, which she used to mop his brow. "We're going to move you to a room where you can stretch out and recover, okay?"

Bill sat bolt upright as soon as he noticed the silence in the room. "Where is my wife?" he asked, looking around. "Where did she go?" The nurse reached out a hand and tried to stop him, but Bill got to his feet without hesitation and turned in a circle. He felt frantic. The spot where Jo had lain in a hospital bed was now just bare linoleum. All that remained in the room was the curtain that had surrounded her bed, a clock on the wall, and a small sink and countertop. "Where is Jo?"

The nurse pushed herself up from her crouching position with a small clucking sound. "Love, we had to wheel her into surgery. It was time."

"Surgery?" Bill felt his heart start to pump blood furiously in his chest. He put a hand to his neck, where his pulse raced. "Why? What's wrong? What about the baby?"

The nurse, clearly weighing her words carefully, watched his face before speaking. "The baby needs to come out now," she said gravely. She'd obviously decided that Bill could not only handle the truth, but that he needed to hear it. "We're doing our best to deliver the baby safely, so I need you to rest and get your wits about you."

Bill bent at the waist, putting his hands on his knees. He almost felt like passing out again, but rather than giving in to the images in his brain —Margaret in a different hospital bed; bright white lights; ejecting from his plane; landing on the cold, hard Korean ground—Bill pushed himself upright again and forced his eyes to remain open. "Can I go in there?"

"Certainly not," the nurse said regretfully. *"But the doctor will come out and update us as soon as possible."*

Bill allowed himself to be led to a room with a vinyl cushioned couch, where he stretched out and took several deep, fortifying breaths. It was in his nature to problem solve, and to make sure that he was never dodging his responsibilities, but the rational part of him knew that there was nothing he could do in that moment to help Jo or the baby. All he would do by barging into the operating room was put his wife and child in danger by distracting the doctor from performing whatever measures needed to be taken in order to save both their lives.

As he realized this, Bill rolled onto his side and pulled his knees closer to his chest. He wanted to let the hot tears flow from his eyes, to get that physical and emotional release, but he knew that this would be about as helpful as storming the operating room. "A man who gives in to tears is a man who is of no use to anyone," *Bill thinks, remembering this nugget of wisdom handed down by his father, a stoic man who'd farmed his way through the Great Depression on a wing and a prayer, coaxing corn from hard-packed dust, and feeding five children on a fistful of coins. Bill respected his father—especially now that he had kids of his own—and he knew that Arnold Booker had always been a man in every sense of the word. So instead of crying, Bill counted his own breaths, pushing each intrusive thought from his mind the way a child might push away a bully who keeps trying to engage him in a struggle on the playground.*

"No," Bill whispered to himself when he thought of Margaret in that hospital bed that seemed too big for her small frame once the baby was gone. Of the tears. The blood. The sheer loss.

"No," he said softly to himself again as he remembered his fallen comrades in Korea, and the fear he'd felt nearly every time he'd tried to fall sleep on foreign soil. The threat of death and danger had lurked around every corner, and that same sensation filled his body again as he waited for word of his wife and child.

"No," he said, this time out loud, as he thought of the worst possible outcome for Jo and the baby. The idea that anything could be wrong with his wife or their child was unfathomable, and absolutely unacceptable.

In the end, Bill spent nearly an hour there, locked inside his own mental battle against these dark thoughts. This only happened to him on occasion, and when it did, he tried to remove himself from whatever situation he was in and find a place to recover. He'd finally calmed himself down and found a peaceful plane on which to exist when he heard his name.

"Mr. Booker?"

Bill opened his eyes immediately, swung his feet around so that they touched the ground, and sat up on the couch. He was ready for whatever was coming his way. A tall, graying doctor in a white coat with a stethoscope dangling around his neck was standing in the doorway. He looked tired and serious.

"Yes," *Bill said gruffly, standing. On the table next to the vinyl couch was a full ashtray, and the smell of stale cigarettes filled the small room. He wiped his hands down the front of his pants, drying his damp palms.* "Is it my wife? Is she okay?"

The doctor lowered his gaze to the floor for what felt like an eternity, then lifted his eyes and looked right at Bill. "Josephine is going to be fine," *he said.* "She's lost a lot of blood, and she went into labor nearly a month early. She was suffering from what's called placenta previa. It's a condition where the placenta covers the cervix—this almost always requires a c-section, which is what we did."

Bill couldn't take it anymore. He felt wild with both relief and terror—terror at what the doctor had not yet said. "And the baby?" *he choked out, barely keeping the emotions he'd so carefully held back from finally breaching the surface and overtaking him.*

At last, the doctor smiled. "She's fine," *he said, giving Bill the same look he must have given to thousands of other fathers over the course of his career.* "Ten fingers, ten toes, and a strong set of lungs. She is a month early, so she's on the small side, but she appears to be quite healthy, Mr. Booker."

"Can I see them?" *Bill coughed into his hand to mask the relief that had already cascaded into tears.* "Can I hold the baby?"

"They were cleaning things up when I left," *the doctor said, motioning for Bill to follow him.* "Let me take you to Mrs. Booker's recovery room, *and you can see her as soon as they bring her back."*

Bill was standing there, pacing the room, when Jo was wheeled back in. He rushed to her side as soon as the orderlies had her bed in place. They locked the wheels so that she wouldn't roll, and then left the room in a hushed, reverent manner.

"Hi," Jo said groggily, holding up a hand for Bill to take. She was pale, her veins blue against her translucent skin. Her eyes were at half-mast. "She's so beautiful," Jo said. Her voice sounded like she'd been walking around in the desert for days without water. "So tiny. So mighty."

"A girl," Bill said, bursting with pride. "Another girl." At home, four-year-old Jimmy was with his three-year-old sister, Nancy, and both kids were being watched by Bill's parents.

"Katherine," Jo said. Her fingers tried to squeeze Bill's, but she was far too weak to do much but twitch lightly. "Kate."

A smile cracked Bill's face as he leaned over the side of the bed and put his lips to his wife's smooth forehead. He ran a hand over her sweat-dampened hair. "How about Katherine Rose?" he offered. "Kate the Great."

Jo nodded, a smile on her tired face.

They'd made it. Bill's wife and daughter were safe. He'd chased away the darkness, avoided disaster, and brought himself back to the present, as he always managed to do.

Now everything would be fine—more than fine. Everything would come up roses.

ONE
may 1963
JO

THE HOUSE IS INTIMIDATING to Jo: it's brand new, entirely modern, and situated in a housing development so freshly hatched that the sidewalks still sparkle with chips of mica, and the palm trees aren't much taller than a grown man. Windows are new and so clean that at least four children have run right into the plate glass on their way outside to play, and the driveways are all peppered with shining Buick Rivieras, wood-paneled Ramblers, and the sleek Corvettes that the newly-chosen astronauts are allowed to lease for one dollar per year upon arriving at Port Canaveral in Florida (this is a cute and clever way of getting around the rule that astronauts can't receive free gifts, in Jo's mind).

Everything feels like it's just come out of shrink-wrap, and it lacks the cozy, homey, lived-in comfort that the Bookers are accustomed to. In fact, Jo's first reaction to seeing Stardust Beach as they'd driven into the town, was to look out the window of their car, stone-faced, and wonder how anyone lived in a flat state without tall sugar maples, white oaks, and black walnut trees. *All these palm trees*, she'd thought. *All this bright sunshine. The whole state feels like living inside of a lemon. But with beaches.*

She wasn't in Minnesota anymore.

In the hallway of the Booker home, which sits on a cul-de-sac of angular new homes, hangs a photo of Josephine and William Booker with their three children, James, Nancy, and Katherine. The photo was taken shortly after Bill Booker was chosen to join the ranks of would-be astronauts at NASA, and was meant to capture the happy family as they embarked upon a journey that would change their lives—and possibly history as well.

Jo passes by the photo with a stack of pool towels in her arms now, pausing as she cocks her head and contemplates it. Her kids are adorable, of course. Bill looks handsome and dignified, and she looks...Jo isn't sure how she looks. Hesitant? Content? Fearful? Lost? Maybe a little bit of everything. The woman in the photograph seems to know that she's the nucleus of the people around her, but also that she'll need to hold everyone together in the face of whatever is coming next. And that right there is the rub, isn't it? Because she has no clue what is coming next. All she knows for certain is that her husband, a decorated Lieutenant Colonel in the Air Force, has been chosen to possibly go to outer space. The very idea of it completely terrifies her.

Jo reaches out to straighten the frame and catches a glimpse of her own reflection in the glass. Her hair is styled, her eyes lightly penciled and coated with mascara. She is not a stranger to herself exactly, but to her own eyes she is an unfamiliar vision. She has done herself up in a way that she thinks is presentable to the other astronauts and their wives, and she's welcomed them and all of their children into her new home so that everyone can get better acquainted. Jo blinks, willing the woman in the glass to come into focus. To be familiar. To be *her*.

In the front room, someone switches the vinyl that's spinning on the blonde wood Zenith console stereo and puts on Roy Orbison's "Pretty Woman." Jo tries on a smile as she tucks her straight brown hair behind one ear, admiring the way it flips up at the ends. She rubs her lips together, making sure her frosted gloss is in place, then —giving the hair at her crown one more quick pat—she turns to take the towels out to the gaggle of children in her backyard who are currently squealing and splashing pool water everywhere while the barbecue sends up smoke and the smell of charbroiled meat.

"Josephine!" a woman says, startling Jo right there in the hallway. "Your home is so lovely."

For a moment, Jo feels as though she's been caught wandering through the private rooms of someone else's house, but no—this is her home; she lives here, tucked into a sunny yellow stucco house with a turquoise kidney bean of a pool right off the kitchen. As a young girl, Jo had always figured she'd live and die in Minnesota, spending her summers at the lake, and her winters laughing and playing in the snow. Never in a million years would she have imagined herself living in a community of NASA people just a stone's throw from Port Canaveral. This was never in the plans. And yet here she is, walking through the hallway of her very own midcentury modern home, holding a pile of freshly laundered pool towels, and listening to her son and her two daughters yelp and holler outside with their new neighborhood friends.

"Thank you," Jo says, smiling at the woman. "It probably looks a lot like yours does. And you can call me Jo."

The woman, tall and willowy with a cigarette in one hand, gives her a grin that makes Jo feel as though they're already old friends, although Jo has been so occupied with unpacking and keeping the kids busy that she hasn't actually met any of the other families until today. Should she have gone around and introduced herself to the other wives in the cul-de-sac by now? Probably. It must seem unfriendly of her, but in truth, she's just out of her element.

Jo inhales and exhales, forcing herself to smile and relax; her nerves are about to get the better of her, and she hasn't even been out amongst the guests for any real amount of time.

"I came in while you were in the kitchen," the woman says, still grinning at her. "You were busy. I'm Frances Maxwell," the dark hair, dark-eyed woman says, extending a slim hand with red lacquered nails. She holds the cigarette in her other hand, elbow perched on her sharp hip as the smoke wafts over her shoulder. "But I only answer to Frankie." She reminds Jo of Sophia Loren, both in figure and in smoldering eye contact.

Jo shifts the towels to one hand and runs a hand over the front of her white linen dress before offering it to Frankie to shake. "It's a pleasure to meet you. I've been so busy getting things sorted out here that I haven't met anyone in the neighborhood yet. I just..." Jo trails off, her eyes darting down the hall nervously. She wants to make a good impression.

Frankie appraises her for a beat, taking a drag on her cigarette and exhaling the smoke upwards through lips the same color as her nails. "Funny thing," she says. "We both go by boys' names. Are you a tomboy, Jo Booker?" Jo shakes her head, though she *does* enjoy fishing, camping, and riding a bicycle. Maybe she is a bit of a tomboy after all. "Me either," Frankie says, putting a hand on Jo's arm. "I wouldn't trade in being a woman for all the tea in China. The dresses, the makeup, the glamour—it all seems like so much more *fun* than being a man, doesn't it?"

Frankie is more plain-spoken and down-to-earth than Jo would have imagined for a woman wearing a bias-cut silk dress in the middle of the Florida humidity, and it's easier than Jo expects to just relax and be herself. She laughs. "I'm a big fan of being a woman," Jo agrees.

"Come over sometime and we'll have a drink by my pool, alright?" Frankie says, blowing smoke over her shoulder again. "You seem like a real peach, Jo Booker, and I think I'm gonna like you." Frankie winks at her as she takes another drag on her cigarette. "I've got to grab a beer for my husband. See you out there?"

Frankie walks down the hallway, hips swinging beneath her sheath of a dress, cigarette held aloft in one manicured hand.

Frankie is obviously going to be a handful, but she seems fun. She's nothing at all like Sally or Genevieve, Jo's closest friends from Minnesota, but maybe that isn't such a bad thing. Maybe a fresh start means jumping in headfirst and trying new things. Meeting new people. Being adventurous. Maybe it means being open to things she previously thought she'd never get used to.

Regardless, Jo thinks she may have just made her first Florida friend.

* * *

The dining room table is pushed up against one wall, and Jo has covered it with platters of fried chicken, a Jello mold with flecks of pineapple and chunks of canned peaches suspended inside of it, bowls of baked beans, a tray of deviled eggs, and the various potluck dishes that the other women have carried in and handed to her as their children raced through the open sliding door and out to the pool. In one green glass serving bowl is a heap of coleslaw; another platter boasts brownies covered in white chocolate icing. Another wife has brought cupcakes, and the family who lives next door to Barbara has contributed a tray of miniature hotdogs stuck with toothpicks that have red, white, and blue plastic flags waving from them. Jo is doing her best to keep track of names and faces and which kids belong to which family, but to be perfectly honest, she's confusing people left and right as she refills drinks and laughs at their small talk and joking asides.

"I really love what you've done with the place, Mrs. Booker," Barbara says, waddling over to where Jo is standing by the dining room table. Barbara has her right hand pressed into her lower back, and her hugely pregnant belly protrudes out in front of her; she looks like she's smuggling a beachball beneath her turquoise-and-white checked tent dress. "I had no idea what to do with this space in my own house," Barbara says, sweeping the hand not pressed to her lower back around to indicate the open kitchen, dining, and living area. "It's just so...modern. I mean, I love it, but I grew up in Connecticut with lots of cherry wood, four-poster beds, and brocade. This looks like a house out of a magazine, doesn't it?" Barbara turns her head to look at Jo as she wrinkles her impossibly small and cute nose. "It'll take some getting used to."

Jo nods and glances over to where Bill is standing with a knot of men who are all dressed as he is: slicked down hair; collared short-sleeve shirts; dress slacks ironed so the crease shows. Each man has a bottle of beer in hand, and even from a distance, Jo can see that Bill is a bit older than the other men—not much, but enough that it's noticeable. Bill has always had a whiff of maturity to him that makes him seem older than other people his age, and in fact, it was one of the things that Jo had liked about him right away.

"You're so right," Jo says absentmindedly, tearing her eyes from the men and bringing them back to Barbara. "It's not what I'm used to either." She tucks her hair behind her ear nervously and points at the sunken living area. "We moved here from Minnesota, and our house there was very traditional: split level, master bedroom upstairs, kids' rooms downstairs. My kitchen was closed off from the rest of the house so I could cook in peace, and the living area was a den with a door that closed. This configuration is going to take some getting used to. It feels like we're all sharing the same space all the time."

Barbara walks over to the edge of the dining space and looks out at the sunken living room where Jo has placed her furniture. She'd assured Bill before leaving Minnesota that her heavy wooden end tables, coffee table, and the dark plaid upholstery on her couch and loveseat were timeless, but now, here in light, airy, sunshiny Florida, it all looks kind of staid and boring. Not to mention out of place—after all, they're essentially living at the beach now, not in some sort of mountain hideaway. There's no fireplace, no heavy wood breakfast bar, and no carpeted stairs in this new house.

Jo follows Barbara so that they're standing side by side as they look at the living room. She sets one hand on her narrow hip as she surveys the room. "I wasn't sure about decorating. Again, our previous home was more traditional, and this house seems to call for entirely different decor. I'm kind of stuck."

Barbara, who is about a foot shorter than Jo, looks up at her with a dimpled smile and dancing eyes. She leans in closer as if she's about to impart a deep, dark secret. "I can give you the name of the lady who decorated our house, Mrs. Booker. You'll love her."

Jo, who has never been one to waste anything—especially the solid, expensive furniture she'd chosen for the house she thought her family would live in forever—smiles with relief. "Please, call me Jo. And thank you so much," she says. "I'm a little lost. This has been a harder transition than I'd imagined, and now that we're here I really want to enjoy our new life. But it's all a bit foreign to me."

"It is," Barbara says, nodding vigorously. "Florida is like nothing else I've ever experienced. Todd and I can't get over this weather," she says, lifting her chin in the direction of the men in the kitchen. "He's the one in the red shirt," she says helpfully. "Sweetest guy you'll ever meet, but he's more at home on a sailboat than he is on a surfboard. And I grew up riding horses and wearing corduroy, so being down here where it's just beaches and bikinis is pretty out there for me."

Jo feels immensely relieved to hear that she's not the only one suffering from culture shock, and she can't help feeling that she and Barbara are bonding—at least enough that she can push their discussion beyond furniture and home decor.

"So," Jo says, looking at the men again. "Is Todd excited to be here?"

"Oh, definitely. He's always wanted to be an astronaut. How about Bill?"

"He's over the moon," she deadpans. The women laugh together. "Sorry, but yes. He is excited. He was a Lieutenant Colonel in the Air Force, and once he heard that there was a chance he could be selected by NASA for a manned space flight, I heard about nothing else. Our whole lives were consumed by his desire to be chosen for this."

"Oh, you're not kidding," Barbara says, bumping Jo's bare shoulder with her own. The central air conditioning is working like magic, but the fact that the kids are constantly going in and out of the sliding patio door means that the sticky May heat is seeping into the house nonetheless. "Todd was obsessed with being chosen. *Obsessed.*"

The women shake their heads in unison, looking at the men as Todd leans back against the counter, listening intently to something Bill is saying. "Looks like maybe our husbands are hitting it off, too," Jo says hopefully. She's already envisioning barbecues by the pool, and having another family to trek to the beach with for picnics. A big part of their lives back home had always been doing outdoorsy things with friends and family, and Jo can't wait to find that kind of community here in Florida. Of course nothing will replace her friendships with Sally and Genevieve, but if she's going to get by here, then she's going to need to forge these new relationships. Her sanity relies on it.

"Hey, we should toast Gordon Cooper," one of the men says, raising his beer bottle in the air. "Cheers to the first man to sleep in space."

"Yeah, but he had to sleep alone!" crows one of the younger-looking men—a guy named Ed Maxwell who Jo has figured out is Frankie's husband. The other men laugh appreciatively.

"I think we can beat thirty-four hours," Todd, Barbara's husband, says with a hopeful grin. "If he did twenty-two orbits, I can do twenty-three."

Barbara leans closer to Jo as the men boast and clink beer bottles. "Lot of bluster for a bunch of newbies, huh?"

Jo says nothing, but folds her arms across her chest as she eyes her husband. Rather than speaking up, he is listening intently to the other men, taking mental notes as to what each of them says.

"Did you hear that Bob Dylan refused to play on *The Ed Sullivan Show*?" Ed Maxwell says. As he speaks, Frankie sidles up to him and slides beneath the arm that he slings over her narrow shoulders. From the way that Frankie looks at Ed, it's clear that they're still newlyweds, or close to. "Said he wouldn't do it if he couldn't sing that song that makes fun of the military and segregation."

This provokes a raucous outburst from the group—military men, all—who boo and shout about Dylan's politics.

"Traitor," a short, stocky man with a square jaw says, tipping his beer bottle to the sky as he chugs. "Can't stand when some famous singer pipes up with his opinion on things he knows nothing about."

"Hey, I have an idea," Barbara says, taking Jo by the hand and pulling her away from the men's discussion. "Let's get everyone dancing."

Jo lifts an eyebrow as she looks pointedly at Barbara's extremely pregnant stomach. "Dancing? I'm not sure that's a good idea."

"Yeah! Come on, let's do it!" Barbara leads the way to the turntable and flips through the stack of records there, choosing "Runaround Sue" by Dion. She sets the needle on it with a fuzzy scratch of static.

Giving a little hip-sway, Barbara starts to dance in the middle of the sunken living room. Jo glances around to see if anyone else is as worried by this as she is. "Do you think you should be doing that in your condition?" Jo calls out over the music, pointing at the way Barbara is moving and shaking. Jo remembers doing a lot of sitting around uncomfortably when she was as pregnant as Barbara is now, but there is a look of total glee and abandon on Barbara's face as she dances.

Barbara laughs merrily. "Absolutely! I hope this knocks the baby loose so she comes out sooner rather than later. I am *done* with being pregnant in this heat. I gotta evict this kid!" She closes her eyes and sways to the music.

Just as Jo is about to insist that Barbara take it easy—maybe sit down and let the other women bring her a cold lemonade—Todd makes his way over to his wife with an appreciative grin on his face.

"Hey, baby," he says, setting his beer bottle on the coffee table and reaching out his hands to take Barbara's. They dance together like they're at a sock hop, and for a moment, Jo blocks out Barbara's gigantic stomach and she can picture this adorable blonde woman wearing Todd's letterman's sweater; she can see them as high school sweethearts in some upscale Connecticut town with green hills, horses, and lots of plaid and leather. As the couple smiles at one another, swinging around (at least as much as they can, considering Barbara's huge belly), Jo admires the ease with which they both seem to do everything. They're cute, cheerful, easygoing people—that much is obvious. Barbara brought Rice Krispies treats, for heaven's sake, and their two little boys are wearing matching navy blue shorts and white polo shirts; they seem like a perfectly nice, friendly family, and Jo loves that. It actually brings her some relief to realize that not *all* the good people in the world are congregated in Minnesota, and that she might encounter more of them out here in the wild.

"Hi," Bill says, coming up next to Jo as they watch Barbara and Todd start to sway together to Elvis singing "Can't Help Falling in Love," which someone else has helpfully added to the Zenith. "How are you holding up?" He puts his beer bottle to his lips and takes a swig, and as he does, his silver watch glints in the sunlight that floods through the skylight over the living room.

Jo nods, but her eyes are still on Barbara and Todd. She wishes that Bill would take her out there and dance to Elvis, but she knows that won't happen. Bill is all business when it comes to meeting his new coworkers and peers, and he'd been nervous all day as they got ready for this party, wanting everything to go well as the families met and mingled for the first time.

"I'm hanging in here," she finally says. "How are you?"

Bill glances back at the kitchen where the other men are now holding paper plates filled with fried chicken, appetizers, desserts, and side dishes. Laughter comes from their little group, and Jo glances at her husband to see if he feels like he's missing out on whatever is being said in his absence. But she knows her husband well enough to know that that isn't what Bill Booker is thinking about at all. In fact, what he's most likely doing is assessing who his biggest competition is, and determining who might be the weakest links out of the other new hires. That would be *so* like him to already be thinking strategy.

"Jo," Bill says, turning his head to look right into her eyes. His face, normally intense and focused, looks oddly relaxed. She has no idea what he's about to say. "You know I've always loved our life, right?"

Jo searches his face for clues. She doesn't know where he's going with this. "Yes?"

"Well, for the first time in a very long time, I think we're right where we're supposed to be. I think this is it." He puts an arm around Jo's narrow waist, pulling her to him; this is as close as they'll get to dancing for the moment.

All around Jo, things are flowing: music, laughter, the sounds of pool water splashing on the concrete outside, the heat of the afternoon. But inside of her, everything has come to a standstill; it's as if someone has pressed the pause button on her heartbeat. Her husband's feelings are completely opposite to her own: he feels at home, in the right place, excited for the future. And in spite of all the pep talking she's been doing in her brain, and all of her attempts to convince herself that she'll find friends and purpose and a new normal in Florida, all Jo wants is to pack up and move back to Minnesota. She wants to spend the summer at the lake with Sally and Genevieve and their families. She wants to look forward to the change of seasons, which she knows she'll miss out on entirely in Florida.

But there isn't time for her to ruminate on the apple cider and fall bonfires and thick blankets of winter snow that she'll be missing, because just as Jo opens her mouth to say something to Bill, a loud "Oh!" rings out from the living room, and Jo spins around to see Barbara standing there, both hands on her stomach.

Barbara's blue eyes go wide in surprise as she stares at the puddle of amniotic fluid that's spreading across the brand-new wood floors, and then she looks right at Jo. "I'm sorry about your floor, Jo," she says breathlessly. "And I don't mean to ruin your party here, but I think we're having a baby."

TWO
bill

BILL STANDS at the breakfast bar in the kitchen, both hands splayed wide on the counter as he taps his fingers mindlessly on the Formica countertop.

"Bill," Jo says gently, pouring a steaming cup of coffee. She's wearing only her dressing gown and a floor-length robe. "Are you anxious about something?"

Bill's tapping stops. "Sorry," he says, pushing himself away from the counter. "I was just thinking."

Jo opens the glass bottle of milk she's pulled from the fridge pours some into her coffee cup. "Are you worried about today?" Her slippers patter across the kitchen floor as she returns the milk to the refrigerator.

"No. I'm fine. Just thinking."

Jo pulls a metal lunch box from the fridge and walks it over to her husband. She stands on tiptoes to kiss him. "Sure you don't want me to make you breakfast?"

Bill gives a single shake of his head as he accepts the lunch box. "No, thank you."

He knows that Jo has come to expect his quiet, serious moods in times of stress. Bill is someone who successfully turns inward for a lot of his processing, and he can keep his own counsel like nobody's business. It's who he is, and who he's always been, though Jo has occasionally complained about feeling like she can't get through to him when he's like this. But if there's one thing Bill admires in a man, it's stoicism and the ability to hold himself together under any circumstance. Nothing wrong with that, in Bill's opinion.

"I'll see you after work, Jojo," Bill says to her, leaning down to kiss her one more time; it's his way of letting her know that while he isn't saying much, he's just fine.

Bill walks through the door to the attached garage, leaving his wife standing in a splotch of bright morning sunlight, holding a coffee mug as her long robe swirls around her ankles.

The drive through the new housing development where all the prospective and current astronauts live deposits Bill right into Stardust Beach as he winds his way down streets so new that they look as if they've been bleached white. The sidewalks are lined with hamburger drive-ins, grocery stores, gas stations, and shops. On street corners women in summer dresses hold the hands of small children as they wait for the minimal amount of traffic to pass, and on the roads other new cars shine under the morning sunlight just like Bill's Corvette does.

He drums his thumbs on the top of the steering wheel as he listens to AM radio, eyes hidden behind a pair of aviator sunglasses. So far, Florida seems like a dreamscape to Bill: all this sun, the way the kids seem happier and more carefree already, and a beautiful house for his family to live in that feels wide open. For once, Bill can breathe. The tightness in his chest is gone, and he imagines Jo bringing dinner out onto the pool deck in the rosy-tangerine evening light, maybe as tiki torches burn from stakes around the pool. It's like they've clicked their heels three times and landed in paradise, but it's also starting to feel like home.

Bill smiles to himself as he hits the accelerator. The car's engine hums to life as the light at the corner of Jupiter Lane and Milky Way (*Clever*, he thinks) turns green.

THE LAUNCH

Stardust Beach is a new outpost in the race to space—the race to the moon, at this point—and it reminds him of the way Los Alamos sprung up out of nowhere to house and entertain the families who relocated to work on the Manhattan Project. Stardust Beach is a cheery, youthful town nestled up next to Merritt Island, right between the towns of Cocoa and Rockledge. Bill looks both ways before turning onto the Port Canaveral property on Merritt Island, taking in the newly planted palm trees, the clean sidewalks, and the perfectly manicured lawns and open spaces.

At the end of the long road that leads into Port Canaveral is a low cement sign—a perfect rectangle—emblazoned with the iconic blue and white NASA logo with its smattering of stars and the jaunty red wing, meant to represent aeronautics. Bill takes a slow right onto the property, keeping his speed low as he approaches the 144,000-acre compound.

With a low whistle, Bill turns down his radio, effectively silencing the Beach Boys for the time being. "Isn't that a sight," he says to himself, ducking his head beneath the sun visor to get a better look at the steel framework of the service structures built onto the launch pads. They rise up from the ground and shoot heavenward, with the blue sky of a late spring morning as their backdrop. Beyond the Space Center is a swath of rich greenery that bumps up against the turquoise waters of the Atlantic Ocean.

Bill parks and leaves the convertible top of the Corvette down, shutting the door with a heavy *thunk*. He makes his way across the smooth, newly-poured asphalt, looking around at the partially full lot. Even this early in the morning, the heat of the day rises up through the soles of his dress shoes. Bill switches his metal lunchbox from one hand to the other, shielding his eyes with one hand as he tips his head to the sky and searches: not one single cloud. Nothing but clear skies, blue waves out in the distance, and a new career as an astronaut.

The whole thing could be a metaphor for his life lately. Bill gives a self-satisfied smile as he crosses the lot in long, confident strides.

He can handle anything that's coming his way—in fact, he's been preparing himself mentally for this for years. The time he spent flying planes in the Air Force had only served to whet Bill's appetite for speed and excitement. He's always wanted to see what else is out there in the universe, and now the opportunity to find out is right here at his fingertips.

Nothing can come between Bill and his chance to go to space.

* * *

"Lieutenant Colonel Booker," a man in glasses says, pacing the room with a cigarette burning idly in one hand. "Thank you for being our first victim."

The other men laugh nervously. There are no windows in this meeting room, and eight men are seated around a long rectangular table with a coffee service placed in its center. Nearly every man besides Bill has an ashtray at his elbow that's already overflowing with a collection of cigarette butts at this early hour.

"Glad to go first," Bill says, sitting up straighter in his chair. "I'd like the other guys to see that it's nothing to be afraid of."

"Do you consider yourself a natural leader, Booker?"

"I do," Bill says succinctly. And he does. In the Air Force, Bill had excelled at decision-making, staying calm no matter what the situation, and guiding the other men through the most harrowing of situations.

The man asking the questions, Arvin North, pulls out a chair at the head of the table and sits. He picks up a manila file and opens it, quietly assessing what looks like a typed list of questions. North pulls a sharpened pencil from behind one ear and taps the eraser against the list of questions.

"I think we should just dive in here, Bill. If you have no preliminary questions for us, then I'd like to begin the actual psychological evaluation."

Bill spreads his hands wide to indicate that he has nothing to hide, and no questions that he's waiting to ask. "I'm an open book," he says, almost meaning it. In fact, he—like any other human being—has things he'd rather not discuss; areas he'd like to leave off-limits. But Bill understands that this particular evaluation will tell the men at the table whether or not he's of sound enough mind to lead a mission into space. And therefore, he's going to answer every single question in the most straightforward way he can; he's going to force himself to be as transparent as possible, and not let a single question that the committee asks ruffle his feathers.

"Fine. Let's begin." Arvin North signals to a man who is running a reel-to-reel recorder. The man, whose hair is slicked to one side just like every other guy at the table, and who is wearing a short-sleeved dress shirt with a white t-shirt visible beneath the slightly opened collar, stands and flicks a switch. The reels begin to spin and he nods at Arvin North that it's safe to begin.

"Booker," Arvin North says, standing up and taking both his cigarette and the list of questions with him as he begins to pace again. "Please tell me about your immediate family."

Bill takes a long, deep breath and begins. "My wife, Josephine, and I have been married for about twelve years. We have three kids: Jimmy, who is eleven, Nancy, ten, and Kate, who just turned seven."

"And Josephine stays home with the children, correct?" Arvin North stops pacing to look at Bill. The only sound in the room is of someone leaning back in a chair that squeaks, and of the reel-to-reel recorder's internal mechanisms clicking and whirring.

"Of course." Bill frowns. He doesn't know anyone whose wife works and leaves the children in the care of others. Not in his circle, anyway.

"Has she previously held a job outside the home?"

Bill is still frowning. "When we met, Jo was a secretary at a dental practice in Minnesota. I was there to get my teeth cleaned." He pauses, his forehead unfurrowing just slightly at the memory. "She was working at the front desk, and on my way out, she took out a bucket full of lollipops and offered me one. Asked me if I'd been good for the dentist." He smirks.

"Cheeky." Arvin North does not smile. "And it's a solid marriage?"

Bill's frown returns and he's jarred out of the reverie of Jo in a tight, pastel pink sweater, smiling up at him from behind a polished wood desk. She *had* been cheeky, and he'd loved it. But that sass—that expectant smile—has been missing of late. For a split-second Bill allows himself to wonder if her cheekiness has been squelched by marriage and children, or whether Jo is simply not as happy with her life as she'd been when they first met.

But what he says out loud is, "Absolutely. Solid as a rock." Jo has always been his rock—that's no lie. From the day they'd met, Bill had known that she was a stand-up girl. She held down a job, went home in the evenings to help her mother care for Jo's aging grandmother, and she even went to church on Sundays. He'd promised her mother that he would make sure that Jo saw the inside of a church at least three out of four Sundays a month, but almost as soon as the ink was dry on their wedding certificate, they'd started spending weekend mornings lounging around in bed with a newspaper and two cups of coffee. Which, of course, led to little Jimmy's birth just ten months into their marriage.

"And how does Josephine feel about you entering the space program?" Arvin North takes a long, slow drag on his cigarette and exhales the smoke towards the ceiling, where a visible layer of gray-blue cigarette smoke already hovers like fog hanging over the land below.

"She is one hundred percent supportive, sir," Bill says, straightening his shoulders. "Always has been."

Arvin North nods as though he's satisfied with the topic of Jo—at least for the moment. "Do any of your children have any special needs?"

"Sir?" Bill's forehead creases.

North clears his throat. "Do any of them have...special needs, like behavior, or mental issues?"

"Oh," Bill says, relaxing. "No. Fit as fiddles, my three. Smart, polite, and obedient." He can say that with all honesty, though he'll leave out the fact that Nancy loves to read books so intensely that she sometimes refuses to go to sleep at night. On more than one occasion, either Bill or Jo have done a bedtime sweep of the kids' rooms, only to find little Nancy sitting in a closet with a book and a flashlight, looking up at them guiltily as she sits beneath the hanging skirts and dresses, giving them a gap-toothed smile.

Arvin North feigns at picking a piece of tobacco from the end of his tongue while his cigarette burns between his first and middle fingers. He looks directly at Bill. "Glad to hear the wife and kids are good." He waits a beat. "We'd like to hear about your first wife now."

Bill's heart hammers in his chest, and his pulse thumps like a heartbeat that's audible to the entire room. With a few moments of soothing, even breaths, Bill pulls himself together and wills the pulsing of his neck veins to stop.

"My first wife," he says slowly, buying himself the tiniest sliver of time by repeating these words. *God, I wish there was a window to look out of,* he thinks. *But this is probably why there aren't any windows: they want to keep us under the microscope and see how we react. Stay cool.* "Margaret Wallings-Booker," he says after a brief pause. "Margaret was my first wife."

"Could you please tell us about your courtship, marriage, and how things ended?"

Bill has the distinct impression that Arvin North and every other man at the table already knows exactly what course his marriage with Margaret took, but rather than assuming that's the case, he starts at the beginning: "Margaret and I were high school sweethearts. She was my date to the senior dance, and we were engaged right after graduation." Bill keeps his eyes on North, who begins to pace the room again. There is a clock high up on the wall over

North's head, and Bill tears his gaze from it. Time does not matter now that he's in the hot seat. His answers are all that matter.

"We got married right after my nineteenth birthday, and Margaret was pregnant with our daughter by the time we were twenty."

"I see," North says flatly to show that he's listening to every word.

"Margaret was always difficult. She was prone to fits of…I don't know. Just fits. She would be silent, then angry, then nearly catatonic. I thought I knew how to handle her moods, but there were times I really wasn't sure what to do. Then, about halfway through her pregnancy, something went wrong." Bill's heart is no longer racing, but instead squeezing itself like a tight fist inside his chest. He swallows gently, knowing that his words will hitch in his throat and cause his voice to break if he goes too quickly. "We went to the hospital, and the baby was born before she could live outside the womb. Her eyes never opened." The ticking of the clock is again audible alongside the reel-to-reel's mechanical spinning sound. "She was so tiny," Bill says softly. He clears his throat and holds his eyes open to stave off tears. "Margaret could not take it. Under the best of circumstances, she couldn't take it, but in her state of mind, she just snapped."

"Meaning she left you?" North prods, though not unkindly.

"No," Bill says. "She did not leave me. She cried incessantly, which is understandable, but something about holding that little baby in her hands…I don't know. Her eyes changed. She turned completely inward. It was like she could no longer hear my voice," he says, looking at the men seated around the table. One or two of them are watching him intently, but the others have their eyes trained solemnly on the tabletop. "I would talk, but it didn't get through. No matter what I said or did, Margaret was locked in a world of her own. Even her parents couldn't get her to speak. She just rocked back and forth and banged her head against things."

"That must have been incredibly difficult." North is watching Bill with his sharp eyes. "What did you do?"

Bill shrugs. "Her parents and I agreed that she needed to get help. We moved her into a treatment facility—a home," he clarifies. "And she stayed there. At first I went every day, then every few days, but eventually just once a week. I kept hoping she'd get better, that she'd see me and remember who I was to her. I thought that maybe the hormones from the baby, or, just...you know?" He looks around the table helplessly, hoping for one of the men to nod his reassurance, but they all stay the course: eyes on table; eyes on the smoke curling from their cigarettes; eyes anywhere but on Bill. "But she never came to. Never spoke to me again. After a year of that, I was ready to have the marriage dissolved, and I'd even spoken to her parents about it. No one was happy about that decision, and my parents begged me not to do it, but I was only twenty-two at that point. I couldn't stay married to a ghost for the rest of my life, and she'd given me no indication that she was still in there."

Arvin North has stopped pacing and is standing behind his own chair, leaning over the back of it to stub his cigarette out in an ashtray. He reaches for the cup of coffee that's resting near his forgotten manila folder and a cup of pencils with clean, pink erasers and sharp points. His eyes lift and land on Bill. "That's understandable," he says, sipping his coffee. "A man that young has his whole life ahead of him."

"I requested a relocation to the Air Force base in Minneapolis in the midst of all of it. I needed a change. And then I went to the dentist one day to get a cleaning, and there was Jo," Bill says, imagining her there again, lips shiny and pink, eyes dancing. "She was offering me a lollipop and a future, and I took both. We were married eight months after we met, and then a year later, James was born."

"And Ms. Wallings?" North prompts him, bringing them back to Margaret.

"She's still in the same facility in Arizona."

"That's a tough decision," North says mildly. There is no judgment in his tone.

"It was. And I'm good at tough decisions," Bill says, lifting his chin an inch. "I can weigh the pros and cons of any situation, and do the things that need to be done."

"Are you in touch with Ms. Wallings?" North has a glint in his eye. He already knows the answer to this question.

The clock on the wall ticks again loudly as Bill weighs the question. "I am. I have, on occasion, made the trip to Arizona to visit her in the facility."

"Any particular reason?"

"Duty," Bill says simply. "I can do the tough things—in any situation—but I am also a man of duty and honor. I may not have been the right husband for her, but I am still a person who cares about her. Her parents have passed, and a part of the expense of her care falls on me." Bill pauses and then goes on. "I didn't divorce her because I stopped loving her...I left because there was no future for us. So I visit when I can, whether it means anything to her or not. It's the right thing to do," he concludes, holding his gaze steady on North's. "And I put a lot of merit in doing the right thing."

"Thank you for your candor, Lieutenant Colonel," Arvin North says, giving him a single nod. "Now we have a few questions for you about your time in Korea."

Bill steels himself and finally allows a single glance at the clock on the wall; the questions are not about to get any easier—they'll just be hard in a different way.

Arvin North slides a fresh cigarette out of the pack he's taken from his breast pocket and puts the end into his mouth. He flicks his lighter and the paper ignites with a hiss. "Let's talk about the mission you led in Korea in December of 1951." His lighter snaps shut. "I want to hear about the casualties."

Bill sighs internally. Putting himself back in Korea exacts an emotional toll on him every time, and occasionally leads to days or weeks of repetitive nightmares. He buckles up mentally, sitting straighter in his chair.

"Okay," Bill says. "The casualties."

THREE

jo

"OH, ISN'T HE GORGEOUS," Jo says, leaning over the hospital bed to peer at the tiny, pink-faced bundle in Barbara's arms.

"His name is Huck," Barbara says.

"Well, isn't that adorable," Jo coos, still admiring the newborn.

Frankie is leaning against the windowsill, her strong, tanned arms visible from beneath a fitted Pucci sheath dress that's a swirl of green, turquoise, black and white. With it, Frankie wears a pair of white wrist-length gloves and matching white heels. Barbara lifts an eyebrow at her shoes.

"It's only a week until Memorial Day," Frankie says to Barbara as the new mother stares at her shoes from her hospital bed, face aghast. "I promise the earth won't tilt on its axis if I wear white shoes a little early." At this, Frankie pointedly sets a potted frangipani plant with blooms of yellow and pink on the table at the foot of Barbara's bed. "Congrats on this little pup, by the way."

"I thought you were having a girl," Jo says, reaching out gingerly to caress the little swirl of silky hair at the baby's crown.

Barbara's smile fades just slightly. "Me too. Well, I'd hoped for one," she says, looking wistfully at her baby. "But I guess I already know all about little boys, so what's one more, right?"

Frankie huffs as she slides her manicured hands from her gloves, unsnapping her purse and dropping the gloves inside. "I don't know about that," she says. "The world is already lousy with men."

"Frankie!" Jo says, turning around quickly to shoot daggers with her eyes. She's still gripping the metal side rail of the bed when two other women enter the room tentatively, arms laden with flowers and presents.

"Hi, girls," Barbara says. "Come in and meet Huck."

The new women cluck over the baby as Barbara holds out a hand. "You also have to meet Jo Booker and Frankie Maxwell," she says, pointing at them in turn. "Jo and Frankie, this is Caroline and Judith."

"Oh!" Caroline says, holding her arms open and pulling Jo into a warm, familiar embrace that is completely disarming. "I am *so sorry* we missed the barbecue at your house the other day! Judith's kids got my kids sick, and then we each had one throwing up that day, so we figured it was better not to come over and take down the entire neighborhood in one fell swoop, you know?"

When she finally lets go, Jo is nearly breathless from surprise at her ebullient greeting. "Well," she says, trying to collect herself from this dizzying onslaught of friendliness. Jo puts a hand to her chest. "Of course—please, don't give it another thought. I'm so happy to meet you both now, and I hope the kids are all better."

"They're healthy as horses and tearing through our houses like a pack of wild bulls raging through a china shop," Judith confirms, holding out a hand to shake Jo's in a more traditional greeting. "Pleasure to meet you both." She turns to Frankie with a small smile and a quick nod.

Frankie is still leaning artfully against the windowsill, watching the entire scene. "Kids, babies, babies, kids," she says, waving a hand in the air. "I have none of them. But what I do have is a husband. Have any of your men done their psychological evaluations yet?" Frankie lifts one perfectly drawn brow as she glances at the other women to gauge their responses.

"Jay's is this afternoon," Caroline says, looking down at the baby. Her eyes flick up and meet Frankie's.

"So is Ed's." Frankie inspects her manicure; her face is neutral.

"Good," Caroline says with just a hint of reservation. "Hopefully they'll get this out of the way and move on. I don't think any of them look forward to sitting down and having a group of strangers grill them about personal details for two hours, do they?"

"I would think not," Frankie says.

Jo knows that Bill had done his evaluation first thing that morning, and she's eager for him to come home so she can hear how it went. But that's for later—right now there's a baby in the room, and their husbands' jobs are rendered momentarily irrelevant. Jo turns back to Barbara. "So, how are you feeling? This is your third time, so it's old hat by now, I'm sure."

Barbara sighs. "I wish. I think every time I'm in the throes of labor is about when I remember how painful the whole thing is. But then, the minute they whisk the baby away to clean him, you just forget, don't you? You forget all the horrible stuff."

"You'd have to," Judith interjects, "or no one would do it more than once, and then the entire species would die out."

The other women laugh appreciatively.

"I remember after finding out about giving birth—I must have been fourteen at the time—I asked my mother, 'Mom, why would anyone do this in the first place? And once they have, why would they do it *again*?'" Jo laughs at this memory as she tells the story. "And she said to me, 'You do it once for love, and then you do it again for love.' It was that simple."

The other women nod, their eyes returning to Barbara, who is the picture of maternal love as she holds little Huck there in her hospital bed, gazing at his tiny nose and his squished-up face.

"If only everything were that simple," Frankie says with finality, pushing herself away from the windowsill. "Ladies, I'm sorry to break up this little party, but Barbara probably needs some peace and quiet anyway. And I need to be on my way."

Jo follows suit and leaves with Frankie, their heeled shoes clicking as they walk down the shiny, polished hallways. The women's steps match perfectly as they pass the rooms of tired but happy new mothers recuperating on the maternity ward.

Once they're out in the hot sun of midday, Frankie pulls a pair of cat-eye sunglasses from her purse and slides them on. This makes her look terribly glamorous, and Jo says so.

"Oh, Jo," Frankie laughs. "I bought them at Neiman Marcus—they're nothing special." She stops and gives Jo an appraising look. "Do you like fashion?"

Jo glances down at her red bandana print blouse, which is tucked into a pleated skirt made of a dark denim fabric. She'd started sewing her own clothes as a teenager, and while she saves time now by shopping off the rack, every so often she still likes to buy a Butterick pattern, lay it on the floor of her living room, and cut into her fabric with the satisfying slice of her sharp pinking shears. She painstakingly pins the fabric and gets everything just so, and then occasionally stays up well into the wee hours of the morning with a pot of coffee, her Singer humming faithfully as she listens to the radio. It's one of those small personal pleasures that she indulges in every so often—sleep be damned—because it gives her such joy to be doing something for herself and without any interruption from Bill or the kids.

"I actually do like fashion," Jo says, blushing as she runs a hand over the blouse she'd made just before leaving Minnesota. "But I don't think my style is very evolved."

Frankie is pulling a cigarette from her purse and she turns her head to look at Jo again, though her eyes are shielded by the dark sunglasses. "It doesn't have to be evolved, Jo—your style just has to be *yours*."

Jo thinks about this as they stand beneath a swaying palm tree in the parking lot of the hospital. She looks up at the reflective, glittering windows of the building, noticing the way the fluffy, white clouds are mirrored in the glass.

"I guess so," Jo says uncertainly. "But where do you get *your* sense of style?" It's probably too hot to be standing around on the pavement, chit-chatting about fashion, but Jo is trying hard to acclimate to the painfully humid weather, so she forces herself to stand there, willing her pores not to sweat.

"My style?" Frankie blows smoke straight up at the sky. "From my mother. She and my father both came here from Italy in 1922. My mother was still a girl then, but her sense of style was already solidified, as was her appetite for life." Frankie flicks ash onto the gray pavement, crossing one arm over her flat stomach and holding on to the opposite elbow as she stands there, looking elegantly cool in the heat. "They had pasta most days, took naps in the afternoon, smoked like chimneys, and ate dinner no earlier than nine. My parents still drink a bottle of red wine every night. In my entire life, I have never once heard my mother complain about the things other women do: she never says she's 'fat,' she simply says she's been enjoying life a bit too much. And then she drinks a gallon of water with lemon each day until she 'feels like herself again.'" Frankie shakes her head, tutting as she very clearly imagines this Italian mother of hers.

"Your family sounds so different than mine."

"How so?"

"Well," Jo says. "For starters, my parents were born here, and they lived through the Great Depression—both of them on Midwestern farms. Because of that, they're extremely frugal. My dad can pinch a penny until it screams."

Frankie chuckles at this. "Until it screams, huh?"

"Oh, absolutely. I wore my mother's wedding dress when I married Bill, not because I thought it suited me, but because it was free. And when I met him, I was working as a secretary. My dad wanted me to be self-sufficient. He told me and my sisters when we were quite young that there were no guarantees in life—about anything. He said we could marry well, but a stock market crash or some other unforeseen disaster could wipe out our families. My dad thought that having daughters who worked was the best way to insulate us from hardship. 'If you can work, you can feed yourself—and your children,' he always said," Jo says, using a deep, faux man's voice.

Frankie nods. "That's true," she says. "But I've already worked and lived on my own, and now I don't want to work anymore." She makes a face. "Not because I'm lazy, but because there are so many other things to *do,* you know?"

Jo does know—of course she knows. A woman can have a wide range of passions and hobbies and pursuits, they just can't jeopardize her obligations as a wife and mother. "Sure. Of course," she says.

"I want to learn French," Frankie says, smoking again as she gazes up at the palm trees overhead. "And I want to bake strudel. I want to take a road trip all the way from Florida to Maine, from Maine to Alaska, and then down to California. I want to see it all—maybe even Mexico."

Jo blinks in response. Her dreams have always been much more pedestrian than the ones that Frankie apparently entertains: she wants to sew curtains for the entire house. She'd like to take the kids to Yellowstone before they all grow up and leave to live their own lives. She wants to read a novel a week purely for her own enjoyment. But road tripping around the perimeter of the country? Learning to speak a foreign language? Thoughts like these have never crossed her mind.

"You know what we should do?" Frankie says, dropping her cigarette butt on the pavement and crushing it beneath the toe of her high heeled shoe.

"What's that?"

"Take a girls' road trip," Frankie says. "Once the men are all settled, we should drive up to Atlantic City and have a weekend of debauchery. See Sinatra at the 500 Club."

Again, Jo simply blinks. Who *is* this woman? She's completely entranced by Frankie—she can admit that to herself—but she's also mystified that such a female creature exists in her orbit. Someone who wants to do things simply for the sake of doing them, not to benefit her own family. A woman who thinks it's perfectly reasonable to just jet away to Atlantic City, of all places, and spend a weekend gazing up at Old Blue Eyes on stage while someone else is back in Stardust Beach holding down the fort.

"That sounds…really fun," Jo says, giving her best Girl Scout-type *I'm game for anything* smile. "But I can't really imagine leaving my children."

Frankie's face falls. She pushes her sunglasses up on top of her head and her brown eyes pierce Jo's. "They'd be fine without you for a weekend," she says. "I promise."

It's on the tip of Jo's tongue to remind Frankie that, as a woman who has no children, it's really not fair of her to say so, but she thinks better of it. After all, she knows nothing of Frankie's personal life or marriage—not yet, anyway—so she bites her tongue.

"You're so right," Jo says agreeably. "I'm sure they would be fine." But she isn't convinced that they would be, nor is she at all sure that Bill would support her disappearing on a road trip with a bunch of other women, so she just keeps smiling. "It was so good to see you today, Frankie," she says, turning to find her car in the lot, which is officially baking in the noon sun like a tray of cookies in the oven. "I need to get home and do some afternoon chores, but I'd love to have you over soon for coffee."

Frankie smiles back, but her eyes are slightly narrowed in consideration. Jo feels scrutinized under her gaze—seen, but not in a good way. Seen, but for who she really is: a dull, staid, boring mom from Minneapolis. Being around Frankie makes her feel as if she doesn't have a glamorous bone in her entire body, but it also makes her feel like she *wants* to be glamorous. Frankie is somehow aspirational for her—almost like the kind of friend a girl has when she's young; the type who drives a little too fast, starts to smoke a little too young, and always has a really good bad idea up her sleeve.

"Definitely," Frankie says, watching Jo as she walks over to the family station wagon. Jo unlocks the driver's side door and lifts a hand in farewell.

Jo backs up with caution, tapping her brakes quickly so as not to nick an old man passing slowly behind her car with a cane, then she puts her car in drive and exits from the lot.

In her rearview mirror, she sees Frankie getting into a convertible Corvette—one that looks just like the car that Bill drives. She registers the carefree way that Frankie settles in behind the wheel with the top down so that she can bask in the Florida sun.

It never would have occurred to Jo to ask Bill if she could drive his Corvette. And she knows in her heart that it never would have occurred to him to offer it.

* * *

"Mommy, Mommy, Mommy!" Nancy shouts that evening as Jo takes a bubbling tuna casserole from the oven, both hands engulfed in giant, well-worn oven mitts. "Can I get the new Nancy Drew book? It's called *The Moonstone Castle Mystery*!"

Jo uses one shoulder to push the long strand of hair out of her eyes as she navigates around her ten-year-old daughter to set the hot casserole dish on a trivet on the kitchen counter.

"Baby, I'm not sure right now," Jo says distractedly, turning to pull a salad from the refrigerator. She takes the lid off the Tupperware container, revealing a chopped head of iceberg lettuce dotted with shaved radish rounds, light green crescents of celery, and chunks of tomato. "Can you get the salad dressing out of the fridge, Nance? Please? And set it on the table," Jo says hurriedly, nodding at the table with its bright yellow placemats and clean silverware set out on folded, ironed napkins.

Nancy sighs, but does as her mother asks. "But, Mom. Please? I played Barbies with Kate *all afternoon* like you wanted."

Jo can hear the annoyance in her middle child's voice over having to entertain her younger sister, but Jo had already thanked Nancy for watching Kate so that she could go to the hospital to see Barbara and baby Huck. Jimmy had been home as well, and while Jo prefers not to leave her children alone, she knows that, at ten and eleven, her two oldest kids are plenty responsible enough to watch television for a couple of hours with their little sister, or to make a snack that doesn't require any cooking. She'd grown up strong and independent and responsible, and she wants that for her children as well.

"Honey, Daddy will be home soon and I want to make sure you're all washed and ready for—" Jo is about to say "dinner," but just then, the door from the garage into the house opens. Bill walks in looking distracted.

"Daddy!" Nancy shouts, flinging herself at her father. She wraps her arms around his waist and hugs him, looking up at him adoringly. "Do you think I can get the new Nancy Drew book since I babysat Kate today?"

"Why did you babysit?" he asks, looking at Jo as he puts an arm around Nancy and pats her shoulder.

"I went to the hospital to check on Barbara and the baby," Jo says, willing her eyes not to travel to the spot in the front room where Barbara's water had broken just days earlier. She'd been able to mostly remove the spot, but the reminder of impending childbirth in the middle of her new house is mildly unappetizing as Jo gets dinner on the table.

"How is she?"

"She's doing just great," Jo says with a smile. "I got to see the baby—little Huck. He's adorable."

"Todd seems pleased to have another boy," Bill says. He gives Nancy a squeeze and lets her go, moving through the kitchen to set his briefcase on a table in the front room. "Listen, I need a few minutes to myself. Why don't you all eat without me this evening, and save me a plate for later?"

For the third time that day, Jo finds herself standing there just blinking at someone without knowing quite what to say. "You don't want to eat with us?"

This is a turn of events; Bill is the one who has always been so insistent on the importance of the family dinner. Though they'd never talked about it much, she'd gotten the impression that Margaret, his first wife, had always felt unwell and never wanted to cook or eat together. It takes very little motivation for a second wife to do the kinds of things that a first wife didn't do—quietly besting the first wife can become a competition, of sorts—and once Jo had gotten that impression about Margaret, she'd made it her mission to have a hot meal on the table each evening, and to have the children washed and ready to eat when Bill walked in the door.

"I'm a little under the weather," Bill says. Jimmy has come in to the kitchen with his face washed and hair wetted down to hold his cowlick in place. "Hi, buddy," Bill says to his son.

"You're sick, Dad?" Jimmy asks, eyes filled with worry. "We can't play catch tonight?"

Bill puts out a hand like he might muss his son's hair, but then pulls it back. Jimmy has just reached the age where he isn't a fan of things like having his hair tousled, or being treated like a baby in any way. As a fellow firstborn son, Bill can understand his son's need to grow into manhood, and he does his best to act as though eleven is right on the cusp of shaving and driving.

"Listen, bub," Bill says as he clears his throat. "I just need to lie down for a bit. I'll see how I feel, okay?"

Without another word, Bill vanishes down the hall and leaves Jo with two of her three children. They're looking to her for cues, but Bill has never once, in their entire marriage, come home and gone directly to the bedroom for a nap.

"What do we do, Mommy?" Nancy asks.

Jo slides her hands out of the oven mitts and tosses them on the counter, then she slips the apron over her head and hangs it on its hook in the pantry cupboard. She runs her hands over her hair to smooth it down.

"Well," Jo says, "I guess we eat. Jimmy, please get the milk out of the fridge, and Nancy, go get your sister. Make sure her hands are washed."

Nancy emits a long, loud sigh, then turns on her heel to walk back to the bedrooms, where Kate is no doubt lost in a land of Barbies or baby dolls. "Fine," she says, her voice ringing out in the giant openness of the modern house. "But I still think I deserve that new book."

It's Jo's turn to sigh out loud as she drops into her seat at the table, spreading her napkin across her lap. She reaches for the serving spoon to dish up some casserole onto Kate's plate, and then makes a mental note for the next day while she's out running errands: *Buy more milk; go to fabric store to find new Butterick patterns for summer dresses; stop at the bookstore and look for the new Nancy Drew book.*

Another day, she thinks, glopping a spoonful of casserole onto her own plate as the children pull out their chairs and sit down with her, *of not learning a foreign language, of not shopping at Neiman Marcus, and of not taking a leisurely nap after lunch. Oh well.*

FOUR
bill

IT ISN'T like Bill to come home, skip the family dinner, and miss out on playing catch with Jimmy in the neighborhood park, but the psychological evaluation that morning had given him a pounding headache that's lasted all day, and holing up in his dark, air-conditioned bedroom is about all he can manage.

Jo and the kids are in the kitchen, and their voices travel through the open house and down the hall to the master suite, where Bill is in bed with one pillow under his head and one on top of it. Closing his eyes and taking long, deep breaths is the only way he can think of to get the sound of Arvin North's voice out of his head.

We'd like to talk about your first wife now...Meaning she left you?...Are you in touch with Ms. Wallings?

Bill puts both hands on the pillow atop his head and squeezes it against his eyes and forehead, trying to push the memory of it all away, but he can't. Instead of North's voice, he sees Margaret's face —the way it was when they'd met in high school. She'd been so lovely then, so sweet, so happy, so untouched by pain. Of course, she'd cried and yelled more easily and more often than any of the other girls Bill had dated up to that point, but he'd just thought she was high-spirited. There was a passion to Margaret that had drawn him in (as it would have drawn in any other young, red-blooded boy), and he had naively assumed that a part of her rapidly changing moods had to do with her wild, untamed love for him.

Oh, youthful ignorance.

Bill flips over onto his stomach and buries his face in the pillow, keeping the other one on top of his head to block out the sliver of sunlight that's still visible beneath the bedroom curtains.

He imagines Margaret on the night of the senior dance: her hair swept into a sleek updo with tendrils of red falling from the sides; her eyebrows the same soft, ginger color as her hair; her dress, a shiny pink confection with a rosebud of fabric at the hip; her blue eyes looking up into his as they'd slow danced to "I Love You (For Sentimental Reasons)" by Nat King Cole. In that moment, he'd known that the only thing he needed—the only thing he wanted in life—was to have Margaret as his bride. And she'd said yes that night as they'd lain in one another's arms in the back of Bill's dad's 1939 Plymouth coupe.

"But is Daddy okay?" Kate's little voice asks now from outside the closed door of the master suite.

"Yes, shhh. Daddy is fine," Jo hushes her. "Let's all go on a walk to the park, shall we?"

Bill hears Jo hustling the kids through a quick after-dinner change into their play clothes. He can picture her standing right outside their door and he wonders if she might pop in, but she doesn't. Instead, Bill hears the echo of feet down the hallway, followed by Jo's sure-footed steps, and then the front door closes and the house is silent again.

Is going into space the right thing to do? Bill isn't even sure; he just knows that it's what he was born to do. The moment he'd heard about the possibility of joining the team at NASA, he'd been so sure—so absolutely convinced, right to the marrow of his bones—that this was the mission he needed to put his life on course, that he'd immediately filled out the paperwork, gotten the appropriate recommendations, and sent it all off without even mentioning a word of it to Jo.

Maybe he'd known in his heart that moving to Florida was going to be a tough sell for his outdoorsy, wholesome, all-American girl, but Jo is a trouper; more than anything, she knows how to shore up a mission and get things done, and that's what he needs from her right now. Bill needs Jo to keep this house in order—in fact, to get it decorated correctly so that they fit in amongst the other families in Stardust Beach—and he needs her to be the rock that holds this family together. She'd been unconvinced before the move that they'd need to change things like their furniture and their hobbies, but now that they're here, he can see she's become more amenable to getting floor-to-ceiling bookshelves installed, and to maybe trading in their old dining table for a chrome one with leatherette chairs. She's even talked to Jimmy and Nancy about taking surfing lessons, and while he can't ever imagine her becoming a lady who lunches poolside at an expensive hotel, he's heard her talk about possibly starting a weekly card game with the other wives, and even that small effort pleases him.

The children are still in the early days of their school experience in Florida, and while they'd arrived in April with less than a month of school to go before summer break, Bill still wants Jo to help smooth the way for them, to make sure they have what they need, and to facilitate their budding relationships with the children of his coworkers. He also hopes that he and Jo can develop some real friendships with their new neighbors, but that's lower on his list of priorities. As adults, their personal happiness is less imperative to Bill than that of his children, and all of that is slightly lower on his scale of importance than him doing well at NASA and being chosen to lead a mission into space.

At thirty-five and with seventeen years in the Air Force, Bill had reached the point where he'd needed to make a bold move. It was time to challenge himself, to elevate his family, and to make his mark on history, and so he'd applied to NASA without hesitation. His own father had died of a heart attack at 49, so Bill figures that he's—at best—in the middle of his life right now, or that—at worst—he's over the peak of the mountain and coasting towards eternity.

These are the kinds of thoughts that keep a man awake at night, that keep him plunging ahead towards his own destiny.

But no matter what obstacles get in his way, Bill knows how important it is to stay the course. He needs to keep his head on straight, and to not let things like a mandatory psychological evaluation dig up the past in a way that forces him to retreat into himself, as he sometimes does when the going gets tough. It takes a lot these days to send him into a dark space where all he can do is curl up in the fetal position, but it's still possible. In the years since Kate's traumatic birth, small things have occasionally caught him off guard, reminding him of Korea, of loss, of pain. But he does his best to always stay aware, and to remove himself from other people when he needs a moment to regroup. He doesn't need Jo or the children to see him in a bad way, and he doesn't like to talk to anyone until he brings himself out from whatever dark cloud is passing over him.

Under no circumstances does Bill like to lose control of his emotions, and he likes it least of all when he's sitting in a room full of NASA employees. He'd held it together all day, and he's pretty sure that he made it through the door of his own house and back to the bedroom without anyone knowing how truly off-kilter he's feeling, which is precisely as he wants it.

Bill rolls over and takes a long, fortifying breath. As he lets it out, his bones rattle and his brain buzzes. He's going to need to stay in the cool bedroom with the curtains drawn for as long as he can—all evening, if possible. He'll wake up tomorrow on the right side of the bed, ready to take on another day.

He wants this so badly that he can taste it. Space travel is—and will be—the culmination of his childhood dreams, his years flying in the Air Force, and the legacy he wants to leave for his family. Coming to Florida was the right choice; Bill absolutely knows this in his gut.

And the sooner he can convince Jo that he was right to bring them here, the better for all of them.

* * *

"Booker." Ed Maxwell is standing in the middle of the small cafeteria on the ground floor of NASA the next morning. There are four round tables with chairs surrounding each of them, and three vending machines lining one wall. One of the vending machines spits out coffee with cream, sugar, or just black, and Ed is standing before that machine, one hand poised to push the buttons.

Bill stops in his tracks as he's passing the open cafeteria area; there is no one else in the shiny-floored room. "What's up?"

"You got a minute?" Ed asks, punching the buttons and then waiting while the white paper cup fills with hot coffee. He picks it up off the dispensing tray and walks across the room to where Bill is standing next to a table, briefcase in hand.

Bill glances at his watch. "Sure. I'm a few minutes early. What's up?"

Ed scans the room quickly even though it's obvious that they're alone. "How'd it go yesterday during your psych eval? Were they tough on you?"

Bill swallows and then clears his throat. "Sure," he says honestly. "They were pretty tough. But I think they have to be. They need to know what we're made of, and what might be lurking in the background that could surface and throw us off track. We have to be cool-headed, and they need to do their due diligence to make sure that we are."

Ed nods; his jaw is clenched and his eyes are on the floor. "You got dark stuff in your past?"

Bill almost laughs at this, because it seems so incongruous to ask a man first thing in the morning what his deepest, darkest secrets are. He wipes the shocked smile off his face. "I have stuff, Ed. Don't you?"

Ed takes a drink of his coffee. "Yeah. Of course. And they dug around pretty hard inside that locked box in my head. I went home feeling like I'd had a long night with an insatiable woman."

"That good, huh?" Bill chuckles.

"No, buddy. Not in a good way. I felt like I got put through the wringer: my head hurt. My back was sore. I felt like I got kicked in the balls."

"Oof."

Ed makes a face. "Exactly." He puts one hand on his hip and brings his coffee cup to his lips again. "Anyway, I just wanted to know if I was alone in feeling like ground beef after it was all said and done." He gives an uncomfortable laugh.

Bill, not normally one for honest heart-to-hearts, gives Ed a sympathetic look. "You're not alone. Trust me."

Ed holds out his hand and shakes Bill's. "Thanks for that."

The men stand there awkwardly for a moment; the transition to sports talk or to breezy conversation about the weather seems like too much effort. "Let's head in and get this day started, shall we?" Bill says, tipping his head in the direction of the offices where they all meet up each morning for a debrief.

Ed claps Bill on the back heartily, nearly spilling his own coffee in the process. "Lead the way, Lieutenant Colonel," he says with a level of good-natured cheer that seems at least partially fabricated after the seriousness of their brief conversation.

The men walk together in companionable silence, their shoes squeaking against the linoleum all the way.

FIVE

jo

IT'S a week and a half after the barbecue at Bill and Jo's house, and the women and kids are gathered in Caroline's backyard. Caroline's kids, Marcus and Christina, are showing all the other children how to jump through their sprinkler (as if there were a right and a wrong way to do so), and Barbara is sitting in the shade, holding newborn Huck to her breast beneath a lightweight blanket as she nurses him.

"You don't even look like you had a baby," Caroline says, walking across the thick sawgrass in a pair of wildly unfashionable, single-buckle Birkenstock sandals. Jo admires the way Caroline bucks convention by forgoing makeup and wearing simple dresses that look as though she whipped them up in twenty minutes on a sewing machine in her rec room. "Drink this, hon," Caroline says, handing Barbara a tall glass of lemonade over ice. "I'd love to spike it for you, but I don't think little Huck is ready for vodka just yet."

The other women laugh lightly and take their Madras cocktails from the tray that Caroline sets on the patio table in the grass. Jo sips hers, unsure about what exactly is in a Madras, but she soon deduces that it's just cranberry, orange juice, vodka, and lime. She also realizes quickly that it's terribly refreshing in this heat and humidity, and that if she's not careful she could easily overdo it. She sets her drink down purposefully and focuses on Caroline.

"I have to ask, Caroline," Jo says, looking once again at the simple floral print A-line dress with a rope belt that Caroline is wearing, "but do you make your own dresses?"

Caroline puts one leg over the picnic bench and sits down to join them with a pleased sigh. "Oh, call me Carrie—everyone does," she says. "And how could you tell—was it the upscale edge stitching along my hem?" She winks at Jo with a smile and holds up the skirt of her dress with one hand, showing them a slightly wonky line of thread.

Jo flushes; she hadn't meant to sound catty—not at all. "No! I sew a lot of my own clothes, and I thought I spotted a fellow seamstress in our group here. That was all."

Carrie reaches out and pats Jo's thigh as if they've been best girlfriends for years. "I'm teasing, Jo. I sew because I never got bitten by the fashion bug, if I'm being honest. I see the things that other women wear and I admire them so much for their style, but it's not for me." She wrinkles her small nose, which is dotted with a constellation of freckles. "But your clothes look so professional. Where did you learn to sew like that?"

"My mom," Jo says with pride. "And thank you. I was a Girl Scout growing up—"

"Of course you were," Frankie interjects, tapping her pack of cigarettes against the wooden tabletop, but not taking one out—most likely in deference to the newborn in their midst. When Jo looks at Frankie she expects to see derision, but instead, Frankie's face is a mixture of amusement and affection. "I know who I want on my team in case of an emergency or a natural disaster, and Barbie doll," she says, turning to Barbara and the baby, "I'm sorry, but it ain't you with your twinsets and pearls."

Barbara looks stunned for a second, but then her face collapses in laughter. "I am actually not offended," she says, switching Huck from one breast to the other beneath the blanket. "My money is on Jo being the one out of all of us who could start a fire without a match. Or build a shelter from twigs and leaves." Huck fusses as he resettles, and then he goes quiet. "But if you ever want someone to keep the score of a golf game in her head, I'm your girl. I also won a limbo challenge in college, and I'm passionate about dressage."

The other women stare at Barbara for a long moment and then they break into collective laughter. "Yeah, I'm on Team Jo, too," Judith, who is overall the quietest of the bunch, says. "But I'd love to see you limbo sometime, Barbara."

"You know," Barbara says, leaning back against the chair she's sitting in next to the trunk of the tree that hangs over them, "when you called me 'Barbie doll' a minute ago, Frankie, it took me back to when I was a little girl. My parents always called me Barbie, and to be honest, most of my friends back in Connecticut do, too."

"Huh," Frankie says, slipping her unopened pack of cigarettes into her purse and snapping it shut. "So most of us have nicknames already—Frankie, Jo, Carrie, and Barbie. Aren't we a bunch of cuties? We sound like a pep squad."

Everyone's eyes shift to Judith, who is sitting there quietly, knitting as she sips her Madras cocktail. She's focusing on her motions—*knit one, purl one, knit one, purl one*—but she suddenly notices that everyone has gone quiet and her eyes flick up to the other women.

"What about you, Moody Judy," Frankie says, lifting her chin at the most mysterious member of the group. "You got any good nicknames? Do people call you Judy?"

Judith pushes her dark-framed glasses up her nose with her forefinger. "Not really. Just Judith."

"Well, Just Judith, I think we'll call you Jude," Frankie says, uncrossing her legs beneath the picnic table and recrossing them. She rattles her ice in the empty glass, having long since drained her Madras.

Judith shrugs. "Suits me just fine," she says, returning to her *knit one, purl one*. She truly does seem like the most easygoing person Jo has ever met, but as the other women move on with their conversation, comparing notes about babies and men, Jo's eyes linger on Judith—or rather, the recently-christened *Jude*—and the way her face remains placid and unbothered.

Jo tilts her head slightly, watching the calm sea of Jude's face. She has given them nothing so far in terms of personality: she hasn't once yelled at her twin daughters, the sweetly-named Hope and Faith, and she hasn't said a single bad word about her husband Vance's long hours at NASA, unlike the other women whose lightly-veiled complaints run the gamut from "He's never home," to "I feel like his head is in space already, but the empty shell of his body is still here on Earth." But not Jude; she just knits and purls and watches as Hope and Faith work out their differences with one another and with the other children, never even raising an eyebrow.

"So we are officially a girl gang now," Carrie says, reaching out and putting her index finger inside the soft curl of Huck's baby fingers now that Barbie has removed him from under the blanket. He is slumbering easily with a belly full of milk, and the women carry on around him. "We've got nicknames and we drink together in the afternoon."

"Yes," Frankie says drily, "we are an extremely tough girl gang, drinking Madras cocktails beneath a palm tree while we run a pre-school here in the backyard." She lifts her chin in the direction of the children—nine in total, aside from baby Huck—and as if on cue, Hope and Faith seem to team up without exchanging words and push Carrie's five-year-old daughter, Christina, right into the sprinkler.

Christina stands up, her face already crumpled into a red, tear-stained mask. "Mommy," she says, walking over to Carrie with both hands held out. Her palms are wet and covered in blades of grass. "I don't like to be messy."

Carrie pulls Christina into her lap and, without batting an eye, lifts the hem of her own homemade dress and uses it like a rag to wipe off her daughter's hands. "See?" she says to the other women. "One of the other beautiful things about not having spent hundreds of dollars on a high fashion dress!" She plants a kiss on her daughter's cheek, wipes both of Christina's eyes with the heels of her hands, and then sets the little girl back on the ground and gives her a loving pat on the bottom. "Go play, lovey," she says.

Jo watches in amazement as Christina, tears now almost a memory, runs right back into the fray of children.

"She's so easy," Jo says in wonder. Kate is way more high-strung than that, and once the tears start to flow, it's nearly impossible to stanch them. Sometimes Jo feels like the worst mother in the world because she can't always figure out how to soothe or redirect her own children when they need it.

Carrie shrugs and knocks back the last of her Madras. "She can definitely be a pill." Her eyes flicker over to Jude, who is still knitting away, seemingly oblivious to the fact that it was her twins who had pushed Christina into the sprinkler and started the tears in the first place. "But for the most part, she's pretty angelic. Her brother is much more of a rough-and-tumble kid, believe me."

"Boys tend to be, I think," Jo says, thinking of the way that Jimmy likes to take things apart without asking and then attempt to put them together again—with varying degrees of success.

"I'll second that," Barbie agrees. "Though I don't have any girls, so I can't really compare raising one to the other. But I can say that I never jumped out of a tree as a kid, and on more than one occasion I've seen Heath and Henry attempting to climb branches and catapult themselves onto the grass. Three and four year olds!" she says, shaking her head. She looks down at sleeping Huck. "I can only hope that this little monster is Mommy's calm and easy one."

"What are your girls like, Jude?" Jo asks, pulling Jude away from her knitting again.

Jude smiles wanly as she pushes her glasses up her nose again. "They're pretty easy. Mostly they just entertain each other and come to me when they're hungry, if I'm honest." Jude sets her knitting on the table and pushes herself to standing. She's a tall, lean woman with mousy blonde hair, and her glasses hide a pair of brown eyes that look like melted chocolate. "Carrie, would you mind if I slipped in and got a refill of juice? I'm still a bit thirsty, and I need to use your powder room."

"Oh, go ahead, honey. *Mi casa es su casa* and all that jazz." She waves a hand at the house and turns back to watch the children as they start a rowdy game of Red Rover.

Jude walks through the sliding door and into the house just as Jo remembers that she brought a recipe card with her for Barbie, but left it in her purse in the living room. "I'll be right back," she says, though the other women are already deep in conversation about when they'll be asked to sit for formal family photos for the NASA press kit.

Once inside the air-conditioned house, Jo takes a moment to wander around. The hallway is lined with black-and-white candid photographs that must have been taken by a professional photographer, but they seem to capture Carrie and her husband Jay and the kids in the most natural of poses. Jo is envious of the way the pictures appear artsy and not staged, like her own family photos. She desperately wants to be as comfortable and as sure in her own skin as the smiling woman in these photos is.

The front room, where her purse is sitting on the couch, is filled with yellow suede furniture—*With children?* Jo thinks—and a huge, state-of-the-art stereo system is set up next to a bookshelf that's covered in hundreds of books and equally as many albums. She walks over and looks at the spines of the novels and the vinyl, pulling *Please Please Me* by the Beatles from the stacks. It's brand new and fresh off the press, and Jo has been wanting to purchase it for herself. There's just something about the Fab Four that turns her into a teenager again, and she loves listening to them sing.

She puts the record back and finds the recipe card for Barbie in her purse, which she presses to her chest as she walks back through the kitchen.

"Oh!" Jo stops in her tracks. "Jude," she says, fanning herself with the recipe card unnecessarily. "I forgot you were in here. I have a recipe that I was going to give to Barbie," she says, holding up the card with her neat handwriting on it, as if this will allow Jude to see the directions for making Beef Burgundy over Noodles. "Don't you think the nicknames we've all got are cute?" she rambles on, slipping the card into the front pocket of her skirt. "People have always called me Jo, but it feels like we're all getting to know each other much more quickly. In fact, if someone calls me Josephine, I assume we're pretty much strangers—" Jo cuts herself off here as she realizes that, for the entirety of her chattering, Jude has been standing there with a bottle of vodka in one hand, poised to pour it into her glass. "Oh, I'm sorry," Jo says, backing away and sliding open the door to the patio. She walks directly to the picnic table and sits down again, the laughter of the other women drowning out the thoughts in her head.

Jo slips the recipe to Barbie as she heads over to the children to hold a stick for limbo at one point, and then she moves the sprinkler to another part of the yard so that Carrie's lawn won't drown in a puddle of water. But all the while, she's glancing back at Jude, quiet knit-purl Jude, who is smiling to herself and drinking her juice with vodka.

Jo is unsure what to make of Jude as she blithely sips her secret cocktail, but before she knows it, they're all consulting their watches and moaning about needing to get dinner on the table in this heat.

Jo gathers Jimmy, Nancy, and Kate, and heads home to put her meatloaf in the oven.

* * *

"Can you come out after the kids are in bed?" Frankie is asking as Jo listens. The phone is wedged between Jo's shoulder and her ear as she turns Kate around by the shoulders and points wordlessly towards the bathroom so that Kate will wash her hands before dinner.

"Uhhhh," Jo says, spinning around in the kitchen and reaching for a bottle of milk that's sitting on the counter. As she tries to walk to the table, she realizes that in all of her turning and twisting and reaching, the long, coiled phone cord has wound itself around her torso. She rolls her eyes and repeats all of her steps backwards until she's free of the cord. "I'm not sure, Frankie." Jimmy and Nancy pull out their chairs and sit down just as Bill comes in the side door and sets down his briefcase. "I might be able to. Can I call you back?"

Frankie exhales, and Jo can tell that she's smoking. Perhaps she's sitting on her lanai with a glass of wine and a French for Beginners book. "Sure," Frankie says. "You can call me. But I think it would do you some good to get out of the house and take a walk. Spin it to Bill like that: just tell him that we're a couple of gals who want to walk off our middle-aged chub after dinner."

Jo nearly laughs out loud; she's thirty-two, and there's no way that Frankie is any older than she is. In her mind, they're far from middle age. "Okay, I'll throw that against the wall and see if it sticks. Listen, I need to get dinner served. I'll call you after."

She hangs up the phone and turns to Bill with a forced smile. "Hi, honey," Jo says, walking over to him and leaning in for a kiss. "How was the day?"

"Can't complain." Bill loosens his tie and slips it over his head. He sets it on the counter, walks over to the fridge, and takes out a beer. "How about you?"

Jo is making tracks back and forth across the kitchen as she brings the meatloaf, a bowl of mashed potatoes, and another bowl of green snap peas to the table. She sets each thing down efficiently, pointing to Kate's chair so that her youngest will sit rather than fling herself at Bill, as she loves to do.

"We went over to Carrie and Jay's house," she says, then remembers that Bill doesn't know all the ladies as well as she does. "I mean Caroline's house. The Reeds have a lovely home." She sits down and unfolds her napkin, keeping her eye on her daughters as she does this to make sure that they're watching. Jo knows she isn't the most fashionable or the most wildly exotic woman on the planet, but she does know her manners, and it's her goal to teach them to her daughters by example. Once she sees that they've both put napkins on their laps, she looks back at Bill. "The kids all played in the sprinkler, and we sat in the shade and had lemonade."

She isn't sure why the lie trips off her tongue the way it does, but Jo fills her plate and avoids looking directly at her husband. Bill has never minded her having a drink here or there, but something about sitting around all afternoon and having cocktails with the new neighbor ladies feels...decadent. And unlike something Jo would do. And yet she'd enjoyed it—immensely. The drink had loosened her up a bit, and the company was good. Catching Jude pouring herself more vodka was still tickling at the back of her brain, but there was no way she wanted to bother Bill with idle gossip like that when she was still trying to make friends with these women.

"Sounds nice. I'm glad you're fraternizing with the other hens," Bill says as he forks a big bite of meatloaf into his mouth. He smiles at his children. "And how about you hedgehogs? Have you been up to anything good today?"

Kate, never one to hold her tongue, nearly bounces out of her seat now that she's been given permission to speak up. "Daddy," she says breathlessly. "Today at the Reeds we jumped in a sprinkler. And then Hope and Faith pushed Christina down and Christina CRIED. Can you believe that? And no one even got in trouble. If Nancy pushed me into the sprinkler, she would get in trouble, right?" Her eyes are wide as she watches her father's face for a response.

Bill looks at Jo as he takes a pull from his bottle of beer. "Help me out here."

"Christina is Carrie and Jay's little girl, and Hope and Faith are the Majors' twins." Jo cuts her meatloaf with a knife, then switches her fork to her right hand and takes a bite. "But I'm sure that Mrs. Majors talked to her girls when they got home, and hopefully it was a lesson for them to be kinder to their friends," she says pointedly, ending the gossip session with a stern look at Kate. "Why don't you tell Daddy about the books we got at the library on our way home from the post office?" she prompts.

Nancy sits up straighter; this is her area of expertise. "Well," she says, tilting her head to one side as though she's preparing to give an important speech. "I spent some time *familiarizing* myself with the children's section," she says, looking at Jo for praise as she stresses the word "familiarizing" (Jo is big on the children using what she calls "five-dollar words" to expand their vocabularies). "But in the end, I think I'll find more to read in the young adult section," Nancy decides. She pushes her mashed potatoes around with her fork. "Even Jimmy got a book," she says, looking at her older brother.

Jimmy, who prefers to eat fast and get outside to maximize his play time with the other neighborhood kids before dark, merely rolls his eyes.

"What did you get, champ?" Bill asks his son.

Since the evening when he locked himself in the bedroom and skipped dinner, Jo has been watching Bill for signs that anything might be wrong. He seems fine at the moment, but she's wary of missing something and she pays attention closely as he talks to the children over dinner.

"A book about Joe DiMaggio," Jimmy says. "Mom made me get it."

"I think summer reading is important." Jo looks at her son as he pushes his peas aside and tries to hide them beneath the edge of his meatloaf. "And getting to choose a book about something you're interested in isn't exactly torture, Jimmy."

Bill sighs. "I wish I had time to read for fun. It's been nothing but work since we moved here, and frankly, I'm envious of you all getting to play in the sprinkler and go to the library."

"Let's go swimming tonight, Daddy!" Kate says. She swings her short legs under the table, kicking the legs of her chair with her heels. "Can we?"

Bill glances out the sliding door that divides the dining area from the pool deck. "We could. It's certainly warm enough."

This is Jo's opportunity, and without thinking, she takes it. "If you all go swimming, would you mind if I went on a walk with

Frankie this evening? She called before dinner and asked if I wanted to get some exercise with her."

Bill glances up from his plate and his eyes fix on Jo. "You two are going out walking?"

Jo shrugs. "It sounded nice. She thought maybe after the kids were asleep, but if you're going to swim with them, perhaps you could oversee showers and bedtime?"

Bill looks at Jo with a surprised smile. "Sure. I'd love to put these monsters to bed. What do you say, guys? Think we can manage it?"

The kids all make excited noises about swimming and breaking the normal routine of Jo supervising the brushing of teeth and story time, and Jo feels an unexpected sense of relief at the idea of getting out of the house on her own. Most days it never occurs to her to escape from the expectations and chores of her life, but every so often, the idea of just opening the front door and leaving it all behind for an hour or two *does* seem appealing. She's never considered going out walking with a girlfriend, and it's refreshing to savor just a touch of independence.

Once dinner is done and the dishes are washed and put away, Jo wipes down the counters and picks up the phone to dial Frankie.

"It's Jo," she says as soon as she has Frankie on the line. "I just need to change my clothes, but I'm up for that walk if you are." She's giddy like a young girl whose mother has just agreed to let her go outside with a friend.

"Meet you in front of your house in ten minutes."

The sun has fallen behind the palm trees, leaving the sky a watery blue. There are pinpricks of starlight all over the evening sky as Jo emerges from the front door of her house in a pair of culottes and a sleeveless shirt. She's got her Keds on, and she's ready to stroll.

"Glad you could join me," Frankie says. She's wearing a pair of high-waisted shorts and a man's white t-shirt with sandals. "Let's check out our new neighborhood, shall we?"

The women walk in companionable silence for a block, looking at the cars in the driveways, and at the families living their lives inside of lit-up homes.

"Think they're all here for the same reason?" Frankie asks, nodding at a family sitting in the front room of their house with the television on.

"Essentially," Jo says. "Aren't we all living in this community because our husbands are working for NASA in some capacity?"

"Do you think everyone here is trying to be chosen for a mission?"

Jo lifts one shoulder and lets it fall. "I think some of the men are probably working at mission control or in some other capacity. I haven't asked Bill many questions yet. I feel…" She trails off here as they walk.

"You feel?" Frankie prompts.

"I feel like I'm in this new place without a husband sometimes," she says, surprising herself at the words that come out of her own mouth. "I mean, not really, but sometimes. You know?" Jo looks over at Frankie's profile.

"I get it." Frankie looks straight ahead as she nods. "Ed is gone a lot, and I don't even have kids to distract me from the silence of the house. It feels different than life before because everything is new to me here, and I don't quite have my bearings yet." Frankie stops walking in front of a house that's completely dark. There are no cars in the driveway, and the porch light is off. She picks a bright red hibiscus flower from a bush in front of the house and tucks it behind her ear, then leans over to pick another one. "But meeting you has really helped me to feel more grounded." Frankie reaches out gently and puts the hibiscus behind Jo's ear so that they're matching. "And the other ladies, too. But mostly you."

"Me?" Jo asks. They start walking again and Jo reaches up to touch the flower. She feels exotic as she breathes in the humid evening air, and she imagines her husband and children cannon-balling into the pool while she explores the neighborhood.

"Yes, you. You're a real breath of fresh air, Josephine," Frankie says. "Can't you see that?"

Jo definitely cannot see that. She thinks of herself as not terribly interesting, and it surprises her that Frankie thinks there's something appealing about her—at least more than the other women in their little group. "I'm just a girl from Minnesota," Jo protests, shaking her head. "Not anything worth writing home about."

"Ah, but that's where you're wrong." Frankie pulls her cigarettes out of the pocket of her shorts and puts the end of one in her mouth. She holds the pack out to Jo, who surprises herself again by taking one. She glances around furtively, as if someone might see her sneaking a smoke and have something to say about it. With one eyebrow raised in amusement, Frankie flicks her lighter and touches it to the end of both of their cigarettes. They each inhale and exhale into the night air before Frankie speaks again. "You're kind of an everywoman, Jo, and there's great appeal in that."

They're walking again, and the nicotine is working its magic on Jo, who gave up smoking as soon as she married Bill. "An everywoman? As in dull and workaday?"

Frankie shakes her head and waves a hand around. "No, no, no—you've got it all wrong. An everywoman in the sense that you sort of have it all. And you do it all—with ease."

Jo barks out a laugh. She and Frankie hardly know one another. "You think I have it all? And I look like I do everything easily?"

"Yes," Frankie says plainly. "I do. Am I wrong?"

This gives Jo pause. They pass by a house where a man is in the driveway, having a cigarette of his own. He nods at them and they smile politely in return, but don't stop their slow, ambling walk. "I have a good family," Jo says carefully. "A loving husband. Wonderful kids. But I get a lot of things wrong. There's something I fail at every day."

The hum of air conditioners working overtime to battle the heat of the evening fills the air as they wander by each house.

"I think you're probably too hard on yourself," Frankie says. She brings her cigarette to her lips and the tip glows orange as she inhales. Jo looks at the flower behind Frankie's ear and the way it's nestled against her dark hair. "I bet your kids think you're amazing."

Jo has plenty to say to this—she's pretty sure that Nancy hates her for making her watch her little sister, that Jimmy thinks she's a stick in the mud for forcing him to read in the summer, and that Kate feels ignored because she's the baby and Jo has never had the time to just be a mom to her and to give Kate her full attention—but instead she just watches Frankie's face as she squints her eyes and looks up at the sky.

"You gave up your whole life in Minnesota to come here for Bill. You uprooted your kids, and you're trying to recreate your family's comfort zone in a place that couldn't be more different than the one you came from. That's big stuff, Jo."

Jo looks at the toes of her white Keds as she walks. "Thank you for saying that. I haven't let myself pause long enough to appreciate the work it takes to keep things going every day. Sometimes it's a lot." Jo takes another drag on her cigarette. "I want to hear more about you, though."

Frankie gives a throaty laugh. "What's to tell? I met Ed in New York City four years ago and we got married in a whirlwind. And now here we are!" She's clearly trying to sound breezy, but it falls flat. "I'm a city girl, and this feels like living in a quiet beach town, but at least it's gorgeous here. And I can work on my tan." Frankie nudges Jo with her elbow as they walk side by side.

Jo smiles, but she's sensing a lot below the surface; there are plenty of things that Frankie isn't saying. "What were you doing in New York when you met Ed?"

"I was a Rockette," Frankie says, sounding wistful. "I went there to be an actress. All I ever wanted was to be on Broadway—I can sing, too." Frankie turns to Jo and grabs her elbow so that they're both standing still beneath a streetlight that's just flickered on. "I had all these dreams, and I didn't want to give them up, but meeting Ed changed things. I'd been struggling to get by, and he swooped in and saved me. I fell in love, sure, but I also saw an entirely different future when I met him. Something traditional; something real. I wanted to give it a shot, to be a wife, to finally grow up and make my parents proud, you know?"

Jo understands the desire to make other people happy and proud. It's human nature to seek that approval, but sometimes it seems like a woman's whole purpose in the world is to make everyone around her happy before claiming any of that happiness for herself.

"And were they proud when you married Ed?"

Frankie starts walking again, but so slowly that it's almost like she doesn't realize she's doing it. She stares ahead into the distance. "Sure. Who *wouldn't* be proud of their daughter marrying a military man who wants to be an astronaut? Remember: my parents are immigrants. They've worked hard to get to where they are in this country, and they want more for their kids than they had for themselves. But do they care about the fact that I gave up on a dream to please them?" Frankie turns her palms to the sky, her rapidly-dwindling cigarette held between two fingers. "I mean, probably not. And once we're married, we spend so much time nurturing the dreams of our husbands, but who worries about us achieving *our* dreams?"

It's a big question, and one that Jo doesn't have an answer to. But they've wound their way through the neighborhood and ended up back in front of Jo's driveway. There are no pool noises coming from the back of the house, so Jo can only assume that Bill has rounded the kids up and is moving them through the bedtime routine.

"Thanks for coming out with me, Joey-girl," Frankie says, dropping her cigarette butt onto the asphalt and crushing it beneath her sandal. She gives Jo a wink and holds out one hand as if she wants to shake. "What do you say we take a vow of silence? Anything we say on our walks stays between us—deal?"

Jo looks at Frankie's hand and then takes it in her own. She shakes. "Deal," Jo says.

Frankie says nothing else, but slips her hands into the pockets of her shorts and walks away, her dark hair glinting under the streetlights as she goes.

Jo pulls the hibiscus from behind her ear and sets it on the hood of Bill's car as she walks up the driveway. He won't know where it came from, but she doesn't care. She's gotten a taste of freedom and friendship this evening, and it feels good.

But a question lingers in her mind as she turns one more time to see Frankie walking up the driveway to her own house: *who worries about a woman's dreams?*

She doesn't know. No one has ever bothered to ask Jo what she wants out of life, whether she's happy, or if she wants to be anything other than what she is. She hugs herself and rubs her bare arms with her hands as if it were cold outside and she had a shiver.

But it isn't a chill that overtakes Jo as goosebumps rise up on her bare skin—it's excitement. It's the thrill of possibility.

SIX

jo

THE ENTRANCE to the Launch Operations Center at Port Canaveral is cavernous and filled with light. Giant windows allow the Florida sun to spill onto the polished concrete floors, and a twenty-foot tall replica of Explorer 1 sits in the center of the oversized foyer. All ten of the newest NASA astronauts' children are trying their hardest to be on good behavior, but the mothers know that the clock is ticking down towards tears, hunger, or boredom, so they're working overtime to make sure the boys' hair is spit-smoothed, and that the girls keep their dresses from getting wrinkled.

"Ladies," a man with square glasses and a camera around his neck says, clapping as he walks into the giant room. His claps echo throughout the space, and the children stop chattering and poking at one another to see who has gotten their attention. "Or should I say, *ladies and gentlemen*," the photographer amends, smiling at the little boys in that way that adults do when they think they're in on the joke with kids.

"Jimmy, Nancy, Kate," Jo whispers to her three, motioning with her hand to bring them all into line in front of her. They obey without question.

"Welcome to the Launch Operations Center," the man says, holding his camera in one hand as he scans their faces. "We're so happy to have you here. We have a lot to accomplish this morning. My name is David Huggins, and I'm the official Port Canaveral photographer, so we'll be getting to know one another a lot better in the coming months as I record your lives for posterity."

Jo takes a deep breath; being photographed isn't her favorite thing, but she knows how important this is for Bill's career. She's even purchased a new dress for the occasion, forgoing the ones she's sewn that would suffice for any other occasion. The kids are all in clean, pressed clothing, and she fed them a big breakfast right before they left the house. They've been warned under threat of no pool time for a week to keep away from any sort of shenanigans—even if the other children in their group are engaging in nonsense.

"I'd like to get some shots of each of the mothers with their children, then some of the entire group of women in front of Explorer 1 there," he says, motioning at the replica of the rocket. "At some point the dads will come out and join us, and then we'll get a combination of shots of the dads with their families, the men and the women together, and then the entire group. Sound good?"

Just then, baby Huck starts to wail and Barbie splits away from the group, hushing him as she walks back and forth across the concrete floors.

"I know that things can get dicey with little ones," Dave Huggins says, "so let's get this show on the road. How about for our first configuration we do each mother with her own children right over here..."

For the next hour, Dave arranges and rearranges the women and the children, and at some point the men file out of a door at one end of the room, walking across the floors as the heels of their dress shoes click on the concrete. The children all wave excitedly at their dads; a few kids can't resist running over and jumping into the strong arms of their fathers, including Kate.

Bill makes his way over to Jo as Kate grips his hand, looking up at him with starry eyes. "How you doing, Jojo?" he asks her, looking at her intently. "You holding up alright?"

Jo puts a brave smile on her face, though she feels more out of place than she wants to let on. Frankie, however, has stolen the show. Like the former Rockette that she is, she grins and poses every time the camera is trained on her, taking direction like a pro whenever Dave asks her to do something different. But as Jo watches Frankie, she notices just a flicker of self-consciousness behind her eyes every time Dave Huggins calls for the women to do something with their own children. It's almost imperceptible, but Frankie looks like a woman wearing a dress without pockets, only rather than just having no place to put her hands, she looks like a woman with nowhere to put *herself*.

"I'm okay," Jo says to Bill quietly, putting her hands on Kate's shoulders as she gathers the kids around her. "You know how stiff I am in photos—I always want to look natural, but I come across looking like a deer in headlights."

"Oh, you do not," Bill says, setting his own hand on Jimmy's shoulder as he leans his head towards his wife. "You look stunning. And I like that dress a lot," he says, giving her an admiring glance. "It reminds me of the day I met you at the dentist's office."

Jo flushes and tries to hide the private smile that tugs at the corners of her mouth. She'd picked the dress out with that specific thought in mind: if this was the color she'd been wearing when Bill had fallen for her, then it should make him proud to pose next to her in these official photos looking as much like that girl as she could possibly look twelve years and three children later. It gives her a shiver of pride to bask in the warmth of his desirous gaze.

"Okay, Booker family!" Dave Huggins says, cupping his mouth so that his words can be heard over the loud echoes of the families chit-chatting with one another in the big, open space. "Let's get Lieutenant Colonel Booker to stand right here," Dave says, pointing at a potted palm tree next to one of the tall windows. The light is coming in at a flattering, warm angle, and the yellow sunshine falls across Jo and her family. The photographs will have a dreamy, softened quality. This relaxes her, knowing that they'll be captured in good light.

"Come closer," Bill says softly, putting an arm around Jo's waist and pulling her to him as the children line up from tallest to shortest in front of them. "Let me show off my wife and children," he says with his lips pressed together like a ventriloquist, smiling at Dave as he squints at them through the lens of the camera. "This is the most exciting time of our lives, Jo, and I want to look back on these photos and remember how it felt to be on top of the world."

Jo's smile falters at his words, but she quickly turns up the wattage and looks directly into the camera. She may not feel the same way her husband does, but she'll be damned if she looks back at these photographs some day and sees her own trepidation and misgivings written all over her face. Come hell or high water, when Jo flips through this photo album in her old age, she'll land on this page and all she'll see is a supportive wife, well-behaved children, and her proud, successful husband.

For the next ten minutes, Jo channels Frankie's confidence as much as she can. She wants the world to look at the Booker family and see the future of space travel. The future of a happy family. The future of America.

* * *

"These kids were amazing today!" Barbie says as the women load the children into their cars in the parking lot under a blazing sun. "I need to put Huck down for a nap, but how about if you all come over after lunch for an afternoon swim at our house?"

The women all sigh gratefully, spared from the necessity of finding a way to spend a hot summer afternoon indoors with their children.

"See you about 1:00?" Barbie says, climbing behind the wheel of her station wagon with all three of her boys lined up in the back.

"Wear your bathing suits, girls!" she shouts as she turns on the engine.

The women wave and drive away in their own cars, eager to get their kids out of dress clothes and to give them lunch so that they can while away the afternoon in the cool water of Barbie's pool.

Jo doesn't have to do any convincing as she puts triangle-cut cheese sandwiches on the table with a bowl of strawberries and three glasses of milk. In short order, all three kids come running into the kitchen wearing swimsuits under their shorts and shirts, and Jo sets them to work on their lunches while she preps dinner and then goes to change into a bathing suit herself.

Standing in her closet, she pulls open a drawer and picks up the orange bikini with its pointy bra cups and white floral pattern. It's daring, and she'd bought it two summers ago at Sally and Genevieve's urging to wear to the lake in Minnesota, but in the end, she'd chickened out and chosen a simple black one-piece for that trip instead. However, something about posing in front of the camera all morning and doing her best to convince herself that she's beginning to embrace this new life is emboldening Jo; she suddenly feels like maybe she *is* the kind of woman who throws on an orange bikini for an afternoon in a friend's pool.

With the bikini on, she stands before the full-length mirror on the back of her closet door, turning this way and that. She's barely over thirty, she reminds herself—not nearly old enough to feel like she can't pull off a two-piece suit. For most of her life, she'd listened to her own mother go on and on about having wide hips and a stretched-out belly, and she knows just looking at herself that she still has years to go before she feels the urge to cover everything up. Jo smooths her hands over the faint silvery lines on her stomach that are reminders of her three pregnancies, proof that she'd been able to deliver and carry three healthy babies. Any scars or reminders that remain are blessings, not curses.

At Barbie's house, Jo shepherds her flock through the front door, instructing them to kick off their shoes near the entryway, as everyone who has arrived before them has done. Jo slides off her own sandals and sets her tote bag next to them.

"Welcome, welcome!" Barbie calls out, striding through the kitchen in a ruby red one-piece suit with a black sarong tied around her waist. "Forgive me if I don't shake and shimmy in the pool like the rest of you," she says, motioning at her mostly covered body. "But I've still got a lot of baby weight to lose before I strut around in just my suit!"

Jo looks at her and sees nothing to hide. It's funny that she herself has just been staring in the mirror and taking stock of her own physical state, only to find that Barbie has been doing the same. Are they all like this—hyper-aware of what they see as their own shortcomings? Does any woman just accept herself at face value, without feeling the need to apologize to the rest of the world in some way?

"You look gorgeous," Carrie says, munching on an apple slice as she walks out of the kitchen. Carrie, for one, looks completely uninterested in whether anyone else thinks she looks good in her bikini. She smiles widely at Jo. "Hi, Jo," she says. "Marcus and Christina are out back, kids—go join them in the pool!"

Jo's three need no more invitation than that, and they dart through the sliding door like convicts escaping from prison. Within seconds, their shorts and shirts have been discarded, and the happy laughter of five kids romping in the water like slippery seals fills the air.

"Should I quiet mine down a bit so Huck can sleep?" Jo asks with her hands on her hips.

Barbie waves this thought away. "Oh, heavens, no. Huck can sleep through a freight train. With two other boys in the house, it's impossible to keep things quiet, and I don't believe in that anyway. Babies and kids need to adapt to us, not the other way around."

"Is Frankie here yet?" Jo asks, following Barbie and Carrie out to the pool.

"No, she called and said she wasn't feeling well," Barbie says as she pulls out a chair and sits down, sliding her oversized sunglasses onto her face. "But maybe the idea of all these kids in the pool was too much. Can't say that I blame her." She says it with a smile and it's not at all meant unkindly, but Jo feels a zing in her heart as she realizes that perhaps that's precisely why Frankie hasn't come.

"Hi, all." Jude walks out the door with Hope and Faith in tow. The twins are wearing matching pink swimsuits, their heads covered by swimming caps covered in daisies. Without further ado, they jump feet-first into the pool and start squealing along with the other children.

There is an open seat next to Jo, and Jude takes it. She's wearing a long shift dress with no sleeves and her feet are bare, but unlike the other women, she doesn't seem to have a swimsuit on.

"So, Jude," Jo says, turning to her. "We haven't gotten to chat much." Barbie and Carrie turn towards one another and start a side conversation of their own, which gives Jo the freedom to talk to Jude one-on-one. "Where did you all live before coming to Stardust Beach?"

"Texas," Jude says drowsily as she pulls her knitting from her bag. "Hot as hell and flat as a pancake. Not much different from Florida, if I'm being honest."

Jo nods politely; she senses that Jude doesn't necessarily want to talk, but something is propelling her forward anyway. She needs to know more. "We came from Minnesota," Jo says without prompting. "It's pretty much the polar opposite of Florida." She frowns. "Except maybe for Alaska—I guess that's the furthest thing from Florida that I can imagine."

Jude is already back to her knitting, but she nods along as Jo speaks. "Sometimes different is good," Jude says mildly. "The sameness of life can be suffocating."

"That's so true," Jo says, accepting a glass of water with lemon in it from Barbie, who has gone into the kitchen, poured the glasses, and come back to hand them around. "Thanks, Barbie," she says as she takes a big, grateful sip. She turns back to Jude. "But there's comfort in the familiar. I miss knowing that I'll wake up and go the same places I've always gone. I miss the friends and family I saw all the time. I miss the traditions and the rituals of life in a place where you've lived for ages, you know? I still think it's weird to go to the grocery store knowing that there's no way I'll run into my mom's best friend from church, or the girl who played the flute with me in the high school band."

Jude stops knitting and looks right at Jo from beneath the brim of her hat. She's not wearing sunglasses, so her piercing green eyes look right into Jo's. "I've been a military wife for a decade, and I was a military brat for the rest of my life before that. Moving and change are all I know, Jo. I meet people, I lose people, I get on with it." She starts to knit again, more furiously this time. "As long as my kids and my husband are happy, then I'm happy."

This proclamation shuts Jo up for the moment. She lets the words sit between them like a leaf floating on the surface of the pool. Finally, Jo speaks. "I think you should be happy, too," she says gently, not looking away from the lemon in her glass as it bobs in the glass. "I think we're more than just wives and mothers, don't you? Or, at least I think we *can* be."

Jude doesn't miss a beat with her knitting needles and she doesn't look up at Jo as she considers this. "I wasn't raised to be anything other than a wife and a mother, Jo, and I'd bet dollars to donuts that you weren't either."

Jo can hear the rush of blood in her ears as she takes in this statement. *I'd bet dollars to donuts that you weren't either...* But is this true? Is it true of all women? Jo chews on her lip and smiles distractedly as Nancy calls out to watch her dive into the pool. She waves at her children and takes a few deep breaths. She's rattled by the straightforward way that Jude has just deconstructed womanhood in one simple sentence.

There's probably some truth to it, but it still bothers Jo to hear it. The idea that wanting more, or that having an opinion on where her family lives is something that's frowned upon nags at her. As she watches her girls playing happily for the rest of the afternoon, Jo can't help but hear Jude's words in her head over and over on a loop.

She decides right then and there that she wants more for Nancy and Kate than these outdated notions of womanhood. Sure, she'd love for them to experience the joys of marriage and motherhood, but what if they want more out of life? What if Nancy wants to be a novelist and live in Los Angeles with her cat and a much-younger Portuguese lover for a companion? What if Kate wants to be a doctor or a fashion designer or an architect and let a nanny help her to raise her children?

Going forward, Jo will do what she needs to do in order to be a supportive wife for Bill because she loves him, she believes in him, and she believes in his career, but she'll also take a bigger piece of the pie for herself, because no matter what the world says about her station in life, her daughters are watching her every move. They're watching her actions and choices, they're taking notes, and she wants them to live exactly the lives they want to, *not* the lives that everyone else chooses for them.

And she'll bet dollars to donuts that they'll thank her for it someday.

SEVEN
bill

THE SHEER AMOUNT of equipment required for a launch is daunting. Bill is well accustomed to the accoutrements of war; he is a military man to his core, and the organizing, carrying, and use of the various parts of his uniform and military load are by now second nature to him. But as he and the other men stand in the center of yet another giant, open space in the Launch Operations Center, taking in the various tables laden with items that are of grave importance to an astronaut, he feels like a kid again, ready to start bootcamp and learn the ropes.

"And this, men, is the Primary Life Support Subsystem," Arvin North says. He has an unlit cigarette tucked behind one ear, and his thick-framed black glasses reflect the overhead lights as he looks at them with both hands on his hips. North has quickly become a huge part of their daily lives, and while Bill associates him with uncomfortable questions, he also sees Arvin North as an authority figure. And no matter what, Bill respects authority. "Your PLSS has the equipment and supplies that you will need to survive in space. I cannot stress enough how important this is."

North walks over to a table and lifts up a large, square pack. "This will hold your oxygen—an obvious necessity. This is what you breathe in during a spacewalk, and the oxygen will pressurize your suit. Each pack comes with a regulator that ensures proper pressurization." North picks up a small, square item and holds it aloft for the men to see. "This handy dandy little item will remove carbon dioxide as you exhale it. You need this." He sets it down and picks up a battery pack with wires coming out of both ends. "This is your electricity. You need this for the suit to work." North sets it down and picks up a small fan. "This will circulate the oxygen through your suit and life support system. Each of these items works in tandem and is integral to your success and to your survival." Arvin North walks around another table and sets both hands on top of two more items. "This is your water cooling apparatus—it flows through tubes known as 'umbilicals' that are connected to your suit, and this is your two-way radio for communication. Any questions?"

"Will we cover the procedures for repairing a pack while we're out there, and will we have a backup plan in the event that someone's pack malfunctions during a spacewalk?" Todd Roman asks, one hand halfway in the air like a Boy Scout asking a question about building a campsite.

Arvin North presses his lips together in a firm line, which Bill takes to mean that he's losing patience for simplistic questions like this. "Roman," he says to Todd, "we will cover so much information in the coming weeks and months that you'll be eating, dreaming, and leaking data about space and aeronautics from your ass every time you sit on the toilet. Got it?"

Todd gives a single nod and clenches his jaw; message received.

"Today I'd like to see each of you put together your own backpack according to the instructions on this piece of paper." North holds up a single sheet of paper with typewritten instructions. "You will each have your own table," he says, pointing at the five separate tables covered with the items he's just shown them. "And when I say go, you will assemble your packs. You have five minutes to complete the task. No one will finish in five minutes. When we've attempted it once, you will dismantle your pack, and we will start again. This exercise repeats until every one of you can put together a fully functioning Primary Life Support Subsystem in under five minutes."

Bill holds in a groan and forces his face to remain completely neutral. Timed drills have always been his personal specialty, but he gets the sense that they'll be running through this exercise a number of times before they manage to get it right. The men have just eaten lunch before this exercise, and while Bill attempts to keep his brain focused on the information being presented, he's having a bit of a drop in energy and could use a hot, black coffee to get through this.

"Find a table, any table," North shouts over the echoey din of the large room as the men speak to one another. "Get in position," he says, consulting a stopwatch that hangs on a black cord around his neck. "Ready, get set, GO!"

Bill pushes the need for caffeine and a ten minute break from his mind and quickly assesses the items on his table, checking them off mentally as he goes: *oxygen, fan, carbon dioxide, electricity, water cooler...*He looks at each item from all angles, comparing it to the sheet of paper that Arvin North has set on his table. It's a fairly easy puzzle to solve, connecting each item to another piece and attempting to fit it all snugly into the pack, but even still, the parts of the backpack are unfamiliar to him, so Bill falters once or twice.

As he's trying to connect the wires of his battery, Bill watches his own hands. They are steady, even. This is his strongest area: calm stability in the face of pressure or danger. He knows that there is no imminent threat, but even still, there is pressure to get the job done in a short amount of time.

Next to Bill, Ed Maxwell is bent over his own table, working quickly to assemble his pack. Bill notices that Ed's got his fan in at the wrong angle, but it's unclear whether or not helping one another is an acceptable move. Arvin North has said nothing about working together, and as Bill glances at Arvin, he sees that there is a slightly bemused, questioning look on North's face. *This is a test*, Bill thinks. *All of this is a test.*

"Maxwell," Bill barks in a confident tone, loud enough that Arvin

North will hear him clearly. "Turn that fan counterclockwise and slide it in the other way."

Ed glances up from the task at hand and looks at Bill with just the slightest trace of annoyance. Still, he rotates the fan, and it slips in easily. "Thanks," Ed says, moving on to the next item.

Bill chooses to keep working on his own pack and not to look back at Arvin North.

When the buzzer goes off, Bill, Ed, and Jay Reed have completed the task. Todd Roman and Vance Majors have not.

"Unpack the items and place them back on the table," North says, resetting his stopwatch. "We begin again in ten seconds." He stares at the stopwatch as the seconds tick away. "And...go!"

When five o'clock rolls around, the men are mentally drained. They've finally completed the task in under five minutes—all of them—and Bill's gone beyond the need for coffee to the need for a stiff drink.

"Let's hit the Black Hole, yeah?" Ed says as they all walk down the linoleum-tiled hallway of the Launch Operations Center that evening, lunch boxes in hand, egos checked by a day of doing and redoing the same task repeatedly.

The Black Hole is the bar right off the property, beachside and open-air to catch the breeze off the water. Bill has been there twice, and to be perfectly honest, he loves it.

"I'm in," Bill says, stopping at the front counter and leaning an elbow on it. "But I need to call home first and let Jo know I'll be late for dinner. Meet you guys there?"

Todd slips on his aviator sunglasses as they hit the front lobby with its tall ceilings and potted plants. "See you there, bud," he says, lifting one hand in the air as he pushes through the front door and out into the hot evening.

Two beautiful secretaries are bustling around and closing things up for the day. They smile at Bill.

"Help you, Lieutenant Colonel Booker?" one of them asks, looking up at him from beneath a fringe of darkly mascaraed lashes.

Her name is Debra, and she's got a pep to her that reminds Bill of the girl who led the cheer squad at his high school. He's heard more than one male employee in the lunch room commenting on Debra's assets and her smile with a knowing laugh, but she seems cheerfully oblivious to the fact that the guys think of her as the unofficial NASA pinup girl.

"Hi, Deb." Bill is still leaning on the counter. "Mind if I borrow your phone to call home and check in?"

Debra, a bottle blonde with smooth skin, an hourglass figure, and a penchant for a flipped bouffant hairdo and slim pencil skirts, smiles at him with her row of straight, pearly-white teeth. "Sure," she says in a breathy Marilyn Monroe voice. "Of course you can." Without taking her eyes from Bill, she pushes the heavy phone across the counter towards him and then walks away to retrieve her purse from the office space in the back.

"Jojo," Bills says when Jo answers. "Hi, hon. The guys want to stop off at the Black Hole for a beer—it's been a day, baby. Mind if I'm a little late for dinner? No, no. You don't have to hold things for me—just feed the kids. Okay. Sure. Love you." He hangs up the phone with a firm hand and pushes it back towards Debra's spot behind the counter. "Thanks, Deb!" Bill calls into the void. The front lobby has emptied out, as business hours are over. Night security will come in soon to man things, but the astronauts and the pretty front desk ladies are done for the day.

Debra comes out of the office with a purse dangling from one shoulder, and a thin cardigan draped over her tanned arm. "Headed to the Black Hole?" she asks conversationally, walking out the front door with Bill. He holds the door for her, admiring offhandedly the way her rear end swings from side to side as she walks.

"Sure. But just for one drink." He squints out at the lot to where his Corvette is parked. "Gotta get home for dinner with the family," he adds. He's just told Jo to go ahead and eat without him, but somehow it feels better to add the fact of his family into this conversation so that Debra doesn't think he has any nefarious intentions with her.

"Of course," Debra says with a smile. "You being a family man and all." She stops walking and stands next to a powder blue 1954 Ford Fairlane. With one hand held over her eyes to shield them from the bright sun, Debra smiles up at Bill, highlighting how much smaller and daintier she is than him. "I might stop by for a drink myself. I've got no one to get home to—aside from my roommate, Cathy, and she doesn't care when I get in."

Bill feels something—a familiar tug, a forgotten sense of promise or excitement—as he realizes that Debra has gone beyond simple friendliness and entered the realm of flirting. He squashes the feeling immediately. "Good on you," he says instead, walking to his car. "A career woman with her independence. Very admirable." Bill tips his imaginary hat to her, and then he turns towards his Corvette without another word.

He's pretty sure that he's leaving Debra standing there in the parking lot wondering if she's said something wrong, but he's also fairly certain that he's deterred her from showing up at the Black Hole that evening looking for witty banter or a free drink. A flirtation of any sort is simply a distraction that he does not need—nor does his marriage need it—and so Bill throws his briefcase onto the passenger seat of the Corvette, revs the engine, and pulls out of the lot without a single look back at Debra.

* * *

The Black Hole has a bar made of polished driftwood that looks like it's been slightly burned in a bonfire. The chairs and stools are all handmade and covered in naugahyde, and paper lanterns in a rainbow of colors hang from the ceiling and above the bar, swaying back and forth in the breeze that comes in off the water through the open walls.

"The ITEMS in this pack are THINGS you need to know INTI-

MATELY," Todd Roman is saying when Bill enters the bar. Todd is standing beside the table where the men are all slouched casually, nursing cold beers from bottles, or holding short, stout glasses of amber liquid. It's clear that Todd is mimicking Arvin North, and the other men hoot with laughter. Vance Majors slaps the table, one eye closed as he laughs heartily.

"Hoo, boy—that's some imitation," Ed says with glee.

Bill walks directly to the bar and orders a Carlsberg. With his beer in hand, he winds through the tables full of NASA employees, local pilots, and women wearing short skirts and bright smiles.

"Pull up a chair, Booker," Ed Maxwell says, reaching out and dragging an empty seat from another table without standing. He pats the chair. "Thanks for helping me out today. Didn't know we could work together on that project."

"I didn't either," Bill says, sitting down and leaning back with a sigh as he takes his first long, cold sip of beer. "But I figured we'd be working as a team in space, so it would benefit us to figure out how to do it with our feet still planted on Earth."

"Good thinking," Ed says, holding up his bottle of beer to tap against Bill's with a muted *clink*. "Hey, how was Sexy Deb?" Ed lifts his eyebrows as he watches Bill's face.

Bill does not smile. "I just borrowed her phone for a sec." This is not an answer to Ed's question, but, as policy, Bill refuses to engage in lowbrow talk. He was one of the few guys in the Air Force who would never shoot the bull about the women he'd been with, and it has always been his modus operandi to keep his private life private. No question. "Hey, don't you have to check in with Francesca after work?"

"Frankie?" Ed frowns. "Nah. She's got her own life. She's probably getting her hair done or having a drink with the girls."

Bill drinks his beer pensively. "What girls?"

"The other wives," Ed says with a shrug.

Bill glances at the men gathered around their table: Vance, Jay, and Todd all have wives and children, and the chance that their wives have gotten babysitters to go out for drinks at dinnertime with Francesca seems low. "Are you sure?" he asks.

Ed's easygoing smile slips a little. "Hey," he says, nudging Bill with his elbow. "Why are you so worried about my wife? Yours doesn't give you enough grief so you gotta start looking for some to borrow?"

Bill holds up a hand. "No, sorry. Not my business. You're right."

Ed visibly relaxes and takes another drink of his beer. "It's fine. I'm just stressed. It's like I need to stop off and have a beer on my way home if I'm going to handle whatever Frankie throws at me—you know what I mean?"

Bill nods to keep the peace, but in truth, he doesn't know what Ed means. He and Jo rarely fight; in a dozen years of marriage, they've not always seen eye-to-eye, but there are no tantrums with Jo. Sure, he usually knows where he stands when it comes to her opinions, but she's the kind of girl who rolls up her sleeves and gets things done. It's one of the things he's always loved most about his wife.

As the guys are sitting around the table dissecting the work day and discussing the intricacies of the backpack they'd spent the afternoon piecing together, a woman in a pastel pink dress walks across the bar and stops in front of the jukebox. She runs a bright red fingernail down the list of songs, finally dropping a dime in the slot and choosing "Big Girls Don't Cry" by Frankie Valli & The Four Seasons. Almost instantly, two other girls in cute, floral dresses join her in the little space in front of the jukebox, where they all start to do a loose, jiggly version of the Watusi. They are clearly at least one round of piña coladas into the evening.

"I think they're looking for dance partners," Vance Majors says, leaning over and slapping Ed on the thigh. "Get your tail out there and be a gentleman, Maxwell."

Ed laughs and shakes his head, putting his beer bottle to his lips. "Nah," he says. "Frankie will have my hide if word gets around that

I'm hanging out at the Black Hole after work and getting seduced by Cape Cookies. No sir."

Vance laughs at this. "I think I'll have one quick dance. No harm, no foul with that. Nobody is getting seduced—it's just dancing."

"Famous last words," Ed says with a smirk.

Vance stands up and sets his empty beer bottle on the table, then joins the three women by the jukebox. They part with cheerful surprise in their eyes, letting Vance dance his way into the center of their group.

"And on that note," Bill says, finishing his Carlsberg and setting the pint glass on the table firmly. "I think I'll say my goodbyes here. See you gents tomorrow." Bill stands and drops a dollar bill on the table for whoever ends up bussing the empties. The other guys are laughing heartily about something Arvin North said that morning, but Bill is ready to separate himself from all of it for the evening. Too many drinks loosen tongues, and they're essentially on NASA grounds; Bill wants no part in getting caught talking about the big boss behind his back.

Out in the parking lot Bill heaves a sigh of relief that the day is behind him. The knots in his shoulders have melted somewhat with the lubrication of the Carlsberg, and he knows that a dinner kept warm in the oven, and an evening with his family await him just a short drive away.

As he slides into the car with its top down, Bill can hear a whoop of laughter from inside the bar, and then the song changes to "Lovers Who Wander" by Dion. He shakes his head.

Bill guns his engine and lets it rev for a second before roaring out of the parking lot and onto A1A.

With the sun sunk low in a marigold sky, he pushes the pedal down hard and races towards home.

EIGHT
jo

THE MASTER BEDROOM is carpeted in a thick, gold shag, and the huge globe lamps on the walnut nightstands are made from a textured yellow glass. Jo sits beneath the covers on her side of the bed in her sleeveless nightgown, smoothing lotion on her hands and up her arms as Bill sets his watch down on the dresser, its face propped up so that he can see it as he passes by.

"You want to do what?" Bill turns to look at her. He's wearing a white t-shirt and boxer shorts to bed, as he normally does, and for a moment Jo is distracted by how good-looking he is. From the first time she saw her husband, she'd found him incredibly attractive, and now, in their thirties, she can see what a solid, distinguished man he's becoming. The lightest dusting of gray is starting to form at his temples, and there are lines at the corners of his eyes that can only be described as *handsome*.

"I want to volunteer at the Stardust Beach Hospital," Jo says, capping the lotion and setting it on her nightstand next to a copy of *The Feminine Mystique*, a new book by Betty Friedan that she'd stopped by the library that afternoon to check out at Carrie's insistence. It's been nearly two weeks since the day at Barbie's house when Jude had laid bare Jo's deepest fears—that the core reason for her existence is simply to benefit others; that she exists to be a wife and mother, but nothing more—and she's thought of little else since.

Bill frowns as he slides under the covers next to her. He looks tired. "Why do you want to give away your time for free when you have so much on your plate already? Help me understand."

Jo wiggles so that she's flat on her back, her soft brown hair fanned out across the crisp white pillow case. She takes a deep breath. "I want to do something that's just for me, Bill."

"But volunteering isn't for you—it's for the people you're volunteering to help, Jojo. That's the whole idea of volunteerism."

She shakes her head emphatically then turns her face back towards the ceiling so that she isn't looking at Bill. "No, it's not. You're missing the point. If I work at the hospital—"

"For free," Bill interjects, holding up a hand that she can see in her peripheral vision, "don't forget that part—you're working for free."

Annoyed, Jo presses on. "Anyway, if I'm volunteering at the hospital, I'm broadening my circle. I'm doing good works, but I'm also making myself a part of this community. I thought that's what you wanted me to do," she adds, reaching over to touch his hand. This part is somewhat calculated, but she knows that convincing Bill she's volunteering for the optics of it will be the tipping point for him. "To integrate myself. To meet people. To do things that will look good on our family resume."

Bill gives a little snort and Jo can feel him staring at her profile in the light of the bedside lamps. "Our *family resume*? What is that?"

Jo gives in and turns her head so that they're looking at one another from their respective pillows. "You know," she says with a slight roll of her eyes. "Our *dossier*. The way we're presenting ourselves to NASA and to the world as a family."

Bill squashes an amused grin. "I'm trying not to find this funny," he says. "But for some reason I do. Just the idea that there's a dossier on the Booker family from Minnesota. And that you'll somehow be raising our profile by changing bedpans in a hospital."

"Why?" Anger rises in Jo's chest, and she puts her arms over the top of the blanket and sheets, hugging the covers tightly against her body. "Why is it so funny to you that I want to reach for some sort of self-actualization, *William Booker*?"

Bill's eyebrows shoot up and the amused smile on his face vanishes. "Oh? We're going with the full name now? Okay. Then let's talk. Your self-actualization is important to me, *Josephine*, but so is the happiness of my family, and the success of my career, which—by the way—is why we're in Florida in the first place."

Jo turns her gaze back to the popcorn ceiling and pulls her arms across her body even more tightly. "Oh, believe me—I'm well aware of why we're here. And I *am* supportive, Bill. I always am. But there was little to no discussion about uprooting our lives and moving across the country. No one asked if this was okay with me, and I know that the kids are just children and therefore they go where we go, but no one asked them either."

Bill sits up and fluffs his pillow with angry punches before flopping back onto it again and reaching for the switch on his lamp to turn it off. "This discussion is ridiculous and fruitless," he says with finality. "We are here to live the kind of dream that almost any family in America would kill to live, Jo, and all you do is complain about it."

Unlike Bill, Jo sits up abruptly, knocking the blankets away. She looks at him in disbelief. "All I do is complain about it? Are you kidding me, Bill? I have made friends, I have the kids doing activities and meeting playmates, and I have been working on the house to make it nice for you," Jo says, ticking each item off on her fingers. "I took Barbie's advice and got a decorator to come in and make some suggestions—did you even notice the fabric swatches on the kitchen counter? I'm choosing new furniture on my own, because you don't seem to care about anything but rocketing off to the damn moon."

It's Bill's turn to sit up and turn to Jo incredulously. He's looking at her with wide, uncomprehending eyes. "Do not swear at me,

Josephine," he says, his eyes flashing at her. "I have more important things to occupy my mind with than whether we choose avocado suede or turquoise leather for the loveseat and barstools."

Jo huffs, folding her arms across her chest as she stares right back at Bill. "You're absent, Bill. Even when you're home with us, you're not really here. I can see it, and I think the kids can, too. It's not good."

"That's why *you* are here," he says, using his hands for emphasis. "And it's why you aren't a secretary in a dentist's office anymore, or volunteering at some hospital. You're here for our kids when I can't be."

Jo's eyes fill with hot tears; he's not hearing her at all.

"I know that. I love being a mother. Nothing makes me happier. And I love that you do things like swim with them, play catch with Jimmy, and let the girls chatter at you after a long day. But Bill, sometimes I need more, too. You leave the house all day and live this whole life that has nothing to do with us. All I'm asking for is a few hours a week where I push a cart from room to room in the maternity ward, offering magazines and snacks to new moms. I just want to be useful to people who I'm not *obligated* to be useful to."

Bill is quiet for a long moment as he assesses his wife's demeanor. Finally, he gives a single nod. "I hear you, Jo. I think you're probably reading too much of that Betsy Friendly," he says, raising his chin in the direction of the book on her nightstand. "But I'm trying to listen to what you're saying."

"*Betty Friedan*," Jo corrects him.

"Right. I think you're probably getting too much crazy talk from that book about how horrible women have it, but I respect the idea that you want to do something that you feel will make you more a part of the community. And, besides that," he says sheepishly, "it *will* look good on our 'family resume,' as you call it."

Jo says nothing, but keeps her eyes on Bill's face.

"So," he says with a sigh, turning his palms to the ceiling. "I guess if it makes you happy to be a candy striper, then I say go for it."

He falls back onto his pillow again and flips onto his side so that his back is to Jo, as if the conversation is finished. "But no more than five or six hours a week, alright?" he adds.

Jo reaches over and turns off the lamp reluctantly, re-situating herself on her pillow in the darkness. Through the slit between their heavy, brocaded curtains, an inch of moonlight pours into the bedroom and falls across the gold carpet.

Jo says nothing more to Bill, but she focuses on the light of the moon as she lets her mind wander. Soon enough, Bill's heavy breathing fills the room, and Jo drops into her own world of dreams.

* * *

"Well, hotdog, girl," Frankie says, exhaling a stream of smoke into the air. She's watching Jo from a seat at the kitchen table as Jo stands at her ironing board, smoothing the wrinkles from Bill's work shirts and hanging each one up on a rack when she's done. "Are you going to wear a little striped apron and cap?"

"I think that's for high school girls who volunteer, isn't it?" Jo says with a laugh.

"No, those are the Blue Teens." Frankie shakes her head. "They wear those cute blue pinafores. I think we'd actually be Gray Ladies now. My mom was a Gray Lady when I was a kid." Frankie takes a drag as her eyes follow Jo around the kitchen.

"Well, I'll wear whatever they want me to wear," Jo says as she picks up another wrinkled white shirt and spreads it across her trusty ironing board. Doing the laundry and filling Bill's closet with freshly pressed clothing each week has been one of her favorite rituals for the entirety of their marriage. There is no doubt in Jo's mind that she is a woman who enjoys domesticity and caring for her family, but the idea that her sense of purpose is now expanding excites her in a way that she can't quite express. "I'm just looking forward to doing something outside the house."

Frankie lays her cigarette at an angle in the heavy green glass ashtray that Jo's placed on the table for her. "I'm impressed, Joey-girl. I am."

"Hey, maybe you should join me? I bet they could use a few more volunteers at Stardust General."

Frankie lifts an eyebrow as she crosses her legs beneath the table. "I'm not sure I'm cut out for bedpans and bedsores, honey." She looks at Jo from under her penciled eyebrows. "I'm more of the 'organizing luncheons for charity' type of gal. So keep me in mind for something like that."

Jo nods as she presses the steam button on her iron and a puff of hot air hits the cotton shirt. "Noted."

"What are the kids going to do while you stripe the candy? Is there a daycare at the hospital or something?"

Jo frowns. "That's the rub. I'm still thinking that through. If I work a few afternoons a week, I can probably leave Nancy and Jimmy in charge of Kate. I don't know how much Bill will like that, though…" She walks over to find a hanger for the shirt she's just finished pressing. The whole ironing process is making the kitchen warmer than it should be, and Jo wipes the back of her hand across her sweaty brow.

"Hey," Frankie says, picking up her cigarette again and holding it in the air. "I might live to regret this, but why don't you let me watch them once a week? Let's just try it out," she says, amending her words quickly. "We'll give it a go, and if they like their old Aunt Frankie, then maybe we can keep it up."

Jo stops in the middle of the kitchen and stares at Frankie. One of the things she's come to love most about her new friend is the way Frankie approaches everything with zeal and amusement, but she has never really imagined "Aunt Frankie" as the babysitting type.

"Oh," Jo says, shaking her head slowly. "I don't know, Frankie… are you sure you're up for that?"

Frankie laughs throatily as she exhales again and then stands up. She walks to the sliding glass door and stares out at the backyard, with its placid turquoise pool, bright yellow patio furniture, and rich green grass. Two mid-sized palm trees dot the grounds. Frankie's back is to Jo as she looks out at the scene. "I'm up for it," she says, turning just her head to look at Jo. "I'm free, and you need someone to watch the kids. What's the biggie, Jo? This is what friends do for each other."

Jo nods, letting the idea warm inside of her. It *would* be nice knowing that the kids weren't left to fend for themselves, but she doesn't want to impose on Frankie in any way. Still, it *is* Frankie's suggestion...

She thinks it over for a moment and then smiles at her friend. "Okay," Jo says, "I would appreciate that so much, Frankie. And I promise they'll be on their best behavior."

Frankie laughs. "I have nieces and nephews, Jo. There's no question in my mind that they'll get into mischief and fight over the last cookie, but I'm prepared to play referee. No need to make any promises you can't keep." She winks.

Jo's first shift at Stardust General is three days later, and after much preparation, she's got the kids cleaned up and fully briefed on what she expects of them while she's gone.

"Now," Jo says, standing before her children in the living room. The kids are lined up like soldiers awaiting Frankie's arrival. "Frankie's word is the law while I'm gone. No television. No arguing. No tricking her into extra snacks." Jimmy makes a face at this. "No hiding from Frankie when she calls for you." Kate looks away guiltily. "And Jimmy and Nancy—I want you both to be nice to Kate." It's Nancy's turn to roll her eyes. "I'll be back by five o'clock, and we'll have dinner together when Daddy gets home at six. Understood?"

The children nod. Jo kisses each of them in turn.

"Good luck, Mommy," Kate says sweetly, running towards the hallway and her Barbie dolls, which are undoubtedly set up on her bedroom floor.

Jo lets Frankie in as soon as she knocks, and Frankie sweeps in, dropping her purse on the new couch. "Ooooh," Frankie says. "It just got delivered?" Jo nods, watching Frankie's face to see if she likes it.

Frankie runs a hand along the long, low orange velvet couch. Jo has also chosen a polished wood coffee table and two chairs that are upholstered with the same velvet as the couch. The whole set-up is slightly outside of Jo's comfort zone, but she's caught herself pausing to admire the furniture more than once. It's growing on her—slowly.

"Looks great, Jo." Frankie glances around with open admiration. "You're really making this place your own."

Jo beams. "Thank you. And thank you again for watching the kids. I'll be back by five," she says, consulting the narrow gold watch on her left wrist. "I need to get over there for orientation."

"Go, go." Frankie sweeps her away with both hands. "We've got this covered, don't we Nance?"

Nancy is standing near the record player, wide-eyed and clutching a library book to her chest. She nods as she watches Frankie with awe.

Jo is nervous as she backs down the driveway in her station wagon, looking both ways to make sure that no neighborhood kids are playing behind her car. She glides through her neighborhood, observing the people who are out walking, planting flowers, or watching their children ride bikes up and down the sidewalks.

As much as she resisted it at first, Jo has started to realize how comfortable it is to be living in a community where people know each other, rather than on a piece of property where you need to put on a coat and lace up your shoes just to walk to the end of the long driveway to check the mail. Now that she's here, she appreciates the convenience of having friends and their kids within walking distance, and the fact that she can run out to the store on a whim for butter or bread rather than having to save up her errands for a day when she's prepared to make a trip "into town." Even the relentless sunshine is bothering her less than it did when they first got to Florida.

At Stardust General Jo walks through the main entrance and

right up to the front desk. She's wearing a knee-length skirt and a light cardigan sweater with a pair of flat, comfortable shoes.

"Good afternoon," she says, smiling at the receptionist. "Josephine Booker, here to volunteer."

The woman points her in the direction of the elevators, and on the third floor Jo is greeted by a cheerful, plump woman who appears to be close to seventy.

"Mrs. Booker?" she says, smiling. "I'm Nurse Edwina, and I'm here to get you oriented." She looks Jo up and down. "You look good. The sweater will come in handy—it gets chilly sometimes."

In short order, Nurse Edwina walks Jo around the third floor, showing her the nurses' lounge, the supply closet where the wheeled trolley is stored, and she shows her how to load up the cart with books, magazines, snacks, and beverages. They work the first few rooms together, and Jo takes mental notes as she watches the way Edwina announces herself at the door to each room, walks in, greets the patient or patients, and just generally brightens things up as she goes.

"You think you can handle this now?" Nurse Edwina asks, pushing the trolley to Jo. "I think you can. You'll be a natural, Mrs. Booker." She smiles at her encouragingly, pats Jo's hand, and waddles back to the nurses' station.

At the first room, Jo wipes her sweaty palms on the front of her skirt and braces herself before knocking. She puts a smile on her face so that it seeps into her voice. "Good afternoon," she says cheerily, pushing the door open slightly. "My name is Jo, how are you?"

An older man is in the bed, the sheet pulled over him as he turns to look at Jo with curiosity. "I'm old, I'm in pain, and my wife and mother are already waiting for me on the other side." His crusty attitude softens as Jo steps into the room with her cart full of goodies. "But when a lovely lady appears before me, I mind being stuck here just a little bit less."

Jo can't help herself; she laughs. "Well, I'm glad my mere existence can brighten your day," she says. "I wish my husband and kids got this excited every time I walked into the room."

"They're damned fools if they don't," he roars, motioning to Jo with an arthritic hand. "Come in, come in. Jo, was it? Short for Josephine, I presume."

"Yes," Jo says. "It is. And you are?"

"Douglas Dandridge," the old man says. He's got to be close to ninety if he's a day. "But you can call me Doug, Dougie, Dandy, Mr. D—call me what you want, young lady, just don't call me late for dinner."

Jo laughs politely. Mr. Dandridge reminds her a bit of her own grandfather. "People call you Mr. D?"

"My students always did. I taught high school math for forty-six years. Retired down here with my wife, but she died within a year. I've spent the last twenty years trying not to acquire a second wife."

"Oh, my," Jo says, laughter bubbling out of her. "Hard to avoid the ladies, is it?"

Mr. Dandridge shrugs and peers at her cart. "You'd be surprised. At a certain age, the women outnumber the men, and they start competing for our affections. You wouldn't understand yet, my girl. For you, the world is still lousy with men." Doug talks loud, and Jo notices a hearing aid in one ear. "But someday they'll be dropping like flies, and you and the other ladies will find yourselves putting on lipstick and hanging around the shuffleboard courts, trying to find an old coot with a little spark left in his plug."

Jo can scarcely imagine herself being old and alone; it seems impossible to fathom, given how little time she has to herself these days. "I'm sorry to hear about your wife," she says.

"Tell me, Josephine." Doug sits up slightly and with some effort. "What does this husband who does not jump for joy every time you enter the room do for a living? Is he a busy man?"

Jo pulls a package of peanut butter crackers and a bottle of orange juice from her cart and sets them on Mr. Dandridge's bedside table. "He's training to be an astronaut. Before that, he was just Lieutenant Colonel Booker, but now he's aiming for the stratosphere."

"A man could do worse," Mr. Dandridge says, looking impressed. "Kind of beats the hell out of teaching calculus to teenagers as a career."

"Oh, no, not at all," Jo promises him. "I think teaching is a wonderful job. Honorable. And you never forget your favorite teachers."

"That's true," Mr. Dandridge muses. "I heard once that being someone's favorite teacher means you get to live forever. Even when you're long gone, you're still in someone's heart. I thought that was nice."

"That's a lovely sentiment." Jo pulls a selection of books and magazines from her cart that she thinks Mr. Dandridge might like. "Could I interest you in a novel or a magazine?" she offers, handing him a stack of *Time* magazines and two Western novels.

Mr. Dandridge looks at them with disinterest. "Eh," he says, motioning for Jo to come closer. She steps up to him and leans over the rail of his bed when he waves his hand for her to do so. "You got any romance novels on your cart there, Josephine?" he whispers. "Maybe one where the girl travels to France and meets a rakish gentleman? Falls in love?"

Jo's eyebrows shoot up, but she turns back to her cart and shuffles through the stack of paperbacks. "How about this one?" She hands him a Harlequin romance called *Doctor in the Tropics* with a blonde nurse on the cover. "It looks like she might get to travel and find love."

Mr. Dandridge takes the book in his shaky hand and passes back the magazines and Western novels. "I'll take it," he says. "And next time you come back I'll give you a full report on this particular piece of literature."

Jo laughs as she reorganizes her cart. "Okay, that sounds like a deal to me, Mr. D."

With a wave, she backs her trolley out of the room and continues down the hall, knocking on doors, introducing herself, and leaving cans of 7UP, little packages of cookies or crackers, and all kinds of reading materials with the patients. She has a great day. At the end of her three-hour shift, her feet are tired, and her cheeks hurt from smiling.

It feels good to do something unexpected. Driving away from Stardust General with a grin on her face, Jo rolls down the car window to let in the hot summer breeze. Florida isn't exactly home for her yet, but she's finding things that are hers and taking tentative steps to plant herself in the fertile ground of Stardust Beach. With a little care and watering, maybe her roots will extend into the ground here; maybe they'll take hold and spread.

Just maybe.

NINE

Jo

IT'S Sunday evening and the kids are in front of the television watching *The Ed Sullivan Show* while Jo cleans the kitchen and puts away the pots and pans that she's just washed by hand.

"I'm glad you're getting something out of volunteering, Jo, but the kids said Frankie took them to the theater to see *Cleopatra* the other day. Do you really think that's appropriate?" Bill is leaning against the counter with his arms folded across his chest.

"It's historical," Jo says defensively as she bends over to slide a heavy pot into a low cabinet. "And it's Elizabeth Taylor—she's a great actress." When Jo stands up and turns to face Bill, he's giving her a long, searching look.

"There are scenes in bed, far too much kissing for my taste, and I hear that Elizabeth Taylor brags about her sexual prowess. I really don't think that's the kind of thing our young children should be seeing."

Jo folds the dishtowel she's been using and hangs it over the handle of the oven before heaving a deep sigh and turning out the light over the kitchen sink. "I bet most of it went right over their heads," she says in a near whisper. "All I heard about was how glamorous Cleopatra was, and Jimmy loved the Battle of Actium scene. He talked about it all afternoon that day."

Bill shakes his head. "Look, I know she's your friend, but I'm just not sure that a thirty-year-old woman with no children who smokes two packs of cigarettes a day is the best babysitter for our children."

Now Jo has gone beyond mildly defensive to fully annoyed. "Frankie is a wonderful woman, Bill. I would never leave the kids with someone I didn't trust. They've had fun with her the few times she's watched them, and in case you haven't noticed, it's been an amazing experience for me so far at the hospital. Not that you've bothered to ask much about how it's going."

Jo walks across the kitchen and makes to turn off the light, which would leave Bill standing there in the dark.

"Jo," he says with a warning in his voice. She stops with her hand on the light switch. "Fine." Bill relents. "How is it going so far? Have you decided to go back to school and become a nurse yet?"

Jo spins back around on him angrily. She would have accepted his belated, solicited inquiry into her volunteerism, but the sarcastic question tacked on at the end takes it a step too far. "Maybe," she says with a tight jaw. "Maybe I *will* go to college and go into medicine. Who knows?"

Bill pushes away from the counter and walks over to Jo, taking her by the elbow. "Me. I know. You're not the type, Jo. You love being a mom," he says imploringly, looking down into her eyes. "You've never once told me you were unsatisfied with being my wife, or with being a mother to our children, and I don't think you are now. You're just...floundering a little."

"But I'm *not*." Jo shakes her head for emphasis. "I'm doing my best to find my footing here." She drops her voice so that the kids won't hear her over the sound of Ed Sullivan introducing his next guest. "I didn't want to move to Florida, Bill. You know that. This place isn't me. I mean, it's beautiful, and having a pool is exotic, but I don't know if I fit in here. I'm mountains, and picnics in the woods, and making my own dresses out of fabric I find on sale. And Florida is bikinis, and beaches, and eating lunch at the Neiman Marcus cafe while shopping for the latest fashions." Jo pauses, exasperated. She flaps her hands in the air and then lets them fall to her sides helplessly. "I'm a fish out of water here, Bill."

Bill's expression softens as he walks over to his wife, putting both hands on her waist. "Jojo, you're not a fish out of water. You are a wonderful, caring, sweet woman, and everyone who meets you sees that. You're already making friends here, and accomplishing good things. I'm proud of you."

Jo's stubborn attitude melts somewhat as Bill pulls her closer. He lowers his face so that their lips are just inches apart, and Jo relaxes into his arms. "Thank you," she says, growing inexplicably teary-eyed. "It's nice to be seen."

"I do see you. This has been—"

"Mommy?" Nancy calls from the front room. "Can we watch one more show?"

Bill shakes his head at Jo and whispers, "No, let's put them to bed and go up on the roof. You want to?"

Jo steps out of his grasp as Nancy pokes her head into the kitchen. "One more show, Mommy? Please?"

"No, sweetheart, not tonight. Dad and I are going to team up and get everyone into bed."

"Awww!" Jimmy calls out from the front room; the other two are clearly listening to see if there's any chance of more television. "Come on, Mom!"

Bill clears his throat. "No ifs, ands, or buts about it, amigos," he says in a gruff voice. "First one into pajamas with their teeth brushed gets to choose which parent tucks them in."

Jo smiles because Bill will be the one the kids angle to have as the parent who puts them to bed. She also knows he's done this on purpose, perhaps to give her a break from the bulk of the child-rearing duties for one evening, but also possibly to butter her up so that they don't turn out the lights and immediately fall asleep with their backs to one another, as they've been doing lately. While Bill shepherds and cajoles the children, Jo takes two bottles of beer out of the fridge and slips a bottle opener into the pocket of her skirt.

"I think we've done it, boss," Bill says twenty minutes later, after a whirlwind of giggles, toothpaste, and bedtime stories. "What do you say we make for the stars?"

Jo carries the beers, one in each hand, as she follows Bill out to the pool deck. He pulls a ladder from the side of the house and sets it against the ledge of the roof, then tests it to make sure it's stable. Bill holds the end of the ladder steady and takes the beers from Jo.

"Up you go, Mrs. Booker," he says, easily gripping the necks of both beer bottles in one hand as he holds the ladder with the other. He's got a handsome, impish grin on his face—it's the same one Jo fell in love with all those years ago, and it charms her still. She can't help but smile back at him as she mounts the ladder, holding on with both hands and carefully placing each flat-shoed foot on a rung before moving up to the next.

Going up on the roof together at night after the kids are in bed has long been a favorite thing for Jo and Bill, but they have yet to ascend to their roof here in Florida. This one is slightly pitched and has a different tile from their roof in Minnesota, so Jo looks around, trying to find a place to sit comfortably.

"Here," Bill says, his head appearing above the ladder. He hands her the beers. "Be right back."

A minute later he returns, handing Jo a heavy quilt. Bill climbs the rest of the way up and spreads the blanket out for them, then takes the beers so that Jo can fish the bottle opener from her skirt pocket. The bottle lids make a satisfying pop as Bill frees them, and they clink their beers together wordlessly, looking up at the clear sky above. It's mid-July, and the moon is full and bright.

"We came here for this," Bill says reverently, watching as the lights of the sky twinkle and dance above them. "Look right there."

He points at a spot off in the distance. "That's the Summer Triangle: Vega, Altair, and Deneb. This little trilogy is only visible on clear summer nights, and if you look really closely, you can see some of the other stars in their constellations. They're faint, but you've got Cygnus the Swan," Bill says, pointing at one corner of the Summer Triangle. "There's Aquila the Eagle, and over there is Lyra the Harp."

As always, Jo is dazzled by her husband's brilliance, and she wishes that she knew something, *anything*, as intimately as Bill knows the stars. Instead of speaking, she sips her beer slowly, not wanting to get dizzy while she's up on the roof.

"Everything might feel vast right now, Jojo, and home might seem far away," Bill says softly, "but when you look at the scope of the heavens, you realize that we're not that far from anyone we love."

Jo turns to look at her husband. His skin is smooth, but the curves of his jaw and cheekbones are sharp. "Do you miss it, too?" she asks, watching him carefully. "Do you miss Minnesota?"

Bill glances at her. "I do. I miss it. That's where the kids were born, and there's always comfort in what's familiar. But I can be at home anywhere, Jo—any place that allows me to be with you, Jim, Nancy, and Kate. That's all I've ever wanted," he says, shaking his head as he searches her eyes with his. "A family and a home. And you give me that."

Jo gets a twinge of guilt as he says this; she *wants* to feel the same, but it's simply taking longer for her to assimilate. She's always been a creature of habit, and leaving her parents and siblings and friends behind for this strange paradise has felt like a radical change. She swallows hard before speaking. "I know, Bill," she finally acquiesces. "Home is where we all are, and this is really a beautiful house. A wonderful community."

He's still watching her, looking hopeful as she speaks. "It is," he agrees.

"The other wives are all great. Well, Judith is proving to be a bit of a mystery," Jo says, biting her lip as she looks up at the Summer Triangle once again. "Bill," she says in a serious voice. "Last month, when we were at Carrie's house, I caught her pouring herself more vodka in the kitchen."

Bill frowns. "Pouring it...like, secretly?"

"Yes! I went into the kitchen and found her there. I think I startled her." It's Jo's turn to frown. "And then we had a slight disagreement another day when we were at Barbie's pool with all the kids. Or rather," Jo says, correcting herself as she fans her skirt out around her knees, "it wasn't so much a *disagreement*, as her telling me that our only purpose as women is to—oh, never mind." Jo waves a hand and wrinkles her nose slightly. "It was just women talking. I don't want to weigh you down with things that aren't worth repeating."

Bill is still watching her, but this time with a puzzled look. "Everything okay between you ladies?"

"Yes, absolutely," Jo says with a reassuring smile. "And now that I've been volunteering at the hospital for three or four weeks, I think I'm really hitting my stride. I won't say that I'm entirely at home yet, but I know where everything is in Stardust Beach, I have friends to meet up with, and when I go to the hospital, I feel useful and needed. I'm not as unhappy as I was, Bill." Jo reaches over and puts her hand on her husband's thigh, squeezing it as she watches his face. "I'm still homesick, and I wish like hell we were back home and camping at Clear Lake right now instead of melting in this humidity, but things are okay. I promise."

Bill visibly relaxes; the tension has been palpable since they arrived in May, and between his long hours at NASA and the physical distance between them in bed at night, Jo has felt increasingly as if she were living at the beach with a stranger. She closes her eyes and leans in closer, turning her face up to Bill's for a kiss, which he obliges. Their lips touch tenderly, and Jo feels something stir in her; she puts a hand to his cheek and deepens the kiss as the moonlight falls on their hair and skin.

Bill pulls away first, but not abruptly. Instead, he kisses her closed eyes, her forehead, her nose. "Did I tell you about the solar eclipse yesterday?" he asks with a boyish eagerness that makes Jo laugh as she accepts the kisses he's planting all over her face.

"It wasn't top secret, Bill," she says, amused. "In fact, you took us all out to the yard with those little glasses so we could look at it."

"No, I mean, did I tell you about the astronomers who chartered a DC-8 so that they could fly along the path of the eclipse up in the Northern Territory of Alaska? They got to see it for forty-four seconds longer than the rest of us knuckleheads here on the ground." He shakes his head. "I'm so jealous."

This makes Jo laugh even more. "When did you get to be such a space nut, sweetheart? Were you always like this?"

Bill looks at her incredulously. "Of course. From my first Air Force flight onwards, all I wanted to do was fly higher, faster, farther." His eyes look slightly glassy while he stares up at the stars, one arm now around Jo's shoulders as he holds her close. "I'm living my dream, Jojo."

The laughter inside of her dies down when she sees how serious Bill is. This is his dream. And Jude may not have been entirely right when she said that Jo's only purpose in life is to be a wife and a mother, but she was at least partly right: it's Jo's duty—it was in her vows, for heaven's sake—to love, honor, and cherish her husband, and that means to fully support him as well. To bolster him, and to help him achieve his dreams. She reaches over and brushes his hair across his forehead. "I love you, William Booker," she says, leaning closer and kissing him on the lips again. "I love you, and your dreams."

In response, Bill lays Jo on her back there atop the roof and kisses her slowly, moving down her throat and kissing her on the hollow of her neck. Jo sighs softly as Bill's nimble fingers work the top buttons of her blouse. She's tempted to sit up and look around to see if any of their neighbors are outside, but then Bill unzips the side of her skirt and she forgets entirely that they live in a neighborhood.

There, beneath the Summer Triangle on a hot July night, Bill makes Jo forget everything. All she can think of as the passion builds between them is the weight of her husband on her. The feeling of his arms. The solidness of *him*.

Jo closes her eyes and arches her back as she bathes in the moonlight.

TEN
bill

"THIS IS JEANIE FLORENCE." Arvin North is standing before the men, who are seated around the long, rectangular table in the same room where the psychological evaluation took place. "She is joining our team directly from MIT. Jeanie is an aerospace engineering technician, and she will be working closely with our team to prepare for space flight." North pauses and takes a long, sweeping look at the five men. In his gaze Bill can see that there is no room for even the slightest lifted eyebrow between the astronauts, so instead of catching the eye of Vance, Todd, Jay, or Ed, Bill looks at the paper on the table in front of him and picks up a pen, as if he might be about to take notes.

Arvin North cedes the floor to Jeanie, who—to her credit—makes eye contact with each of the men separately. She steps up to the green chalkboard hanging on the wall and picks up a piece of chalk. Without hesitation, she turns her back to them and begins to scrawl her name and job title in cursive, and it's then that Jay catches Ed's glance and they share a look that travels between one another and Jeanie's rounded behind, which is outlined in her slim pencil skirt. Bill notices this exchange, but then studiously goes back to looking at his paper.

"It's a pleasure to meet you gentlemen," Jeanie says, dropping the chalk in the tray and turning back to them as she brushes her hands against each other to release the chalk dust. She smiles at the group with just the slightest hint of hesitation. "Mr. North has given me a brief introduction, and I'd like to immediately address the obvious in order to dispel any rumors that might start amongst you: I am, in fact, a woman."

There is silence in the room for a full ten seconds, and then Vance laughs. "I was kind of thinking you might be," he says with a playful smile. "Thanks for clearing that up."

Jeanie puts her hands on her hips. "I've encountered more pushback than you can possibly imagine during my brief time in the world of engineering, but I want to be clear with you all up front that I've got what it takes to work with you. Mr. North has been extremely forward-thinking when it comes to selecting me for this team, but I understand that there can be—on occasion—some disbelief about women working in science." She lets her hands fall from her hips and her attitude shifts, her face softening. "I have spent my entire life looking up at the heavens and wondering what's out there. When I applied to MIT, the female students only accounted for about one to two percent of the entire population, so any jokes or comments you can think of are ones I've undoubtedly already heard. I'd like to ask you to treat me just as you would any other team members, and to put your faith in my work, just as I put mine in yours."

The room is silent, and Bill glances at Arvin North, who is standing off to the side of the chalkboard, arms folded over his stout chest. He's nodding at everything Jeanie says. "I assume that there will be no issues whatsoever," North says, addressing the men again. "If you have anything you'd like to discuss, my door is open. But my expectation is that we will work in lockstep as a team, and that there will be no issues." His tone leaves no room for misunderstanding: he expects them to put their nonsense aside and behave professionally, and Bill, for one, is ready to do that.

Jeanie is watching Arvin North as he speaks, and when he's done, she steps forward again. "I'm sure you all heard about the engineering test in Seattle this past weekend," she says, eyebrows lifted like a teacher who is waiting for her pupils to jump in and join the class discussion. "Five engineers at Boeing undertook what should have been a thirty-day test of the life support systems that would sustain a crewed space station. They were working in their space chamber, which was the first of its kind in the U.S. It included all the necessary life-support equipment that would have been required for a multi-person, long-duration mission." Jeanie looks around at the men, who are listening with interest; at this point, Bill starts jotting notes on his paper. "This project was built for NASA's Office of Advanced Research and Technology, and the crew simulated some very unique and specific problems of spaceflight. These issues included environmental control, waste disposal, food preparation, and how to address the personal hygiene needs of the crew."

Bill is watching Jeanie as she talks, as are the other men. She appears to be in her early to mid-twenties, with rich, chocolate brown hair and eyes, and her skin is rosy and untouched by makeup. Her round eyes are slightly magnified by the thick, tortoiseshell-framed glasses she's wearing, and her skirt is a plain navy blue, with a white blouse tucked into it neatly. It's simple and appropriate for work. Jeanie is clearly a beautiful girl, but unlike Debra at the front desk, Jeanie Florence looks freshly scrubbed, devoid of the time-consuming constraints of fashion and makeup, and as if perhaps she'd fallen asleep the night before with a physics textbook open on the bed next to her. Her schoolgirl charm combined with a brilliant mind makes her undeniably attractive.

"Unfortunately," Jeanie goes on, pacing back and forth in front of the chalkboard as Arvin North continues to watch her, "this weekend the test came to an abrupt end after only five days when the crew and engineers realized that they were working with a faulty reactor tank. This was obviously only a test situation, but it underscores the fact that we have light years to go when it comes to reaching our ultimate goal of sustained space travel." Bill glances at Jeanie's hands, which are now clasped lightly in front of her: no rings. He drags his eyes back to her face. "I am extremely honored to be amongst you all as we reach for the stars, and work toward someday having an international space station—a time when astronauts of both genders will be out there exploring the universe."

Jeanie is swept away to an office after this introduction, and the men are quickly engaged in a day-long training about aircraft flight readiness, broken up only by their daily one-hour Russian language class. Over lunch in the break room with its humming vending machines (tuna on white bread for Bill, with a shiny red apple and a thermos of chicken noodle soup), there are a few comments about Jeanie, but they're mild and mostly whispered.

Bill tries to focus on reading his copy of *The Florida Star*, folding the newspaper in half and tucking it beneath one corner of his lunchbox as he holds his sandwich.

"Cute *and* smart? She'll get nabbed by a recent college grad. Probably give birth to a few little future astronauts, and then forget all about being an engineer," Vance Majors predicts as he bites into a banana.

"I'd like her to tutor me in astrophysics," Ed says in a mocking, lecherous tone. "I wish my high school teachers had looked like her. I bet my grades would have been top-notch."

The other men laugh.

It's on the tip of Bill's tongue to defend Jeanie, to remind the other guys that a woman can be more than a teacher or a mother to future astronauts, but he himself isn't immune to thinking or saying the wrong thing on occasion, so he keeps his mouth shut and flips to the sports page.

"You think she'd like to join us at the Black Hole?" Ed goes on. "Maybe get to know the team on a more personal level?"

Bill scans the news, reading casually about the US Women's Golf Open that coincided with the solar eclipse the previous Saturday. Mary Mills won her first title by three strokes ahead of runners-up

Louise Suggs and Sandra Haynie. Jack Nicklaus won the PGA championship the next day, and the photo of him holding up a ball and his club, his sandy blonde hair loose in the breeze, dominates the page. By contrast, the column on the US Women's Golf Open is small and has no accompanying photo. Bill's brow furrows as he compares the two articles.

He's never been one to think too deeply about the differences between men and women—or the differences in their lives, for that matter—but raising two daughters has given him a whole new perspective on things. Bill wants nothing more than for Nancy and Kate to be able to do anything they want to do in life. He turns the sports page and finds a brief blurb about NASA's announcement the day before that Dr. George Mueller would succeed D. Brainerd Holmes as the head of the Apollo program, something he's already heard about.

Bill chews his tuna sandwich thoughtfully as he looks out the window at the midday sky. He's spent his entire life reaching for the next goal—the next thing he wants to achieve. He climbed the ranks in the Air Force, becoming a Lieutenant Colonel and flying the F-104, and the F-4 Phantom II. He wanted to be an astronaut, and he reached for that goal. He has a beautiful family, and a happy life, and never once has he been forced to choose between his own dreams and anything else. So why is it so hard to imagine that Nancy and Kate, or Jeanie Florence—or even Jo—should have the same right?

"Booker," Ed Maxwell says, slamming his metal lunchbox closed with a *clank*. "I'm hitting the latrine. Meet you back in there?"

The two men have been partnered up for an afternoon training session. Bill nods at him absently, turning back to his lunch. He shoves the last bite of sandwich into his mouth as he closes his own lunchbox and then takes the apple with him. The break room has emptied out as he sat there, thinking his own deep thoughts. Bill tosses his apple in the air and catches it in one hand just as Debra passes by the open door of the break room, flashing him a bright smile.

The thought that has been tickling his brain as he eats has gotten away like a butterfly escaping from a net, but a seed has been planted there nonetheless. He isn't sure about Jo and her crazy feminist books and ideas, but he *is* sure that she has the right to be happy and fulfilled.

* * *

Jo is waiting at home that evening with a pinched look around her eyes. She's dishing up a chicken and green bean casserole and pouring iced tea into glasses, but she is also clearly avoiding making eye contact with Bill.

"Hi, kiddos," he says, setting his briefcase down just inside the door from the garage. "How was your Monday?"

Jimmy is sorting through a stack of baseball cards, putting the most important ones to the side and reading the stats on each one as he goes. "Good," he says simply, not looking at his dad.

"I read a whole book this afternoon," Nancy boasts. "It was about a girl who went to stay with her grandparents all summer on their farm, and she became friends with a horse and a rabbit."

"Sounds like a great story, Nanny-goat," Bill says, reaching out to ruffle his middle child's hair. "How about Kate the Great?"

Kate tips her head to one side and looks up at the ceiling like she's sifting through a million things and choosing the most important items to share. "WELL," she says. "I played with my Barbies and then Mommy let me swim for a while and then I had to wash the cor-teen out of my hair," she says.

"*Chlorine*, ding-dong," Jimmy corrects his kid sister.

Kate rolls her eyes. "Whatever," she says. "And then I was going to ride my bike in the driveway but for some reason I laid on my bed and I just FELL ASLEEP," she adds dramatically, shrugging like it's one of the great mysteries of the universe.

"Wow," Bill says, still eyeing Jo and wondering what's eating at her. "I wish I would have gotten a midday nap."

"It wasn't a nap, Daddy," Kate insists. "I just closed my eyes and slept like it was night time."

"That's pretty much a nap," Jimmy says drily, still looking at his baseball cards.

"What's for dinner?" Bill asks Jo, though it's obvious at that point what they're having.

"Casserole and applesauce," she says, flicking a glance at the kids. "Go wash up, and put your baseball cards away, Jimmy," she says with a touch of impatience. "Dinner will get cold while I'm waiting on all of you."

Bill sits down in his chair and rests his elbows on the table. As soon as the kids are down the hall, washing up in their Jack-and-Jill bathroom, he clears his throat. "What's going on, JoJo?"

Jo picks up an envelope from the counter and walks it over to him, dropping it on the placemat in front of her husband without making eye contact. "You got a letter today from Desert Sage."

Bill's heart drops; the envelope is still sealed, but they both know that any correspondence from Desert Sage is going to be about his first wife, Margaret. He picks up the envelope and taps the edge of it against the tabletop. "I should open this later," he says.

Jo gives a single-shouldered shrug. "Whatever you think is best," she says with a touch of frost in her voice. Jo is possibly the most even-tempered woman Bill has ever known, but when she's got something stuck in her craw, it's not exactly a well-kept secret.

In general, Bill knows that the less said about Margaret, the better, but he also knows that the less said, the more likely Jo is to ice him out over the coming days. He sighs, accepting that he probably can't win this one.

"Or I can open it now," he says, feeling a hundred years older than he had when he walked in the door just minutes earlier.

Again, Jo shrugs just the one shoulder. "Do what you need to."

Bill slips a finger under the flap and opens the envelope, sliding the single sheet of paper out and unfolding it so that he can scan it quickly before the children come back to the table.

Dear Mr. Booker,

We are writing to inform you of your ex-wife's status, which you have requested that we do at any time if there are major changes. With the passing of her parents, you have agreed to be her next-of-kin, and though we understand that you and Margaret are no longer legally married, you are the only person she can count on in this world.

Bill pauses and rubs his eyes tiredly before reading on.

In the past week, Margaret has become something of a danger to herself and to the nurses on the ward. We have reassessed her needs, and determined that she will be better served by moving from the second floor up to the third floor, where patients are in locked rooms that have been prepared without anything that can be used for potential harm to self or others. This means no bedsheets, nothing with wires or blades, no bath tub, no windows that open to the outside. It may sound restrictive, but, Mr. Booker, this is absolutely necessary to ensure Margaret's safety.

With this increase in care will obviously come an increase in cost, and I am happy to speak to you about this over the phone so that you are aware what the change in monthly fees will be. Please call me at your earliest convenience so that we might get this worked out and agreed upon before the August bill comes due.

With best wishes for continued partnership in Margaret's care—

The kids come skittering back into the kitchen just as Bill finishes, and he shoves the letter back into the envelope, passing it surreptitiously to Jo as she walks by. He gives her a single nod, meaning that it's okay for her to read the letter, and so she steps into the living room as the kids take their seats, reads the letter, and returns with it tucked into the pocket of her apron.

"Well," Jo says with faux brightness as she takes her seat at the table. "Daddy is all caught up on the day." She turns a high-wattage smile towards Bill that he can tell is clearly not a true reflection of her mood. "So I think we should eat dinner here, and then after I clean up, I think he should do an evening swim with you guys again so that I can take a walk with Frankie and get some exercise."

The kids hoot and holler with joy as Jo surely knew that they would, and Bill catches her eye across the table. He knows from the look on her face that this is her way of saying she needs to process the letter and that they'll talk about it later once the kids are asleep. Making any sort of grumbling noises about her going out walking with Frankie will only exacerbate things, so Bill takes it all in stride.

"Good for you, Jojo," he says, accepting the bowl of applesauce that she passes. "Getting out there and walking in the evenings. You and Frankie are quite the duo."

Every word between them seems loaded with some sort of unspoken meaning. They had talked about Bill's feelings towards Frankie as a sitter for the kids while Jo volunteers at the hospital, but they'd tabled that discussion and not brought it up since. Digging that up now might only make things worse in the face of this issue with Margaret's care, and the increase in monthly fees that comes with it.

"Frankie and I do get along," Jo says with a tight smile. "Like birds of a feather."

The rest of dinner is just chitchat and listening to the kids talk about their new friends in the neighborhood, and Jo quickly washes the dishes and sets the kitchen right again before changing into shorts and Keds and a sleeveless shirt.

"I'll be back in a while," she says to Bill, kissing each of the kids in turn. "You three get to bed and don't give Dad any trouble, you hear?"

Bill watches as the front door closes behind his wife before rallying the troops for their evening swim.

ELEVEN

jo

THE SUN HAS VANISHED behind the trees but the stars aren't out yet when Jo meets Frankie at the end of the driveway. Instead of shorts, Frankie is wearing a long, loose caftan with bright orange and blue swirls. The tip of her cigarette glows as she inhales. She reaches up to push a stray piece of hair behind her ear; the rest of it is loosely clipped into a messy chignon. Frankie looks like she's been lounging around all afternoon, reading Mary McCarthy's *The Group* on the couch and drinking gin and tonics as she works her way through a pack of cigarettes.

Jo frowns at her. "You okay, Frankie?" she asks, stopping at the edge of the driveway as Frankie smokes but does not move.

Frankie tilts her head to one side. "Yeah," she says in an offhanded way, waving her cigarette around. "My monthly visitor showed up today. I'm just low on energy. How about you? You look like you've got a bee in your bonnet, and you sounded that way on the phone. Did Bill come home hot under the collar about that new woman engineer?"

Jo grabs Frankie by the elbow and starts dragging her down the block. "No," she says, puzzled. "What new woman? I thought only men worked at NASA. Except for the secretaries, of course."

Frankie tugs her arm from Jo's grasp and slows their pace, putting her cigarette to her lips again as she shrugs. "Beats me. Ed was just ranting over dinner about how this young girl is an engineer and how she got the floor today to introduce herself like she was some grown man with decades of experience. He thinks it's strange that Arvin North let her have so much control. Maybe she's his niece or something."

Jo stops walking. "Frankie," she says. "Maybe she's just a brilliant scientist. Maybe she has every bit as much right to be there as our husbands do. Maybe she's going to be a top-notch engineer."

Frankie exhales a stream of smoke as they pick back up their slow walking pace. "Or maybe she'll go into space with one of our husbands, closed up in a tiny rocket ship where they have to share oxygen and a bed."

Jo shakes her head. "I don't know. I don't think there'll be a woman in the space program anytime soon, and if there ever is, I'm sure they'll get their own beds."

Frankie looks unperturbed by the entire discussion. "I think there will be a woman on the moon."

They amble in silence for a minute or two as the sky fades from blue to lavender to plum, with a line of creamy golden orange hovering along the horizon. If there's one thing Jo can say for sure about Florida, it's that the sunsets here are top of the line.

"Can I tell you a secret?" Jo reaches for Frankie's cigarette, which Frankie gives her.

"Josephine Booker has secrets?" Frankie says with a smirk. "Wait, is this like your mom's secret apple pie recipe or something? Because I cook strictly out of the *Betty Crocker's Picture Cook Book,* and I only do that just barely." She takes her cigarette back.

Jo shakes her head, watching Frankie's face. She truly feels as though they've become friends over the past couple of months, and while they've spent more time on the phone, taking their evening walks, and hanging out in each other's kitchens than they have with any of the other women in their group, there's still a lot they don't know about each other. "No," Jo says, "it's a real secret. Although if I gave you any of my mother's best recipes, she'd tan my hide."

"Those Minnesota broads and their secret recipes." Frankie watches Jo with interest to see where she's going with this.

"Anyway," Jo says on a sigh. "I need you to promise me you won't tell anyone—not even Ed—what I'm about to tell you."

Frankie stops walking and leans against a Cadillac that's parked at the curb in front of a darkened house. She pulls a pack of cigarettes from the pocket of her caftan and lights a new one, passing it to Jo. Then she lights another for herself. "I promise," Frankie says. She keeps leaning against the car, with her eyes trained on Jo.

"Okay." Jo paces back and forth, smoking like a chimney. She's never told anyone about this—not even Sally and Genevieve, who have always been her closest friends. "Before Bill and I were married...he had another wife."

Frankie waits. "And what? Did he kill her or something?" She snorts at her own joke.

"No, he locked her up in a mental facility."

Frankie's laughter dies instantly. "Jo. What the hell?"

Jo scuffs her tennis shoe along the pavement, kicking the tire of the Cadillac gently with her toe. "Her name was Margaret—*is* Margaret," she corrects herself. "And they were high school sweethearts. They got married really young, and Margaret was always a little..." Jo lowers her voice to a whisper, as if the palm trees might overhear the discussion and spread it around the neighborhood. "She was always a little *crazy*."

"Aren't we all, honey." Frankie is smoking like her life depends on it as she watches Jo intently.

"So Bill and her parents put her in this home, and eventually he asked for a divorce. When we met, I was twenty and he was twenty-three, and we got engaged and married as soon as we could."

"And did Margaret agree to the divorce or is she, like...totally medicated and out of it?" Frankie looks awed.

Jo shrugs. "I'm not sure. I've never met her. She's in Arizona, which is where they grew up. Bill was stationed in Minneapolis at the Air Force base when I met him, and we lived there for our entire marriage until we came here. He doesn't talk about Margaret much. Actually, he doesn't talk about her at all, and I usually don't even think about the fact that he was married to someone before me."

Frankie gives a low whistle. She pushes away from the Cadillac when the front door of the house swings open and a man stands there, watching them.

"Evening," Jo says to the man with a wave and a half smile. She grabs onto Frankie again and starts walking, dragging Frankie with her once more.

"So why are you telling me this now? Did something happen? Did you guys fight about Margaret?"

"He got a letter from Desert Sage today—that's where Margaret lives—and they want more money. Apparently, she's become a danger and she needs a higher level of supervision."

"Jeez Louise, Jo." Frankie is totally animated now; she seems to have snapped out of the lazy funk she'd been in earlier. "I really didn't think you had anything juicy like this in your past."

Jo sits down on a curb and lets her head drop dejectedly. "I wouldn't say it's in *my* past, exactly—this is more Bill's secret, and therefore I probably shouldn't have told it, but it's definitely seeping into my life today, and now I can't stop thinking about this poor woman. She's probably locked up somewhere in Arizona in a room with no bedsheets, possibly scared and certainly confused." Jo looks up at Frankie, who is standing over her and looking at Jo with concern. "What if she asks for him? What if she doesn't remember that they're divorced? I've basically got someone else's husband, Frankie. I *stole* someone's husband."

Frankie sighs and sits on the curb next to Jo. "Honey, he's yours now. After a dozen years and three kids, he's definitely yours."

"I feel that way most of the time," Jo says. "I would say ninety-nine percent of the time I don't even remember that Bill was married to someone else before me, but then it comes crashing back, and I just have visions of him...with another woman. You know," she looks at Frankie pleadingly. "*With* another woman."

Frankie's eyebrows shoot up. "Oh. Right. Okay." She taps her cigarette pack against her hand. "I think I'm gonna need another smoke for this conversation."

"It's just...can you imagine, Frankie?" Jo drops her voice. "Picturing your husband with someone else—knowing he's been with another woman?" She gives an involuntary shudder. "I know a lot of men are more experienced than their wives, but I guess there was a part of me that always thought that whoever I married would be having their first time on our wedding night as well."

Frankie chokes on her smoke. "Oh, Jo," she splutters. She's laugh-coughing as she bends forward at the waist, putting her forehead against her knees while they sit there together. "Wait—was your wedding night your first time? Actually?"

Jo blinks at Frankie. "Of course." Realization dawns over Jo. "Wasn't it yours?"

Frankie stares back at her, looking like she's waiting for the punchline. "No, darling. No, no, *no*."

Jo flushes in the twilight. Her cigarette is long gone, so she has nothing to do with her hands, and instead wraps her arms around her shins. "It's just how I was raised, I guess." She averts her gaze. "I'm not judging you or anything."

"I'm not judging you either," Frankie volleys back, still chuckling as she takes a drag on her fresh cigarette.

The women sit in silence, their shoulders nearly touching. Two boys about Jimmy's age ride by on bikes with playing cards stuck in the spokes of their wheels. The *click-click* sound of their bikes fades off into the distance as the boys turn a corner together.

Jo is lost in thought; Frankie smokes and looks off into the distance. The notion that she and her new friend are from different worlds is not a new one to Jo, but she realizes as she sits there that

Frankie has had a whole wild life in New York City, while Jo has essentially just gone from her parents' house to her husband's house, and spent the intervening years raising kids. Meanwhile, Frankie has done interesting things, cavorting with actors and dancers, drinking in smoky bars, and—obviously—having sex with men she never married. While Frankie was dancing on Broadway, Jo was taking secretarial courses at Miss Smith's Typing School and then working at the front counter of the dentist's office. It had not occurred to her to let her prom date get past second base, nor did she even once consider taking things further with Bill before the wedding, though she understood that there was a whole school of thought surrounding the testing of sexual chemistry between two people before making a lifetime commitment. But the very idea of that had seemed completely foreign to her as a twenty-year-old—the kind of thing that other girls did, but that Jo never would.

"You know," Frankie says, finally breaking the silence between them. "It might be nice to never know anything different than being with Ed. But I also think I learned some important things about myself before I met him."

"Like what?" Jo turns her head and looks at Frankie, who smiles knowingly and taps the ash of her cigarette onto the pavement.

"Oh, like what pleases me. I knew some men who were, shall we say, not very interested in the satisfaction of the women they were with, and I discovered that I did not like that. I prefer a lover who takes his time. Someone who cares about me and about how I feel in bed."

Jo is about to say something, but the reality of her unworldliness is almost palpable to her. Instead of speaking, she just nods.

"I appreciate a man who appreciates me is all I'm saying," Frankie goes on. "And let me tell you, Josephine Booker, not all men appreciate women. Some are quite cruel. So if you have a man who loves you and kisses you and treats you like a whole person, then you are way ahead of the game."

Bill has never treated her any other way than what Frankie is describing, so again, Jo says nothing. The two boys on bikes circle the block once more, passing by Jo and Frankie without looking at them. It's after dark and Jo wouldn't like Jimmy out here on his bike at this time of night, but these aren't her children, so she lets it go.

"Anyhow," Frankie says, bumping Jo with her shoulder. "This is a bigger talk than either of us bargained for, but I still liked it. Most days I don't get to talk about anything *real* with anyone. I remember, in New York, I had three roommates, and sometimes we'd split a cheap bottle of wine and talk late into the night. Sometimes it got real like this, and I always fell asleep thinking how great it was to have girlfriends. I mean, men are nice and all, but women really *get* each other, you know?"

Jo nods. "I do know. I had some great friends in Minnesota, and I miss them." She thinks of the girls she'd grown up with; they'd been there for one another through the births of all their children, they'd shared secrets about nursing babies, about talking to their husbands, about fighting with siblings. But in all the years she'd been friends with Sally and Genevieve, they'd never peeled back the most intimate layers of their lives and talked like *this*, which makes Jo wonder whether they'd ever really known each other at all.

"Call them," Frankie says. "Or send a letter. Don't lose your old friends, but don't discount your new ones. In each stage of life, we need people who understand where we are. And right now, you and I are in the same place."

This makes perfect sense to Jo and she locks eyes with Frankie. "You are so right. This is a new and different stage. None of my old friends would understand this at all, but you do. You're here, and you get it."

Frankie shrugs and goes back to smoking in the dark. In the distance, a woman's voice shouts for Daniel and Paul, and Jo guesses that these are the boys on the bikes, because they do not ride by again.

"We both have husbands who want to travel into the unknown.

They have a dangerous passion, and we're on the world's stage watching them try to achieve their dreams. I get all of that—all five of us wives are in that same boat together. But beyond that, our lives are different, and that's okay."

"Yeah," Jo says, nodding slowly. "That is okay." She slings an arm around Frankie's shoulders and touches her head against her friend's for a moment. "I appreciate you."

"I appreciate you too, Joey-girl."

* * *

"So, how much is it? The increase?" Jo is back from her walk with Frankie, the kids are all in bed asleep (save for Nancy, who is most likely reading a mystery book under her blankets with a flashlight, something Jo pretends to ignore in the summertime when no one has to get up early for school), and Bill is flossing his teeth next to her in the master bathroom.

"I need to call tomorrow," Bill says. "You saw the same letter I did—there were no concrete details." He tugs his dental floss through his molars and leans in closer to the mirror to look at his teeth.

Jo smears cold cream over her entire face as she stands there in a pair of pink satin tap shorts and a matching tank top. They are both facing the mirror, and when they make eye contact with one another, it's through their reflections. "How much does it cost each month right now?" Jo is careful not to phrase it like *How much is it costing us*, because she knows that Bill earns the money and that Margaret is solely his responsibility, but certainly there is the feeling that the money comes out of their family budget.

Bill is running the floss between his lower front teeth when he glances at Jo in the mirror. "About thirteen hundred dollars."

Jo stops smearing the cream on her face and turns her whole body to face Bill. "Thirteen hundred *dollars*?"

Bill spits into the sink and reaches for his toothbrush. "I'm in charge of the funds her parents left her when they died, so between that and her welfare payment for being disabled, I only send a check for about five hundred dollars a month out of our account."

Jo is still breathless. "Five hundred dollars. *A month*." She feels as if her chest is heaving. "That's...so much money, Bill."

"Well, it's about to be more." He squeezes toothpaste onto his brush and runs it under the tap. "Right now she's overseen by nurses and they bring her meals to her room. A higher level of care will entail full-time oversight. I'll know more after I call Desert Sage tomorrow, Jo. There's no point worrying about it now."

Jo reaches for a washcloth and runs it under the warm water, looking into her own eyes in the mirror. She's been blithely volunteering and making dinner and taking her children to the library while her husband spends a good portion of his paycheck to support a woman in another state who will never again be able to support herself. A woman of thirty-five. A woman who might live another forty or fifty years. This thought actually *does* make Jo's heart palpitate. God forbid anything should happen to Bill; if he died, would she be responsible for Margaret's care? And if not her, then who?

Bill comes up behind her then, having brushed and rinsed and wiped his face on a hand towel. He puts his hands on her bare shoulders and leans down, pressing his lips to the warm crook of Jo's neck and kissing her there. She shrugs her shoulder to push him away—not because she dislikes his kisses, but because it tickles.

"I don't want you to worry about this, Jo. This is my problem, not yours."

"Bill," Jo says incredulously, wiping away the cold cream with her washcloth. "How can you say that? Anything that affects our family is definitely *our* problem. We're a team." She swallows hard and Bill remains where he is, hands on her shoulders. "Do you think I should get a job? I mean, one that pays? I could look for something that starts when the kids go back to school. Maybe the school needs a secretary—I could do that. Something to help out financially."

Bill's hands fall from her shoulders and he takes a step back.

"Jo," he says, his face serious. "No. Margaret's care is not for you to worry about. I appreciate your concern, but I don't want you to even consider that option. Aside from the fact that the kids are young, how would that look? I'm working for NASA, making plenty of money, and my wife takes a job answering telephones?" He shakes his head. "How would we even explain that to the kids?"

Jo scrubs at her face roughly with the washcloth. "They should know the truth anyway. Do you think it's reasonable for them to never know that their father was married to someone before their mother?"

Bill's jaw drops. He is aghast. "Jo. There is no reason for them to know that. It is not relevant, it does not apply to their lives, and frankly, I don't think it's any of their business." Without another word, Bill turns and walks out of the bathroom.

Jo tosses her washcloth into the laundry basket, flips off the bathroom light, and trails after him. "How can you say that?" She throws back the covers of their bed and climbs in next to her husband. "Our lives—who we are—is what makes them who *they* are."

Bill shakes his head firmly. "Wrong." He flops back onto his pillow angrily. "*Their* choices make them who they are."

Jo reaches for the hand cream on her nightstand and begins to rub it into her hands and elbows with vigor. "I disagree, Bill. I think they watch and learn from us. I think knowing who their parents are will help them become fully-formed people."

Bill huffs and reaches for the switch on his bedside lamp, clicking it off abruptly. "This discussion is over for now," he says, turning his back to Jo.

She sets the lotion on her nightstand and turns out her own light with resignation. Jo's frustration has given way to sadness as she lays there in the dark yet again, trying to fall asleep with an unresolved issue wedged in between her and Bill there in their bed. Since moving to Florida, they've spent more time at odds than they have in all the years of their marriage combined, and all Jo wants is for it to end.

Jo wants her husband back, and she wants to squelch the thought that he still belongs to someone else—some phantom woman who lives in Arizona—before the idea takes up residence in her heart.

TWELVE
bill

BILL MOVES through his day with thoughts of Jo in his mind. Well, of Jo and of Margaret, who he no longer thinks of as his wife, but he does think of as his responsibility. Their relationship—while a youthful one—had been passionate, and their bond was real. They'd come of age together in a small Arizona town, driving around the desert at night under a bright moon as they talked about seeing the world. When Margaret had agreed to be his wife, Bill was ecstatic. He'd wondered how one guy could get so lucky, how one simple eighteen-year-old kid with designs on a career in the Air Force could ever find a girl so pretty and so adventurous and so willing to be his. In Bill's eyes, Margaret was the total package.

And then things had gone south. At first, her moods had been charming, and he'd chalked them up to female tendencies: her jealousy, her need for constant reassurance. Things had calmed a bit during the preparations for their wedding, and Bill had secretly hoped that perhaps wearing his ring had given Margaret a sense of comfort that erased her need to give in to flashes of anger or despondency. And it had worked—for a while. Shortly after the wedding Margaret had gotten pregnant, and that shift in hormones had caused a wild ricocheting of her moods once again.

One day Bill would come home to find his pregnant bride stroking her growing belly with a beatific smile, singing lullabies to herself as she cut potatoes in the kitchen. The next day he might find her curled up, fully clothed and in the bathtub, crying about a dead bird she'd seen on a walk that morning. Sometimes he'd walk in to find her poised and ready to throw things at him (a tomato, a pillow, and once even a teacup, which had shattered upon hitting the doorframe, just narrowly missing his head), but Bill could hardly figure out what had angered her before her rage morphed into something else. More often than not, these bouts of anger dissolved into passion, and they'd find themselves coupling heatedly on the tile floor of their tiny kitchen, all but erasing whatever had come before.

But the baby...the baby had been the thing that destroyed Margaret. When she lost Violet (they'd called her that in hopeful anticipation, and then never spoken her name to one another again), Margaret had become a shell of her former self. At that point, Bill and Margaret's parents had come together and agreed that she needed more help than any of them could give. But it had broken Bill's heart to do it. Driving his young, scared wife to Desert Sage and checking her in was the first time that Bill had been confronted with life's fragility. No matter how strong he was, no matter how much he gave of himself, no matter how stoic he was in his life and in his job, the universe sometimes had other plans. He'd vowed then and there to hold himself to the highest standards, to keep his chin up, and to never let his guard down again—at least not entirely—just to make sure that nothing would ever again break his heart the way that leaving his wife at a lockdown facility had done.

"Booker," Arvin North says that afternoon, intercepting Bill as he carries a paper cup of coffee from one meeting room to another. "Speak to you for a moment?"

Bill follows North into a small office, ducking slightly—though it isn't necessary—when he walks through the doorway, which feels low. At six-foot-three, Bill is accustomed to being the tallest man in the room, but Arvin North can't be much more than five-foot-six, so Bill feels particularly oversized in his presence.

"Sit, sit," North says, flapping a hand at a chair across from his own. There is a wooden desk between them, and North sits, lacing his fingers together over his slightly rounded stomach as he leans back and assesses Bill. "I wanted to talk to you about Jeanie Florence."

Bill sits up straighter. "Sir?"

Without breaking eye contact, Arvin North speaks. "I've noticed—and I'd anticipated—some level of pushback from the men when I decided to bring a female engineer into our pod, but I think it's an important thing to do."

Bill, well-versed in the art of listening to his superiors without speaking, simply nods once.

"I did notice, however, that you were completely without a visible response when Jeanie came into the room. You listened to her without reacting, and I would imagine that you also refrained from making the kind of…perhaps inappropriate comments that the other men would have made over beers at the Black Hole."

"Sir," Bill says again, this time as an acknowledgement of Arvin North's words. On the wall above North's head is an industrial-looking clock whose secondhand sweeps smoothly as the seconds tick by.

"Jeanie Florence is a brilliant scientist," North goes on, hands still folded on his stomach. "Not to mention the fact that the future of NASA is here in front of us now. As a man of a certain age, I can tell you that I have spent many years in the workplace without women in skirts swishing around us—except maybe to drop off a fresh cup of coffee—but that's all changing, Booker. I have three daughters of my own, and I want them to have every opportunity that my son has. If they want to work at NASA, then I want them to work at NASA. Perhaps you feel the same way."

Bill holds his gaze steady until he's sure that North is ready for his response. "I do, sir. I have two little girls of my own. They're still pretty young, and I can't envision them going to the moon just yet, but I want them to do that if that's what they want. And a female scientist has just as much to offer as a male one, in my opinion." Bill stops talking, confident that he's gotten his message across.

"Good." North gives a single nod and pats his hands on his tidy desk. "I'm glad we're on the same page with this. I want to be sure that I can count on you to encourage the other men to treat Miss Florence with the utmost respect, and while the adjustment might take time, I'm confident that it will happen. Before we know it—although perhaps not during my tenure at NASA, given my age—this building will be split equally between men and women, and everyone will behave as though it was never any other way."

Bill isn't entirely sure that it will be as easy as North thinks it will be, but he doesn't disagree. Times are changing, and while female golfers might not get as much coverage as their male counterparts, Bill feels strongly that a wave of strength is building beneath the women he knows, and that whether he and his male contemporaries want to admit it or not, that wave will break sooner rather than later and bring massive change to every part of their lives.

"Thank you for speaking with me," North says. "You should head into the Russian lesson so you don't miss too much."

Bill stands up crisply and stands at attention for a moment; he's never entirely shaken off his tendencies towards military precision. He gives North a long look in parting before he turns and walks out, coffee still in hand.

* * *

The Black Hole is crawling with Cape Cookies that evening, and many of them are wearing skirts so abbreviated that they leave nothing to the imagination. Bill politely averts his gaze as they dance over by the jukebox, sipping drinks, and making flirtatious eye contact with every handsome young man in the bar.

"Who invited *her*?" Vance Majors nods at Jeanie Florence and another woman who is stuck to Jeanie's side like glue.

Bill lets his eyes linger on the women. They look out of place in a bar dominated by male astronauts and pilots. "I'm not sure if anyone did, Vance," he says drily. "I think bars are widely considered to be accessible to both genders."

"Funny." Vance gives a sarcastic bark and tips his beer back. "Who do you think the other broad is?"

Rather than answer, Bill sets his drink on the bar and cuts through the crowd without even looking at Vance again. When he reaches Jeanie and her friend, they stop talking to one another and look up at him almost reverently. "Bill Booker," he says, holding out a hand to Jeanie. "I was in the group you spoke to the other day."

Jeanie stares at him appraisingly before offering her own hand and giving Bill a surprisingly firm shake. "I know. Lieutenant Colonel William Booker. I know who all of you are."

Bill feels somewhat ashamed at this admission; Jeanie has obviously done her homework and she takes the men—and her job—seriously. He wishes he could say the same about his fellow astronauts. "Very impressive education you've had, Miss Florence."

"Please—Jeanie," she says, a tentative smile spreading across her face. *She looks so young and hesitant*, Bill thinks. "This is Eleanore Welter," Jeanie says, turning to her friend. "She's been working for NASA in Houston for the past three years, and they've just transferred her here."

Eleanore holds out a hand and gives Bill a similarly impressive handshake. "Nice to meet you, Lieutenant Colonel," she says in a surprisingly gruff voice.

"Call me Bill," he says to both young women. "And please come join us for a drink. I know that fraternizing between the sexes in the workplace can come as naturally as a bunch of boys and girls mingling at a middle school dance, but I think we're all reasonably smart, accomplished adults. We can do this."

The women laugh—albeit somewhat nervously—but Jeanie does not hesitate. "We'd love to," she says, holding her chin high.

Bill takes a deep breath and leads them back across the bar, making a silent prayer that Vance, Ed, Todd, and Jay will be on their best behavior.

As Bill makes the introductions, he realizes that the men are at least partially fascinated by having women in the mix of their daily work lives, and perhaps the rest of their attitude comes from being uncertain about how the women will react to them. In a sense, it does feel *a bit* like a middle school dance, but Bill heads back to the bar and orders another round of beers, which he carries over on a tray and passes around.

As the evening winds on, everyone relaxes. There is laughter, there are questions and answers, and there is even a short debate about music, which ends when Ed squires Eleanore over to the jukebox and they each choose a song to see which gets the most favorable response from the rest of the bar patrons. Through it all, Bill finds his eye traveling to wherever Jeanie is, gauging her comfort level, her joy, or her amusement at whatever is happening or being said. Rather than seeing this as a red flag, he lets himself be entertained by her curiosity and happiness, and when he catches her eyes dancing as she laughs at something Jay is saying, a smile spreads across his own face. In a way, he feels as though he's simply done what Arvin North has asked him to do: he's shown the other guys how to behave like gentlemen, and how to break down the barriers and misconceptions between the sexes. Maybe Jo would even be proud of him for this little feat of social engineering. She's been so tetchy lately, and so defensive of womanhood, that perhaps she might find this olive branch that he's extended towards his female coworkers to be a kindness.

But as Bill watches Jeanie sip her second beer, tossing her long hair over one shoulder and pushing her glasses up her small, cute, freckled nose, he knows that Jo will not see this in the same light as he's attempting to cast his actions. She will not find it charming, sweet, or generous. She will find it suspect.

And as Bill's heart does a weird fluttery thing in his chest, he understands on a visceral level that Jo would be right not to see this as entirely innocent. He has done nothing wrong, but his head and his heart are giving off flashing warning lights and whistles to let him know that he's in uncharted territory and that a storm is approaching.

Bill finds somewhere else to look while he finishes his beer, and then he says his goodbyes and heads home, appropriately sobered by this realization.

THIRTEEN

jo

"GOOD MORNING, MR. D," Jo says to Douglas Dandridge as she wheels her cart into his hospital room on a rainy August afternoon.

Douglas is staring at the threatening clouds gathered outside his window. "It took me some time, Josephine," he says without turning to look at her directly, "but I've come to love these summer storms in Florida. They really clear the air, don't they?"

Jo has to agree with him: they do clear the air, leaving behind a freshness for a short while, and sometimes clearing out just in time for the bruised but hopeful evening sky to dissolve into sunset.

"How are you today?" Jo asks him, choosing two novels from her cart and setting them on his bedside table. In the time that Jo has known Douglas Dandridge, he's worked through at least three or four Harlequin romance novels a week, and he's showed no sign of slowing down. In fact, the hospital cart has run out of books for him, so she's taken to asking her friends if they have any he can borrow, and she slides them onto his nightstand without letting him know that she's had to seek them out on her own time.

Douglas finally turns to look at her, and Jo gasps at the sight of his forehead. "What happened?" she asks, rushing over to him with one hand outstretched. She stops short of gently touching the deep purple bruise over his eye.

Mr. Dandridge puts his own shaky hand to the knot that's formed there, and Jo notices a string of stitches over his eye. "I fell," he says simply. "It's not unheard of for a man my age, you know."

Jo pulls up the chair next to his bed and sits on it as she reaches for his hand and clasps it between both of her own. In the past two months, she and Mr. Dandridge have become fast friends, and seeing him like this brings a sharp pain to Jo's heart. "How did you fall? Was the nurse here? Did you slip in the shower?"

Douglas chuckles and squeezes Jo's hand with his long, cool fingers. "Don't you worry for a minute, Josephine. I'm fine. I got out of bed one evening thinking I could make it to the bathroom on my own, and lo and behold, I could not." He laughs again, but this time it's tinged with embarrassment. "Some things about being an old man are not so wonderful," he says with a little shrug.

Jo smiles at him sympathetically. "Promise me you'll call for the nurse next time, will you?"

He's about to respond when there's a knock at the door of his room. Jo turns in her chair and sees an unfamiliar doctor in a white coat standing there. Her first instinct is to jump up and retrieve her cart, as she feels like she's just been caught sitting down on the job, but Douglas does not let go of her hand.

"Hello, Mr. Dandridge," the doctor says with a wide smile and a Latin accent. He turns to Jo with a puzzled smile when he sees the familiarity between her and Douglas. "I'm sorry, I didn't know Mr. Dandridge had family visiting."

Jo pats Douglas's hand and stands up, smoothing down her skirt with both hands. "I'm Josephine Booker," she says. "I'm actually a volunteer, but Mr. Dandridge is one of my favorite people here."

The doctor's smile widens. "He's everybody's favorite. I'm Dr. Chavez," he says, extending a hand to Jo. "I'm new to Stardust General, but I've already become a big fan of this guy." He tips his head at Douglas, who makes a *pshhh* sound and waves a hand at the doctor. "He acts like he doesn't like me much, but let me tell you: when no one else is here, we can talk baseball for hours."

"My son is a baseball nut, too," Jo says as she looks back and forth between the two men. "He's dying to go to New York and see the Yankees play."

"I can understand that," says Dr. Chavez. "Seeing the Yankees play is truly an all-American thing to do."

There is a brief silence in the room and Jo gathers herself, realizing that Dr. Chavez most likely wants to check up on Mr. Dandridge or ask him some personal medical questions. "I should move along," Jo says, taking her cart by the handle and steering it toward the door. "I'll see you Thursday, Mr. D," she says to Douglas, turning back to him regretfully. "No more falling down, you hear?"

"I hear you, Josephine," he says, shaking his head as though he's put out by her words, but from the look on his face, Jo can tell that he loves having someone worry about him. "Take good care of those kids."

With a wave at Mr. Dandridge and a nod and a smile for Dr. Chavez, Jo pushes her cart out into the hallway. She's about to knock on the next door when she hears Douglas chastising Dr. Chavez. "You just had to butt in and scare off the only pretty girl who comes to see me, didn't you?"

Dr. Chavez's booming laugh echoes out into the hallway, and Jo smiles as she blushes. She enjoys Douglas's company, too.

Jo finishes visiting the last rooms in the hallway and is making her way towards the elevator when Dr. Chavez spots her and lifts a hand for her to wait.

"Mrs. Booker," he says, his eyes landing on her left hand ever so briefly to confirm that there's a ring there. He looks back at her. "Thank you for taking the time to sit with Mr. Dandridge. I think it really makes a difference in his care to have someone he looks forward to seeing. As far as I know, he's entirely without family here, and I truly think you brighten his spirits."

Jo's cheeks get hot again and she looks down at the neat rows of books on the top shelf of her cart. "Well, I enjoy visiting with him—and working here. Or, rather, volunteering. I know I don't *work* here. Not for a paycheck anyway. Not like a real nurse or a doctor." Jo can hear herself stammering nervously. To her own ears she sounds like a moronic nitwit, and she bites her bottom lip to keep any more words from tumbling out.

Dr. Chavez smiles kindly. "Make no mistake: you work here. Spending time with patients in a non-medical capacity is just as important to their overall care as a nurse coming in and taking their stats, or a doctor doing a progress check. When Mr. Dandridge—and, I presume, everyone else on the ward—sees you walk into the room, they undoubtedly experience some very positive feelings and physical responses."

"Oh," Jo says. She's entirely flattered and far too flustered for her own liking. "Thank you. I just bring books and snacks."

"You bring hope, friendship, a friendly smile, and, for some of them, the only news they get from the outside world. Don't discount that, Mrs. Booker."

"Call me Jo," she says, knotting her hands together nervously. "And thank you. It's nice to be appreciated."

Dr. Chavez watches her with open curiosity. He has dark black hair with bits of silver shot through at the temples and his dark brown eyes are framed by friendly-looking crow's feet that crinkle every time he smiles. Jo can tell from the butterflies in her stomach that she actually finds Dr. Chavez quite handsome, though she doesn't often have this kind of physical response to men anymore; it's been years since she's had a giddy crush on anyone other than Bill.

As if he's just realizing how much time he's spending talking to a hospital volunteer, Dr. Chavez takes a step back and gives Jo a friendly nod. "I'll see you around, Jo," he says with a twinkle in his eyes. "It's been a pleasure meeting you."

"Thank you. You as well, Dr. Chavez." Jo punches the button for the elevator and the doors slide open instantly. She backs up into the elevator, pulling the cart with her. The doors close on Dr. Chavez, who is standing there with both hands in the pockets of his white lab coat.

As soon as she begins to descend to the floor below, Jo catches a glimpse of her own reflection in the mirrored doors in front of her. Her cheeks are pink like she's just gone for a brisk evening walk with Frankie, and her eyes are shining with something that looks suspiciously like happiness. Of course she's worried about Mr. Dandridge getting out of bed and falling and needing stitches, but as the doors slide open once again and she pushes the cart back out into a new hallway, she straightens her shoulders with purpose. A doctor—and a handsome, gregarious, friendly one at that—has recognized her for something good. It's very validating.

Aside from being with the children, or taking walks with Frankie at twilight, Stardust General has become Jo's favorite place to be. For the rest of the afternoon, she smiles at everyone she passes, glowing with pleasure over finding something that she's good at. Something that makes her feel useful. Something that feels distinctly like a step on the path to finding out who she truly is.

* * *

"Mr. Huggins—please, come in." Jo steps aside as she opens her front door the next morning. David Huggins, the official NASA photographer, has requested a day where he can drop in on each of the five families to take some candid shots of their mornings. From the kitchen, the children can be heard talking about an episode of *The Bugs Bunny Show* as they pour milk into their cereal bowls.

"Thank you for having me," Dave says, stepping into her open living space and looking around. Jo had spent the evening before dusting, vacuuming, and otherwise preparing the house to be photographed, though Bill had assured her more than once that everything looked just fine. Dave Huggins sets his camera on the couch and puts both hands on his hips as he looks around. "Love what you've done with the place."

Jo tries to look at the house through objective eyes: the furniture now is modern and airy, and the colors she's chosen have the fresh, juicy feeling of citrus. The sunlight from the slanted skylight pours in, bathing the jade plants and the African violets near the windowsill in morning sunshine.

"Thank you," she says. "Bill is about to leave for work, but we thought maybe you'd want some shots of us all having breakfast together?" Jo clasps her hands in front of her, trying to hide how nervous she feels about having her life and her family photographed for public consumption.

"I want to capture some truly candid moments, so please just go about your morning as you would if I wasn't here at all." Dave turns to his camera and begins to fuss with the buttons and switches.

It's like she's on stage, performing her life for a live audience, but Jo tries to push that thought aside and act normally. "Honey," she says to Bill, approaching him with a pot of coffee as he sits at the head of the table. "Coffee?" It both sounds and feels stilted, but Jo wants her family to make a good impression.

Bill holds out his coffee cup and she fills it before filling her own and sitting down. A big family breakfast is an activity usually reserved for the weekends, but Bill had agreed that they should get up early and make themselves more camera-ready for Dave Huggins than they normally would be. In fact, Jo was accustomed to pouring coffee and packing Bill's lunch while wearing a robe over her nightgown, then kissing him goodbye at the door before going to wake the children for the day. But there is something nice about having everyone up and dressed before eight o'clock. It feels organized. Productive.

"So, what are you all up to today?" Bill asks, setting a napkin on his thigh as he reaches for a piece of buttered toast from the plate that Jo has set on the table.

"Beach," Kate says decisively. "Mommy said she would take us there for a picnic because she doesn't have to go to the hospital today."

"Oh," Dave Huggins says. His voice is somewhat jarring in the middle of their family breakfast even though they are, of course, aware of his presence. "I wanted to come to the hospital with you for one of your shifts and get some footage of your good works there, if that's alright."

Jo smiles nervously, holding a piece of toast over her plate. "Oh," she says, trying to look unbothered by the idea of having to explain why a photographer is following her around Stardust General. Thus far, she's been able to get by without sharing much detail about her personal life, but she fears that her days as a quiet, mild-mannered volunteer are about to end. "Of course. I can arrange that. I have a shift tomorrow afternoon, if that works."

"That would be great, wouldn't it, Jojo?" Bill says encouragingly, looking at Jo with a kind of goofy pride. He's done a night-and-day turnaround when it comes to her volunteerism, packing away any of his prior reticence as he's come to realize how good the hospital has been for Jo, and—as she'd predicted—how good it looks to NASA for his wife to be integrating herself into the community in this way.

Jo chews her toast slowly and then takes a sip of coffee. "It would be great," she says carefully. "I'll just need to let my supervising nurse know so that no one is surprised."

"Actually," Dave says, moving his camera away from his face so that he's looking at Jo. "I already called the hospital and explained the situation, and I've gotten clearance to be there."

He at least has the common sense to look slightly chagrined at stepping into Jo's life without permission, but she pushes down her annoyance and puts a cheerful smile on her face. "That's wonderful."

The rest of breakfast is easy and lighthearted, and the children do most of the talking as Dave Huggins walks around, taking photos of them laughing and smiling from all angles. He packs up his camera after Bill leaves for work, thanking Jo and leaving to do the same thing at Frankie and Ed's house, minus the children.

Jo slips her feet out of her flat shoes as she cleans up the breakfast dishes. The children sit under a tree in the backyard, just beyond the kitchen window. She knows they're talking about ways to convince Jo and Bill to get them a dog, but she's been pretending for days not to know what they're scheming and planning. Jo doesn't have the heart to tell them that she isn't sure she's ready for that kind of commitment, because no matter how much they promise to do the lion's share of the work when it comes to walking, feeding, and cleaning up after a pet, Jo harbors no illusions about who will truly be on the hook for the heavy lifting when it comes to dog care.

She rinses the platter that held the scrambled eggs, setting it on the drying rack as she watches her children through the window over the sink. Kate jumps up from her spot on the grass, gesticulating wildly. She's doing the majority of the talking while her older brother and sister listen. This makes Jo smile, as her youngest is a born leader and a true charmer. She has no doubt that Kate will do great things in life: she could be a teacher or a politician or a business owner...anything, really. Jo mourns the limitless possibilities of youth as she watches her kids' faces turn pink and shiny from the August heat. Even being young enough that physical discomfort doesn't matter when you're in the midst of playing or talking or doing something interesting—she misses all of it. There's a beauty to still having the story of your life mostly unwritten.

The phone on the wall rings just as Jo is wiping her hands on a dishtowel and admiring her sparkling clean kitchen. She unclips an earring and sets it on the counter, holding the receiver to her ear.

"Good morning, Booker residence," she says without curiosity. It will undoubtedly be the hospital calling to ask her to take a different shift, or maybe Frankie wanting to complain about Dave Huggins not catching her in the best light as he snapped her and Ed sharing a pot of coffee and the newspaper on their living room couch, or perhaps even one of the other wives, looking to have a get-together with the children.

"Good morning," a crisply efficient woman says. "May I please speak to Mr. William Booker?"

"I'm sorry, Mr. Booker is at work. This is his wife, may I help you?" Jo frowns. This woman on the phone sounds official. Busy. Serious.

"This is May Ogilvy from Desert Sage in Tucson, Arizona," the woman says. "I really do need to speak with Mr. Booker directly. Is there a time when I might call back and reach him, or is there perhaps a work number I could call?"

A wave of something rises inside of Jo; it's not anger, and it's not frustration, but it's something that is almost tangible. "Mr. Booker arrives home at six o'clock," Jo says formally. "You may try to call him again then."

Because they have plans that night, Jo knows that Bill will actually walk in at six o'clock rather than stopping at the Black Hole for a beer, and sure enough, the garage door opens and closes just when she expects it to. Bill walks in and sets down his briefcase, just as he does every day, and the kids come rushing in to greet him.

"You should have a phone call coming here soon," Jo says. The smell of fried chicken fills the kitchen and she tosses a green salad with a wooden spoon and fork.

Bill gives her a puzzled look. "From whom?"

Kate and Nancy have been arguing all afternoon about a dress that Nancy has outgrown and that Kate wants to wear, and Jo has very little patience left in her at the moment. They've got a babysitter arriving in an hour to watch the kids, and she really needs to get everyone seated and started on dinner. Jo blows her hair off her forehead impatiently. "May Ogilvy from Desert Sage."

It's almost as if her words summon the ringing of the phone, and Bill reaches for it, plucking the receiver off the wall.

"Yes," he says. "This is Bill Booker. I see. Yes. Thank you. I can handle that tomorrow. Thank you for letting me know. Of course. I'll do that. Thank you." He hangs up after this short exchange.

Jo busies herself with setting the table. She is quite literally biting the tip of her tongue to keep from asking questions, though she certainly has them.

The topic of Margaret's more expensive care has not come up again since the night they'd gone to bed in silence, and Jo is not eager to go into the evening ahead with this sitting between them. She sighs as she washes her hands at the kitchen sink. "Is everything okay?"

Bill pulls out his chair distractedly and sits. He doesn't even take off his tie or unbutton his short-sleeved shirt. Bill sets a napkin in his lap as the kids sit down gloomily, the residue of their day-long battle over the stupid yellow dress still hanging over their heads like a storm cloud. Without looking at Jo, he clears his throat. "I need to make a trip to Arizona," he says brusquely. And then, without further comment: "Jimmy, please pass the corn on the cob."

They eat dinner in relative silence, and Jo's mood is further aggravated by the fact that she's been battling menstrual cramps and moodiness all afternoon. She stabs her fork into her pile of salad and glowers first at Bill, and then at the girls. Jimmy is the only one of them with whom she has no quibble at the moment, and he eats his fried chicken lustily, seemingly oblivious to his sisters' drama, his father's dark frown, and his mother's raging hormonal storm.

The evening ahead promises to be a fun one.

* * *

"Can we get through this as a team?" Bill asks as he swings the Corvette into the lot of the bowling alley, where a bright neon sign advertises twenty-five cent games on Thursday nights. The sun has almost set, and the palm trees outside the bowling alley stand against the watercolor painting of a sky. Jo puts her hand on the door and stares out the windshield. In the parking spot next to theirs, Carrie and Jay close the doors of their car and interlace their fingers as they walk towards the building. Jo can only dream of being that in tune with Bill again; at one point, every day felt that easy between them, with stolen kisses, hand-holding, and being on the same page about things.

Jo turns her head and looks at him directly. "Of course we can. We're a team, Bill. Always. But I need to know why you're going to Arizona."

He lets out a loud, impatient exhale and bangs his palms against the steering wheel. "Dammit, Jo. Isn't it obvious? Margaret. Things are a mess out there, and I need to get it sorted out so that she can stay on at Desert Sage. If I don't, they're going to ask for her to be moved."

A lump forms in Jo's throat as a pair of headlights swing into the lot and illuminate her and Bill in the front seat. His knuckles are white as he grips the steering wheel, and her fingers are knotted together in her lap. "You mentioned once that she has an aunt in Phoenix." Jo stabs wildly at this notion, hoping for another solution. "Maybe she could handle Margaret's care? I mean, this isn't really your job anymore, Bill."

Bill closes his eyes and keeps them that way as someone parks on the other side of their car. He waits for the couple to close their doors and walk away before he speaks. When he does, his words are measured and careful. "Margaret's aunt is elderly and has no money. She cannot handle this." He pauses. "And as much as you don't want to think about it, I was once married to Margaret. I loved her. I vowed to love her 'in sickness and in health,' and then I broke that vow by divorcing her and marrying you."

Jo lowers her chin as she watches his profile. "Is that honestly how you feel? As if you shirked your *real* responsibility to marry me? Do you see me as the cause of your broken vow?"

"No. Jojo. Of course not. But you know who I am. You know I'm a man of my word, and that was a promise I didn't keep. A part of me will feel that way forever. But what I *can* still do is look after her from a distance. I can do that, and I will do that."

Even through the fog of her hormonal rollercoaster, and in spite of the way his words land in her heart, Jo has to admire this about her husband. He is a good man. He has never accepted a responsibility that he hasn't taken seriously, and he gives his all to everything he does. She just wishes that Margaret had never existed. Or, rather, that Margaret had been someone *else's* wife and not Bill's.

It's her turn to sigh in exasperation, but only because she can't find the right words to say to make things better. "Look, we can't solve this tonight, and there's no point in sitting out here and discussing it when we could be inside blowing off some steam." Jo opens her car door. "Let's go in and play a few games with everybody and see if we can relax, yeah?"

Bill opens his door and gets out, slamming it more forcefully than is necessary, in Jo's opinion. They walk in side by side, but neither reaches for the other's hand.

Inside the bowling alley, Carrie and Jay are just putting on their rented shoes, and Jude and Vance are already claiming a lane for their group.

"Hi!" Frankie calls out, standing up from her seat at the end of the lane. She waves at Jo. "Over here!"

Jo lifts her hand half-heartedly. She's mentally preparing herself for socializing and bowling—neither of which she's entirely in the mood for.

"Hi, you two." Frankie stands up and gives Jo a relaxed kiss on the cheek. Frankie is wearing a pair of capri pants in a pink and white checkered pattern, with a tight pink top and a pair of white bowling shoes.

"Do they rent those here?" Jo points at the clean white shoes. "Because I want those ones." Jo, never one to fuss over such things, suddenly wants the glamour of the white shoes as opposed to the regulation bowling alley ones with the inevitably broken laces.

Frankie hands Jo a glass of beer that she's poured from a pitcher. "Nope. These are mine. One of my many secrets and surprising talents: I was once in a bowling league, and I have my own shoes and my own ball." Frankie nods at the line of bowling balls, and Jo guesses immediately that the marbleized pink one is Frankie's.

"Okay," Jo says, accepting the glass of beer. "I am surprised. And impressed. I never imagined you as a bowling alley babe."

"Alright, alright. Go get your shoes." Frankie gives Jo a playful little shove. "I'm ready to clean up this entire alley with our high scores. We're teaming up."

Jo had assumed that the evening would be each couple paired up against the others, but in the end, a part of her is thrilled to partner with Frankie instead of with Bill. She goes to get her rental shoes, handing over her sandals and taking the size sevens that the young girl pushes across the counter to her. The whole alley is filled with the echoing sound of falling pins, and the shouts of glee as people get strikes, spares, doubles, or turkeys ring out up and down the lanes. Everything smells like beer and stale popcorn, but it isn't unpleasant. In fact, the change of scenery is somehow refreshing for Jo. She feels like, if she plays her cards right, she can hide out in their little group all evening and not have to think about Margaret, or about Bill's impending trip to Arizona.

Jo slips on her shoes and walks back to their lane, where Bill is talking animatedly with Ed. He slaps Ed on the shoulder as they laugh about something. Jo sinks into the empty chair next to Frankie and picks up her glass of beer again. This evening out with friends is a first for Bill and Jo since they've been in Florida, and it's only been made possible by the fact that Carrie had met the Wilson triplets at the library in town. Paula, Vicki, and Christina Wilson are sixteen, and as soon as Carrie discovered that they were all experienced babysitters, she'd gotten their phone number and then called the other women excitedly.

Barbie and Todd have opted to sit this one out (baby Huck had passed a cold on to the older boys, and they felt like three sick kids—one just an infant—was too much to put on a teenaged sitter), so Paula, Vicki, and Christina have been split up amongst Jo's kids, Carrie's son and daughter, and Jude's twins, allowing the adults to all have a night out on the town together.

"Team One," Ed announces with mock outrage, "will be myself

and Lieutenant Colonel Booker, as our ladies have jumped ship and decided to partner up against us."

The other two couples turn to Jo and Frankie with encouraging cheers. "You can take these two old geezers for a ride," Vance says, clapping his hands together as he nods at them. "You got this, girls."

"Next," Ed says. "We have Vance and Jude. Then Carrie and Jay. We'll let our traitorous wives take the last turn," he says, winking at Frankie to let her know that he's playing around.

Frankie plays into this by giving her husband a sassy look as she sips her beer, but Jo sits back in her chair and stifles an eye roll. She's not even close to being in the mood for this, and yet here they are, out on the town without kids. Jo wants to enjoy this, but she's going to need to finish this beer and relax a little if that's going to happen.

Someone finds the jukebox in the corner and puts on "Will You Love Me Tomorrow" by the Shirelles as Jo slings one leg over the other. She looks like a woman who is in no hurry to rack up a strike.

The other couples banter and take turns sending their balls down the lane while Jo watches the people around them. In the next lane over, a busty redhead giggles every time her date rolls his ball, then she stands and holds out her hands to put on his cheeks and pull him in for a big kiss. Jo remembers feeling this way about Bill—wanting to kiss him and touch him as much as possible, regardless of where they were and who was watching. She folds her arms over her stomach and takes a few deep breaths.

It's been ages since Jo and Bill had their first date, and she watches him now, remembering the way he picked her up at her house all those years ago.

"Hello, sir," he'd said to Jo's father, stepping up to the porch and offering his hand to shake. "I'm William Booker."

Jo's father, a man who had lived through The Great Depression on a farm in rural Minnesota, stood there in suspenders and a pair of pants that Jo's mother had fixed on more than one occasion. "You'd like to take my daughter out?" Jo's father, Herman White, had said, eyeing Bill warily.

"I would, sir. Josephine is a wonderful girl, and I'd like to take her into town for a movie."

Jo, stationed inside the house with her mother, chewed on the side of her thumb nervously as she waited for her father to give his final approval. The men talked for another minute or two, and finally Herman White had acquiesced, stepping aside and motioning for Jo to come to the door.

"You two have a nice time," he said, shooting Bill a long warning look. "And we'll see you back here no later than ten o'clock."

Driving away from her house that night, Jo had felt the indescribable sensation of promise bubbling inside her stomach. Little pinpricks of joy tingled up and down her spine all evening as Bill sat next to her in the theatre, and she'd smiled stupidly at the movie screen in the dark when he'd taken her hand in his.

Now, twelve years later, she watches him and wonders whether *that* Jo—the young, inexperienced girl she'd been—had any clue at all what she'd been getting into. Dating a man who'd already been married, one who was three years older than her and with five years of military experience already at that point...well, she'd been out of her depth and she hadn't even known it.

"Heyyyy!" Ed shouts, punching a fist in the air as Bill bowls a strike. The two men high-five as Carrie writes down the score. Jo slides further down in her seat, her arms still folded over her stomach. She has yet to say much of anything to anyone.

"Hey, bucko." Frankie leans her head closer to Jo and speaks in a low voice. "I'm thinking of having a cigarette here before we take our turn. Want to join me?" Jo shakes her head. "Okay, let me rephrase that: join me outside for a cigarette." Frankie grabs Jo by the elbow and hoists her up. "We're headed out for a smoke," she says to everyone else, pulling Jo along with her.

Outside, Jo leans against the wall, putting the bottom of one flat bowling shoe against the wall.

"So, what's your damage tonight, chickadee?" Frankie says,

lighting up. She takes a long drag and passes Jo the cigarette. "You and Bill on the outs?"

Jo waves the cigarette away. "Kind of. Remember how I told you about Margaret, his first wife?"

Frankie squints out at the purple evening sky as she exhales up towards the awning that hangs over the building. Behind them, they can hear the sound of cheering and of pins being knocked over through the open front door. "Of course," Frankie says. "Yes."

Jo sighs and waits as a young couple walks past them and into the bowling alley. "Well, now it's not just more money that they need for her care at that home she's in, but there's something going on and he needs to make a trip out there. To Arizona." She turns to Frankie and waits for a response.

Frankie ponders this silently as she smokes. "Hmm," she finally says, flicking her ash onto the pavement. "Well, this is a tough one, Jo. I think he needs to do whatever he needs to do in this situation, and while you might not like it, he's kind of being a stand-up guy by looking after her." Frankie shrugs helplessly. "We can hate that he was married before, but we can't hate him for being a gentleman and a caring human being. Right?"

Frankie's eyes are on Jo as she stares up at the neon sign at the edge of the parking lot. "I guess," Jo says like a pouty child. "I mean, yes, of course I respect him for that. I just wish he didn't have to go out there. It's like, we already pay every month for her care, but I can usually pretend that she doesn't exist. And now it's like every time I'm starting to get my feet under me in Stardust Beach, there's a letter or a phone call about Margaret." Jo shrugs one shoulder. "And I don't want him to leave us here in Florida without him," she adds in a small voice. "Wow, that sounds childish now that I've said it out loud."

Frankie drops her nearly-finished cigarette and crushes it, then puts an arm around Jo's shoulders. "Nah," she says reassuringly, giving her friend a light shake. "Not childish. You feel what you feel, and that's okay. But if he goes—when he goes—I'll keep you company, okay? We'll plan things and the days will go by fast. Promise."

Tears prick the back of Jo's eyes. She's about to make a joke about her own wildly swinging emotions when the old familiar sensation of a cramp in her lower abdomen nearly doubles her over. She purses her lips and blows out a long breath. "I think I just started my period." She laughs as she swipes away a tear.

"Well, that explains a lot." Frankie squeezes Jo's shoulders with a loud laugh. "Why don't you go and do what you need to do, and I'll bowl our round for us?"

As Jo walks through the bowling alley towards the restroom, everything suddenly looks different: the couple in the lane next to theirs seems sweet and hopeful rather than too kissy and annoying; the pitchers of beer at the various tables look frosty and appealing, not warm and flat; and Bill looks like the same handsome, earnest man she married, not a stranger who has dragged her across country and who now wants to abandon her here while flying off to see his ex-wife.

Jo almost laughs at herself in the bathroom mirror as she washes her hands and checks her mascara for tear streaks. She was being silly and hormonal; she can handle this situation. She's got a strong, upstanding husband, three amazing kids, and some great new friends. She reaches for a paper towel, drying her hands as she smiles at her reflection confidently.

"Well, I think he's a hunk," a woman says to her friend as they walk into the restroom together, ignoring Jo completely. "I think they all are. Have you seen them? I'm going to do everything I can to land me an astronaut."

The other woman giggles and shoves her friend's bare arm. "They're all married, I think."

The first woman shrugs as she chooses a stall and locks herself inside of it. "Well, if their wives let them hang out at the Black Hole all the time, then they can't be *that* married, can they?"

Woman number two has come to stand next to Jo at the sink, and she smiles at Jo distractedly as she pulls a tube of lipstick from her pocketbook and purses her lips in the mirror seductively. She's chewing gum, and her hair is like a cloud of blonde cotton candy around her head. "I think you gotta watch yourself, Annie. You don't want some old broad coming to find you at work and starting trouble for you in front of your boss."

From inside her stall, Annie flushes the toilet and laughs cattily. "*Some old broad*," she says with a cackle. "That's true."

Jo wants to say something, but she can't find the right words. She's always known that Bill is a good-looking guy—and that he's made even more so by the addition of his flight suit or Air Force uniform—but she's always let herself believe that other women would respect the bonds of marriage and steer clear of flirting with a man who is clearly spoken for. But hearing these two women makes her think otherwise, and the very idea of younger girls hitting on her husband at the Black Hole makes her stomach lurch.

Actually, it infuriates her. In fact, Jo has some sharp words for these ladies and she'd love nothing more than to let them know that they're acting in a way that not only tears down other women, but tears themselves down as well. Fortunately, she quickly remembers where and who she is before she even opens her mouth: Jo is no longer just a Midwestern mom, but the wife of an astronaut whose family is in the public eye. So rather than saying the kinds of things that could spark rumors and get spread around, pegging her as a hotheaded, jealous wife, Jo takes a deep breath and straightens her blouse.

Instead of waiting for Annie to emerge so that Jo can at least make meaningful eye contact, she balls up her paper towel and throws it into the trash can, and then walks out of the bathroom with her head held high.

FOURTEEN
bill

"THINGS ALRIGHT AT HOME, BOOKER?" Vance asks, clapping Bill on the shoulder heartily.

Bill has been a bit testy at work of late, and he knows it. He gives Vance a quick, curt smile. "Things are fine, thanks."

The men are working together on a mathematical problem that's written across a series of chalkboards that cover the entire wall of a long conference room. They're debating the issue of the necessary trajectory from Earth to various points in space. Jeanie Florence is there, her hand furiously moving across the board as she works a problem with the tip of her tongue held between her teeth.

"You've been looking rough, my friend," Vance goes on, trading in the broken piece of chalk in his hand for a fresh one from the box on the table. "You look like Jo's been making you sleep in the backyard or something."

Involuntarily, Bill's eyes skate over to Jeanie; she appears not to be listening to the conversation.

"Yeah?" Bill says mildly. He's trying to extricate himself from this conversation without going into any sort of detail. Talking about his personal life with coworkers is something he simply does not like to do. When it comes to combat zones and outer space, in Bill's mind there are more important things to focus on than whether the wife is haranguing you about something, or if the kids are misbehaving. "I'm good. I just haven't been sleeping well."

In truth, Bill has been sleeping fine, but he's under a lot of stress. He's already asked Arvin North for three days off to make the journey out to Arizona and check on Margaret's situation, and while North took the whole situation well, it was clear that he would have preferred it if Bill applied his "no personal life at work" policy across the board. He'd waved both hands and shaken his head back and forth as Bill explained the barest outline of the situation in his office.

"Say less," North said gruffly. "Permission for travel is granted, and we'll tell the other men that you're ill and under doctor's orders to stay away from NASA for seventy-two hours. Deal?"

And of course it was a deal Bill had taken—gladly—but there was still the tension at home surrounding the trip. Just that morning, Jo had taken out her ironing board and started pressing shirts and slacks.

"For the trip to Arizona," she'd said, not meeting his eye. Bill had taken his lunch and coffee and left with a small salute, because what was there to say to a woman who'd taken hold of something and refused to let go? What could he possibly say to make her less angry with him?

The conference room clears out for coffee break, and Bill stands there, chalky hands on the hips of his gray pants as he unwittingly leaves dust marks all over himself. Jeanie watches him with a wry smile.

"I can tell someone was never kept after school to clean the boards and erasers," she teases.

"Sorry?" Bill is squinting at an unfinished math problem; the next step is tickling at the back of his brain and he reaches for a discarded piece of chalk as he walks over and starts writing figures and fractions on the board.

"It's just, you have chalk...everywhere," Jeanie says, motioning to his shirt and the front of his pants as she breaks into a charming laugh. She puts one hand over her mouth like a schoolgirl giggling at something the teacher has done wrong.

Normally this would put Bill off—being laughed at is not something he's accustomed to. No one laughs at the Lieutenant Colonel, and no one laughs at their father, unless he's being intentionally funny. And, come to think of it, nothing he's done of late has made Jo laugh, or even smile.

He looks at Jeanie for a long moment. She's young, and without makeup she looks even younger. Today she has a pair of large glasses perched on her nose, and her long, straight hair is tied back in a navy blue ribbon that matches her dress.

"I guess you're right," Bill says, giving in to her laughter. "I never did get in much trouble at school. You?"

Jeanie's smile drops away and she looks surprised. "Me? Oh, no. My dad would never have put up with that. I'm a military brat, and my dad was very strict with us. No messing up at school, no dating, no goofing off."

Bill respects this. He thinks of himself as more relaxed with his own kids—though his expectations for their behavior and success are still quite high.

"I can understand that. The military instills a certain level of perfectionism in you, and that extends to the people around you." Bill tosses his chalk in the tray and brushes his hands together. The dust floats through the air, caught in a beam of afternoon sunlight from the windows that face to the west. "But I like to think that other people might have different understandings about right and wrong, and certainly not everyone is going to live their daily lives as if someone is going to drop in and check their beds for hospital corners."

Jeanie tucks a stray piece of hair behind one ear. "Mmm. Hospital corners." She winces. "You're giving me flashbacks to my childhood, Lieutenant Colonel!"

Bill chuckles as he leans his hands on the back of a chair. They are the only two in the conference room, though Ed and Jay are standing right outside, drinking their coffee and talking about sports.

"And do you find that you uphold those same standards for yourself as an adult, or have you gone in the other direction?"

Jeanie wrinkles her nose. "Maybe half and half. I still can't fall asleep if my kitchen isn't spotless, and I have a routine that I stick to: wash my sheets on Saturday, vacuum my apartment on Sunday, and then every day I do something else, like water the plants on Monday, dust on Tuesday, etcetera."

"Sounds both regimented and wise," Bill says with admiration.

Jeanie tosses her hair in an unselfconscious way. Though it makes Bill think of a young girl, there is nothing intentionally comely or seductive about it. "I suppose. I just don't like to live in filth. However, I refuse to adhere to a color scheme." She holds up a finger in warning. "If you ever see my apartment and the first thing you feel like saying is 'nothing matches,' well, don't." Her smile spreads like a sunrise.

Bill startles slightly at the suggestion that he might see her apartment. He looks away.

Jeanie's sweetness makes her seem like the kind of girl who loved science and math so much in school that she forgot to ever like boys, and is therefore unaware of the effect she has on men. As she's talking about her yellow corduroy couch, her shaggy orange beanbag, and her mismatched dishes, Bill is wondering whether she's ever been in love. It's hard to imagine a girl like Jeanie Florence slowing her thoughts down enough to close her eyes and accept a kiss. Bill can't picture her sitting quietly in a movie theatre, or singing her heart out at a concert. Without even asking, he can tell that she's not a part of the wave of young women who've been swept up by the tide of madness that the press are referring to as "Beatlemania."

"I'm sure it's a perfect bachelorette pad," Bill assures her as the other men start to trickle in. For some reason, he takes a step back, putting more distance between himself and Jeanie, although he hadn't been standing too close and nothing untoward had happened between them.

"Okay," Arvin North says as he enters. He stops and consults the board as he smokes a Pall Mall. "Well, friends. I'm looking at this mess on the board, and I'm not sure we'll ever make it farther than New Jersey at this rate."

The men have the good sense to stifle their laughter, and Bill rubs his temples. It isn't that they're a bunch of dimwits; quite the contrary—these are the best of the best, and he knows that their collective knowledge and abilities are fairly powerful. But there comes a time in the training and preparations where their synapses begin to fray, and their focus wanes. And four o'clock on a Friday is about that time.

"Listen," North says, turning to look at the room as he holds his cigarette between his fingers. His watch glints in the light from the windows. "It's only four, but let's call it a week, yeah? I'm beat. You're all killing me." He waves his hand in the air and a trail of smoke follows. "Get your lunch pails and cut out. Have a good weekend, and we'll start again Monday morning. See you." Without looking back, North leaves the room and the guys punch the air or look relieved.

"Black Hole," Jay says decisively, pointing at the door with both hands. "Last one there buys the first round!"

* * *

"Sir," a flight attendant in a tight blue skirt, a matching buttoned jacket, and a little triangular hat pinned to her carefully coiffed hair bends at the waist and sets a white-gloved hand lightly on Bill's knee. "We do strongly suggest that your seat belt is fastened for takeoff."

Bill is reading a magazine and has forgotten to buckle his lap belt. He tucks the magazine into the pocket of the seat in front of him and reaches for the straps as he watches the young, blonde flight attendant do the same to the other passengers. He notes that while she touches the men lightly on the knee, she lays a hand on the women's shoulders politely, and if a man and a woman are seated together, she always speaks to the woman first.

Human nature is not Bill's area of expertise, and he assumes that Jo might call him obtuse, but he likes to think that noticing details about how people behave is what's gotten him this far. Rather than delving into the *whys* and *hows* of other people's actions, Bill simply notes them and lets his observations inform how he handles any given situation. It certainly helped him in the years he spent in the Air Force, and it will undoubtedly help him as he navigates his work at NASA.

Once they're safely above the clouds, the small troop of flight attendants begin to circulate. Their gloves are off, as are their hats, and each woman stops and smiles at every passenger, looking them in the eye as they bend forward to make sure they're hearing each request. By the time the blonde flight attendant returns to Bill, he's halfway through his *Popular Science* magazine, and he closes it, letting it flop onto his tray table so that the cover is facing up.

"You like fast cars?" the flight attendant asks him with a knowing smile as she cracks a can of beer and pours it into a plastic cup for the man sitting across the aisle from Bill.

"Sorry?"

The flight attendant glances at his magazine. "The cover story." She sets a manicured hand on the back of the seat in front of him as she rests for a moment, bathing him in her bright smile. On the cover of the magazine is a blurry, fast-moving red car, with the title "The Fine Art of Fast Driving" above it.

"Oh, right," Bill says. "I like cars. But I was actually reading this article." He taps his finger against the top corner of the magazine. "Wernher von Braun's got a piece in here about Mars."

The stewardess lifts one perfectly-groomed brow as she leans a hip against the seat in front of him. "Like outer space? Are you an astronaut?"

Bill is well aware of the intrigue surrounding his job, and he nods proudly. "I am. Yes."

Immediately, the smile on the young woman's face brightens. "Wow!" she says, openly appraising him as her eyes dance down to his left hand, which rests on the tray table. Her smile dims only slightly when she sees his wedding ring, and then she turns up the wattage again, pushing herself away from the seat and putting both hands back on her beverage cart. "That's incredible. I'm sure your wife is really proud." With a more guarded smile, she offers him the drink of his choice as well as a bag of salty peanuts, and then winks at him before moving on.

Bill sips his vodka and orange juice as he pops a peanut into his mouth and chews. He glances at the window that looks out onto the blue sky and thinks about Jo. Is she proud? Does she think of him as an astronaut and glow with wifely pride? Or is she just struggling every day to reconcile the new life he's created for them? A part of Bill wanted to believe that Jo would just fall into their changed circumstances without a hiccup, but he can see now that this was never realistic. Jo, who loves nothing more than waking up at a campsite early in the morning to brew a pot of coffee over an open fire, was never going to be the kind of woman who relishes getting her hair done and posing for photographs. But she *is* trying; he can see that. Bill admires her work at the hospital, though he'd at first been uncertain about it, and she's really making a nice home for them in Stardust Beach.

But this trip to Arizona has thrown a wrench in the works, for sure. He finishes his screwdriver in one long pull, and catches the eye of the pretty blonde stewardess as he holds up the empty cup, hoping she'll get the message and bring him another. She does, and he smiles gratefully as he takes it.

Bill returns his attention to the fluffy clouds beneath the wings of the airplane, and tries to stay positive about this visit to handle

Margaret's care. He *has* to stay positive—this is his responsibility, and handling it is not optional, no matter the fact that Jo wishes it were otherwise.

* * *

Desert Sage is a low, single-story stucco building in the desert. Bill steps into the dry heat from the car he's rented, folding the paper map and tossing it onto the passenger seat before it blows away in the wind.

He runs a hand through his disheveled hair and pushes up his aviator sunglasses as he looks around. It's been years since he was here, and nothing has changed except the cars in the small parking lot. Bill walks to the front door and goes through the motions of announcing himself, signing in, and shaking hands with the director of the facility.

"I'm so glad you could make the trip, Mr. Booker," May Ogilvy says, smiling at him like the kindly grandmother she most likely is. "I'd like to take you to visit with Margaret, and then perhaps we can talk in my office."

Bill hasn't been sure what to expect during this visit, other than a discussion about Margaret's care going forward, but seeing her right out of the gate makes his heart race. "Okay," he says amiably. "I'm game."

The facility director leads him down a sunlit hallway. Through the open doors on that floor, Bill can see residents sitting peacefully in rocking chairs that face windows. Many of them have plants growing and flourishing on their windowsills, and he takes stock of their clean rooms and crisply made beds as he walks by them. So far, so good.

May Ogilvy leads Bill through a set of double doors that she unlocks with a key that hangs on a giant ring attached to her belt. She holds it open for him and he follows, sensing the slight shift in energy as the doors close behind them.

"This is our elevated care unit," Mrs. Ogilvy says, avoiding his gaze as she leads him directly through the unit and to another set of doors. She repeats the key process, only this time they encounter a big, burly man in white scrubs, who insists on inspecting their pockets and patting them down. Bill is growing alarmed. "And this is our intensive care unit—not to be confused with medical intensive care," Mrs. Ogilvy adds. "This is where we have moved Margaret, and I'd like to bring you to her if you're prepared."

Bill feels his eyes widen as he nods; he is suddenly far less certain about seeing his ex-wife. "Okay," he says, swallowing. The idea of space travel and potential oxygen leaks seems more manageable in this moment than sitting down across from a woman he'd once loved but who would now, most likely, not even recognize him.

May Ogilvy leads Bill to a room where two male attendants stand against one wall. Bill's eyes graze the room, landing on a woman with long, curly, wild hair. She is standing at the window with her back to him, her face turned up towards the sun that bathes her in hot white light. May Ogilvy stands near the door and nods at the woman standing at the window.

For a long moment, Bill just stares. Finally, he collects himself and clears his throat. "Margaret?" he says.

She turns around slowly—so slowly that Bill isn't even sure she's heard him until she's fully facing him. The moment their eyes lock, everything comes rushing back: school dances; her warm skin under his eager hands; the smell of roses and antiseptic when he'd visited her in the hospital after the miscarriage; the taste of her hot, salty tears whenever he'd held her and tried to kiss away her pain. "Margaret," he says again, this time not as a question.

Margaret looks older but not old; wiser but not wizened; a little frightened, but not frightening. She stares at him. Narrows her eyes. Looks him up and down from head to toe, lingering on his broad chest, his close-cropped hair, and on the wedding band that wraps his left ring finger in yellow gold. Their matching wedding bands had been white gold, with a tiny chip of a diamond embedded in Margaret's. Now her hands are bare, and her face free of makeup.

"I wasn't sure you'd come, Bill," she says to him in a soft, slightly raspy voice. Her eyes fill with tears. "I thought you forgot about me."

Bill shakes his head wordlessly, clears his throat, finds his voice. "I didn't," he says. "I didn't forget about you, I just didn't know how to save you."

FIFTEEN

jo

BILL IS GONE. *He's in Arizona.*

Jo wakes up to these mental reminders as she rolls over and stretches in her giant, empty bed. She puts on her robe and slippers and pads out to the kitchen, where she puts on a pot of coffee and looks out the window over the sink at another bright blue, humid Florida morning. The grass is still slightly dewy, and the pool filter hums loudly as she steps out onto the back patio through the sliding door.

The kids are still asleep, so Jo opens the front door and brings in the newspaper, the eggs, and the glass bottles of milk that have all been delivered just after dawn. Unlike in Minnesota, it's imperative to get the eggs and the milk in and stored safely in the cool refrigerator as soon as possible so that they don't fry and boil on the front porch in the hot morning sun.

Jo drops the newspaper on the kitchen table as she pours her coffee, and the headlines blaze up at her: *There's going to be a march on Washington at the end of the month; A freak escalator accident kills a man and his eight-year-old daughter at a racetrack in New Jersey* (Jo's hand goes to her heart as she skims this one); *Hurricane Arlene passes* *directly over Bermuda with eighty-five mile an hour winds...*Jo sits down and reads on, sipping her coffee in contemplative silence.

She's trying to focus on the news of the world, but her brain keeps jumping back to the late night phone call she'd received from Bill before going to sleep the evening before: he'd arrived in Arizona, gotten a car and driven straight to Desert Sage, and had seen Margaret for the first time in many years. He'd delivered it all so dispassionately—and Jo had certainly tried to receive the details the same way—but beneath their words there was an undeniable current of discomfort. A frisson of angst. In the end, they'd talked about the children briefly, Jo's shift at the hospital, and the fact that Frankie was staying with the kids again. Bill told her about the motor hotel he'd booked near Desert Sage, and that he missed them all terribly. The call had lasted less than five minutes due to the exorbitant cost of a long-distance phone call, but hearing his voice had both soothed her and riled her up, leaving Jo with a weird bubbling sensation in her chest that had kept her awake well past midnight.

When Frankie shows up to watch the kids that afternoon, she's carrying an overflowing bag full of feathers and sequins, but Jo is so distracted that she barely notices her girls' excitement.

"Mommy!" Kate says, dancing around as Jo clips on her pearl earrings and smoothes her skirt before leaving for the hospital. "Did you know Frankie was a dancer on New York?" She's looking at her mother hopefully.

"It was *in* New York, dummy," Jimmy says to Kate.

"James," Jo corrects, frowning at him. "Do not call your sister names." She turns back to Kate. "Yes, I did know that, sweetie. She told you that?"

Frankie is standing in the front room, pulling things out of her bag and laying satiny dresses over the back of the couch. "The girls wanted to see some of my costumes from my days as a Rockette," she explains to Jo. "I hope you don't mind."

Jo fingers the canary yellow feathers of a short dress as Kate sits on the floor with a pair of well-worn dancing shoes, trying to slip her feet into them as if they aren't several sizes too big.

Since Bill is out of town, Jo figures it can't hurt to leave the kids in the hands of a woman who wants to dress them in sequins and beads and teach them how to can-can. "Sounds good to me," she says, dropping a tube of lipstick into her purse. She leans over with a smile and kisses each of the children on their cheeks on her way out of the house.

Jo is uncharacteristically self-assured at the moment; it isn't often that she's alone and in charge of everything on the home front, and if she's being honest with herself, she manages it quite well. Waking up and drinking her coffee in the quiet of the house as she reads the paper, shepherding the kids through their meals and playtime, and running laundry as she sings to herself suits her just fine. Even her simpler dinner plans are like a little vacation to Jo: that night she's promised the kids fish sticks and oven french fries followed by a swim, and the night before she'd let them eat their franks and beans quickly and spend the evening watching television.

Of course they'll go back to business as usual when Bill returns, but for now, sitting by the pool and watching her kids take turns doing cannonballs as the sun sets and the dinner dishes languish in the sink sounds just about right.

"Good afternoon, Josephine," Nurse Edwina says as Jo passes her in the hallway, pushing a freshly stocked and organized cart full of goodies. "Having a nice day?"

"I am," Jo says with a nod. "And you?"

Edwina blows out a long breath as she looks down the hall in one direction and then in the other to make sure they're alone. "You know, Josephine, it's been a long day. Anytime there's a full moon things get crazy around here."

"So that's true then—about full moons and more accidents and births?"

"Oh, definitely." Edwina nods as she clips a ballpoint pen to the chain that hangs around her neck. "There's more of everything, but always more drama."

Jo keeps this in mind as she floats from room to room, handing out bottles of juice, packets of pecan sandies, and reading materials to the various patients—some familiar faces, and some new since her last shift. When she gets to Mr. D's room, she pauses, pulling the two new books she's brought for him from the bottom shelf of the cart. She's hidden them there beneath a pile of discarded magazines so that no one would see them and ask to read the books she'd earmarked for Mr. Dandridge.

"Good afternoon," Jo says, peering in as she knocks. She pushes the door open tentatively. "It's Josephine."

Mr. Dandridge is fast asleep. Jo is disappointed; visiting Mr. D has quickly become her favorite part of coming to the hospital. Since she's already finished the entire floor and has been saving Mr. D's room for last so that she can sit and visit, she creeps all the way in, leaving her cart near the bathroom door and taking the seat next to his bed. She takes the time to breathe in and out, sending good and positive thoughts towards Mr. Dandridge as he sleeps, and hoping for him to make a full recovery from whatever ails him.

"Ah, an angel has fallen from heaven while I slumbered," he says, startling Jo from her meditative state.

"Oh! Mr. Dandridge!" Jo stands up from the chair, tucking her shirt in and making sure she's presentable. "I didn't mean to wake you."

"You didn't," he assures her. "Please sit again. Waking up and finding you here has been the best part of my day—maybe even of my week. Wait—let me think about it for a second," he says, putting a finger to his lips as he considers the week and all that it's entailed. "Yep. Best part of the whole week." Mr. Dandridge looks right at Jo with a big grin. "And how are things for you, Josephine?"

Jo exhales as she sinks back into the chair, putting her hands between her knees. Her shoulders roll forward. "Things are challenging right now," she admits. "My husband is out of town, and I'm just..."

Mr. Dandridge frowns and looks as though he's trying to sit up in his bed. "You're afraid to be alone, Josephine? Are you worried you're not safe?"

Jo's insides melt. Sweet Mr. Dandridge, with his shock of white hair and his mottled and spotted skin, is ready to climb out of bed and do his duty to protect her and make her feel safe, and she can hardly stand it.

Jo puts out a hand and touches his arm. "No, no—it's not that. The children and I are getting by just fine on our own. In fact, we're having a bit of fun," she admits with a quirk of her lips. "We're eating what we call 'fun food' for dinners, and watching TV together in the evenings. It's like we're on a campout or a vacation. Do you know what I mean?"

"Of course, of course," he says, waving his gnarled hand at her. "Everyone feels that way when they get a little change to the routine. Naturally you miss the person who is always at your side, but the beauty is that you *get* to miss them, and then they come home and things go back to normal. Whenever my darling wife used to leave to visit her sister in California, I'd go down to the nearest ballpark where the kids played baseball, and I'd order three hotdogs and sit on the bleachers and eat them all for dinner." He grins like a naughty little boy admitting a secret. "Then I'd go home, take a package of cookies and a stack of comic books to bed with me, and I'd read until I fell asleep. Of course I always cleaned up before she came back home and I told her I ate the meatloaf and peas or the chicken cutlet dinner at the diner in our town every night, and she was never the wiser." Mr. D reaches out and taps his closed fist on Jo's hand like they're co-conspirators. "I bet your guy is the same way: if you left town, he'd eat hot dogs for dinner and drink a beer in the bathtub. So you letting the kids have a bit of fun is just par for the course."

Jo smiles at him. "Thanks, Mr. D. I know he'll come home and things will be back to normal before I know it, it's just...he's gone to Arizona."

"Hot there this time of year," Mr. Dandridge says noncommittally.

"Mmm." Jo nods as she chews her bottom lip. "It is. But...I hate dumping my personal life on you. In fact, I shouldn't." Jo stands up resolutely, ready to hand Mr. Dandridge his books and make her exit so that he can rest.

"You sit yourself down, miss," Mr. Dandridge says in what Jo imagines was his commanding teacher voice from his years in the classroom. Without argument, Jo sits. "You are not bothering me with your personal life. In fact, I have come to relish our friendship, and I appreciate you trusting me with the details of your lovely life." He looks at her and holds her gaze. "Now, what is going on with your husband in Arizona."

Jo sighs and lets go of the tension in her shoulders. "He was married to someone else before he met me." She looks at her lap and twists her wedding band in circles as the story spills forth. When she's done talking, Mr. Dandridge is still watching her from his hospital bed. He turns and looks out the window for a long moment.

"I see," he says, thinking. "Well. Never underestimate the power of first love." As if realizing that he may have said something to offend or upset Jo, he turns quickly to look at her. "Which is not to say that he's there because he *still* loves her, but Jo, the first person you give your heart to is always special. They stay with you. They linger."

She knows he's right, but there's always been a dark, jealous, petty little corner of her heart that hates Margaret for getting there before she did. The grown up part of Jo is ashamed of this, but she can't help the fact that it's true.

"Who was your first love?" Mr. Dandridge asks her.

Jo blows out a breath that lifts her wispy hair away from her forehead. "Oh, jeez," she says with a laugh. "Ralph Putnam."

Douglas Dandridge looks at her expectantly. "He sounds like a dandy. Go on."

Jo giggles. "He was definitely not a dandy. He was the star basketball player at my high school, and I thought for sure we'd get married and have children and live happily ever after."

"And yet your last name is Booker, so…"

"Precisely." Jo shoots him a knowing look. "So Ralph Putnam asked me to be his date to the winter formal when we were sixteen, and of course I said yes and then immediately started choosing what song we'd dance to at our wedding."

Dandridge gives an amused huff. "I spent far too many years around teenagers not to have seen this play out a time or two."

Jo nods. "So then you can imagine what happened: Ralph picked me up for the dance, and I'd gone all out. My mother had made me a pink chiffon dress with a gathered waist, and I had an orchid in my hair. I'd practiced dancing with my younger sister for weeks, and I was ready for the most magical night of my life."

"Oh no." Mr. D winces as if he's in physical pain. "Not the most magical night of your life then?"

Jo shakes her head sadly. "I found out that he'd only invited me to make Suzanne Wimmer jealous. They'd been dating for a year and she broke up with him, and he thought taking me to the dance would be the thing to get her back."

"And did it?" he asks hesitantly, as if hearing the truth might break his heart.

"As it turns out, Suzanne had broken up with Ralph because she was in love with our Algebra teacher, Mr. Simpkins, who had just finished his teaching degree. He was twenty-two, and he waited for her to graduate high school and then they got married."

Mr. Dandridge shakes his head and tsk-tsks at this turn of events. "A tale as old as time," he says. "An ugly one, but still. It happens."

Jo shrugs. She's almost cheerful. "I hate to say that I kind of felt like Ralph Putnam got exactly what he deserved in that situation, but…I wasn't the least bit sorry for him."

"So what happened to old Ralphie in the end?"

"Joined the Coast Guard, last I heard. I think he was stationed up near Alaska. A friend of mine from back home was close with one of his sisters, and she heard he dated a bunch of different local girls up there, but was still single."

"And yet, after all of this, you still call Ralph Putnam the first love of your life?" Mr. Dandridge frowns at her.

"Oh, yes." Jo nods enthusiastically. "The amount of time I spent daydreaming about him in class, going to basketball games and pretending I cared about school spirit, and walking past his house hoping that he would notice me and ask me to the dance—I loved him. For sure. He even kissed me that night before I found out about him just asking me to make Suzanne jealous." She makes a face now at the memory of the kiss, which was lukewarm, at best, though at the time she'd ascribed much more meaning to it than it had deserved. "But what about you—first love—was it Mrs. Dandridge?"

He turns and looks out the window again wistfully. "Oh, sure, sure. You could say that. First girl I really and truly gave my heart to. But first love? The kind of love you're talking about, where you wish and hope and dream...and never forget the heartache?" He glances back at Jo with a twinkle in his eye. "Mrs. Shane."

"Mrs. Shane?"

"My best friend's mother," he says with a bad boy laugh. "Oh, she was a beauty!"

Jo is scandalized; her hand flies to her mouth and she can't find a single thing to say.

"Diana Shane," Mr. Dandridge says. His eyes are misty with the memory of her. "Tall and leggy and brunette. She had my best friend, Chester, when she was only sixteen. So you can imagine that when I was a twelve-year-old boy, she was a gorgeous woman still in her twenties."

This sounds slightly more reasonable, and Jo lets her hand fall to her lap as she listens. "Wow," she says, shaking her head in awe.

"Wow, indeed." Mr. Dandridge laughs again. "Chester and his

mom lived with her parents on the outskirts of town, and anyone who didn't know them always assumed she was his big sister, which he didn't bother to correct. I remember this one time, I went over to their place on my bicycle, and Mrs. Shane was outside in a pair of jeans! That was outrageous, Josephine, for a woman to be wearing jeans held up by a bit of twine in the late 1800s. They belonged to her father, and she'd borrowed them so that she could build a chicken coop. So I pulled up on my bike, and there she was, in jeans and a dirty white shirt, sweat on the back of her neck and dirt on her hands, and oh, was I in love. I wanted to marry Diana Shane and build her a million chicken coops. I wanted to be the husband she never had. You know, it never once occurred to me that marrying her would make me Chester's stepfather." He chuckles at his younger self as he talks. "Silly kid stuff." Mr. D grows serious. "But love is love, and you never discount it. Never call it stupid or brush it away, you understand?"

"Sure." Jo nods fervently. "I agree. It's important to love and to suffer through heartbreak and loss. It makes real, lasting love even sweeter."

"Aha!" Mr. D says, pointing a finger in the air like he's made his point. "There you go. A+ work, Mrs. Booker."

"Ohhhh." Realization dawns on Jo.

"You see? You don't get to discount Mr. Booker's first love or brush it away, because for him, the heartbreak and the loss of it makes his love for you even sweeter."

Is she an idiot that she needed a ninety-year-old man in a hospital bed to state the obvious for her? "You are *so* right."

Mr. Dandridge's raised hand falls to his lap and he sighs. "Okay, now pass me those romance novels and some extra cookies, and I promise not to tell the nurses who gave them to me." He winks at her and points at the door. "And then you go out and spread your cheer around this place so that you can go home and have beans on toast with your children."

"Fish fingers and french fries tonight," Jo says with a smile as she hands Mr. D three packets of pecan sandies and two paperback books.

He flips the books over to inspect them. "*Her Lonely Heart,*" he reads. "*Under the Willow Trees,*" he says, glancing at the other book. "They sound lovely, dearest Josephine. Now, off with you." He waves at her and opens the cover of *Her Lonely Heart*. "I have my books to read."

Jo backs out of the room with her cart and the promise to come by next time she's on duty, and she's still smiling to herself when she nearly bumps into Dr. Chavez in the hall.

"Josephine!" he says, smiling widely with those big, square, white teeth set against a deep tan. "Good to see you!"

"And you as well," she says. She's about to offer Dr. Chavez a packet of cookies for lack of anything better to say, when Nurse Edwina approaches them with her face red and her eyes worried.

"Dr. Chavez," Edwina wheezes. "You're needed in triage immediately. Potential head injury. Young female, unresponsive."

"Any idea what happened?"

"She fell and hit her head on the edge of a pool, and was apparently in the water for a couple of minutes before her neighbor was able to pull her out."

The smile vanishes from Dr. Chavez's face and he turns and walks towards triage without another word.

Jo watches him go, his white coat flapping behind him and his shoes squeaking importantly down the length of the hall.

SIXTEEN

jo

JO GOES about her afternoon as usual, but the thought of a young woman with a head injury lingers in the back of her mind. She's about to put her cart away in the closet where she stores it when she sees a familiar figure standing at the nurse's station with Dr. Chavez: it's Vance Majors, Jude's husband.

Jo takes her time putting her cart back and gathering her purse and lightweight cardigan, then closes the door behind her and waits unobtrusively for Dr. Chavez to walk away.

"Vance," she says, approaching him carefully. "Is everything okay?"

Vance turns to her with surprise. His eyes are tired. "Oh, Jo. Hi." He runs a hand through his hair and exhales. "Things are not really okay." He looks like he might cry. "Jude slipped today and hit her head."

Jo inhales sharply; she never imagined for one second that the young woman with the head injury could be a friend of hers. "Oh, Vance. Oh, I'm so sorry. How is she?"

Vance's eyes follow Dr. Chavez as he sets a clipboard down on a desk and walks into another patient's room. "I'm not sure, to be honest. They think she fell into the water and was there for a minute or two before our neighbor could get over there and pull her out. She's had a pretty good knock to the head, and being in the water for a minute or two wasn't good. She hasn't woken up yet, but her heart and brain activity are normal so far. They think there might be some swelling to her brain...we just don't know."

"Oh my god, the children," Jo says on a sharp inhale, putting one hand to her chest. Where are Hope and Faith?"

Vance's eyes look incredibly tired. "The neighbor girl is watching them. Our parents and siblings are all in New York and Texas—like you, we don't have anyone here."

Jo makes a snap decision. "I'm done with my shift now. I'll stop and get the girls, and they can come to my house. I'll watch them until you know more, or until you can come get them. They can sleep over if they need to."

"Jo, that's really kind of you...I can't ask you to do that."

"You're not asking." Jo puts a hand on his arm.

"But Bill is sick—won't he mind?"

Jo is momentarily puzzled. She's about to say that Bill isn't sick when she remembers that he'd told her Arvin North had approved his absence for a few days with the excuse that a doctor has told him to take the time off.

"Right, right," Jo says, thinking on her feet. "No, he won't mind. He's shut himself away, and I'll keep the kids busy. I'll go get the girls right now if you want."

Vance appears to relent. "Okay, if you think it'll work for your family. That would be so helpful. It would take one thing off my plate."

"Absolutely," Jo pats his arm. "I was going to do something easy for the kids tonight for dinner, so I'll just make a few more fish sticks and then let them swim. Don't you worry about a thing, and call me if you need anything."

With that decided, Jo drives over to Vance and Jude's and collects Hope and Faith, along with enough provisions that they can swim and even sleep over at the Bookers' house, if necessary.

The evening is almost made easier for Jo with the addition of two more children; the change in dynamic makes her three behave differently—better—and Nancy takes on the informal role of babysitter to her younger sister and to Hope and Faith. For his part, Jimmy largely ignores them all. As the kids are playing, Jo cleans up the dinner dishes and calls Frankie.

"No!" Frankie shouts immediately. "Jude fell into the pool? Oh my god!"

Jo recounts the entire story to her, ending with the fact that Hope and Faith are currently at her house, and that she hasn't heard any updates from Vance as of yet.

"I wonder what happened. Have the girls said anything?"

Jo looks out the window to the spot in the thick-bladed grass beneath a tree where all four girls are tossing a ball back and forth, giggling each time one of them misses it. Jimmy is laying under a different tree with a comic book, ignoring them all.

"No, they seem kind of unaware, to be honest," Jo says as she watches them. "I went to pick them up, and the teenager from next door was watching them. They haven't said anything at all about their mother."

"So then maybe they weren't there when it happened?"

"That's a possibility. But where would they have been? And, Frankie," Jo says, interrupting her own train of thought, "how lucky is Jude that a neighbor happened to be close enough to rush over and save her?"

Frankie flicks her lighter on the other end of the phone line and Jo can hear her take the first inhale of a fresh cigarette. "Indeed." She's quiet for a moment. "It's all very mysterious, but of course, terribly tragic."

"She's going to be fine though," Jo says, mostly to reassure herself. The look on Dr. Chavez's face as he'd spoken to Vance that afternoon had been worrying. "She has to be fine."

"You'll keep me updated?"

"Of course. I'll call you as soon as I know anything."

In the end, the girls do end up sleeping over, and Vance comes to retrieve them first thing in the morning. "Thank you so much, Jo," he says sheepishly from her front doorstep. "I owe you one."

"You owe me nothing." She's put on a pair of capri pants and a blouse, but the only makeup she's had time for is a swipe of lipstick after brushing her teeth. "Come in for a cup of coffee?"

Vance wipes his feet on the doormat and follows Jo to the kitchen, where he looks slightly out of place. He waits to be pointed to a chair, and without thinking, Jo gives him Bill's spot. "The kids are still sleeping," she says as she pours him a steaming mug of coffee. "I can wake your girls if you like."

Vance's eyes are rimmed with dark circles and he looks like he hasn't slept. "Actually, do you mind if they sleep a bit more while I run home and take a shower?"

"Of course not. I'll get them breakfast."

"Thank you so much. I'm just going to have to piece things together while Jude is in the hospital. I got a couple of days off of work here, and my mother has agreed to fly in from Houston."

"Oh, Vance," Jo says. She slides into her usual seat at the table with a mug of coffee in her hands. "Why don't you leave the girls here again today while you handle things. Seriously, they're fine. And if we need a change of scenery, we'll go to the library, or call Carrie and see if her kids are interested in a trip to the beach or something."

"Jo, you are a lifesaver," Vance says. He looks relieved. "Bill is a lucky man."

Wordlessly, Jo sips her coffee. She'd like to believe that Bill is a lucky man, but her attitude lately has left something to be desired, and she's well aware of that. Why is it that she's so willing to step in and be there for someone else's husband in his hour of need, but she has such a hard time doing the same for her own? Of course, the answers are not so simple—there are emotions and feelings and plenty of tangled thoughts involved in her own marriage, and right now all she's doing is being a friend to Vance and Jude, which is so much easier.

STEPHANIE TAYLOR

"Thank you," she says to him, looking at her placemat instead of at Vance's face. "Vance, I have to ask, is Jude okay? Not just presently, but in general?" He's quiet, and this forces Jo to look up at his face, which is set in stony silence. "I mean, there was this one day when all of us girls were together, and I didn't want to gossip about it so I haven't mentioned it to anyone, but I found Jude in the kitchen… drinking Carrie's vodka."

Vance says nothing, but stares into his cup of coffee for the longest minute Jo has ever lived through. When he finally looks up at Jo, there is worry in his eyes. "I think it's a bit of a problem," he says. "But I need to get her well before I think about trying to get her to stop drinking."

Jo bites her lip as she nods. "Absolutely. And I'm not trying to be nosey, Vance, I was just worried." She wants to tag on something nice—a compliment about Jude being a great mom, or a good friend, but truth be told, she doesn't have those kinds of feelings about Jude. Not yet, anyway. But she wants to know the woman better; she wants to help her, if she can.

"Thank you." Vance takes a long drink of coffee and then pats the table his hand. "Okay," he says, standing up with the bone-weary type of exhaustion that comes from spending a sleepless night in the hospital. "I'd better shower and get this day started. I want to get back to the hospital as soon as possible and see if there have been any changes."

"Don't you worry about a thing here, alright? If the girls need anything from home, we'll just swing by there and they can run in and grab it."

"The front door is unlocked," Vance says, patting his pockets for his keys and wallet as he makes his way to the door. "And, Jo?"

Jo is in the living room, escorting him to the door. She pauses. "Yes?"

"Thank you again. I really appreciate this, and your discretion about…everything."

"You got it, Vance."

* * *

"And then we put on the dress and Frankie played a song and we all danced," Kate is saying to all the other children as she stands in the sand in her little flowered swimsuit. "And I think someday I'm going to dance on New York, too!"

Jimmy looks like he hears his sister's grammatical mistake again, but rather than correct her, he turns to Marcus instead. "Want to go in the water?"

There are three years between the boys, but Marcus is an easygoing kid who is always up for whatever Jimmy wants. They frequently ride their bikes around the neighborhood, play catch together, or talk about sports. With a shrug, Marcus follows Jimmy to the water.

"I want to hear more about this whole Rockette business," Carrie says from her spot on the giant blanket as she watches Frankie with awe.

Jo has gathered all the women and children—minus Jude, of course—that afternoon for a beach picnic, and the little girls are playing together in a group while Marcus and Jimmy do their thing. Barbie is nursing Huck under the blanket that she has thrown over one shoulder, and her toddlers are happily digging in the sand with shovels.

"Oh, *pshhh*," Frankie says, waving one hand and not looking at any of them. "That's yesterday's news. I was on stage dancing, and now I'm just an old married broad."

Carrie huffs. "Old, my behind. You look like a movie star."

Frankie finally looks her in the eye. "Well, I've done some things that might seem glamorous on the surface, but I'm no brainiac. Not like those girls who are working with our husbands now."

"Come again?" Barbie has been watching Heath and Henry build a sandcastle as she nurses Huck, but she turns back to them now. "What girls?"

Frankie sighs. "They got a whole slew of female engineers who just started. I heard they like to go to the Black Hole after work with our boys. What do we think about that?"

"We do not like it," Barbie says defensively. "We do not like it at all. And Todd hasn't even mentioned it."

Jo feels trouble brewing, so she tactfully changes the subject. "Tuna or egg salad?" she asks, holding one of each sandwich in the air for the children to choose from. They all make their picks, and then she hands bottles of soda around to the women as they take a sandwich or politely pass.

"Dieting," Barbie says with a sad smile. "I need to lose some baby weight, otherwise I'd love an egg salad."

"Oh, honey. You don't need to lose a pound," Carrie says. She's dressed in an oversized dress made of lightweight fabric, and she's hiked it up to her thighs so that her legs are basking in the sun. She adjusts the wide-brimmed hat on her head as she watches the children playing together. "You're all stunning. In fact, *we all are*. We need to stop letting men and society tell us that we aren't good enough."

"Forget about the rest of the world. Before I even leave the house, my mirror tells me I'm not good enough," Frankie says drily.

Carrie reaches over and swats Frankie's bare leg with a rolled-up magazine. "Stop it! And you all mark my words: we might eat celery sticks and starve ourselves now to fit in, but someday there will be a lot of pushback to this. People will understand how hard it is to be a woman, and they won't expect us to give birth and then immediately have a tiny waist again."

Barbie switches Huck to the other breast as she shoots a disbelieving look in Carrie's direction. "I don't think so," she says with a sad look. "My mom has been on me since I was ten to stay skinny. She told me no man would want a fat woman, and I've never seen anything to say otherwise."

Jo frowns at this, but she sees both sides of the coin on this issue. She wants her girls to grow up in a world where they don't look at every bite of food and wonder whether it will go directly to their hips (and if it does, who cares!), but she also knows that there are zero messages coming from society at large that don't have to do with being slim, pretty, and feminine. It's a tug-of-war in her own heart; she's already absorbed all the messages herself. Without even thinking about it, Jo can substitute coffee for breakfast, or skip dessert even when it looks mouthwateringly delicious.

Jimmy and Marcus come running back from the water's edge with handfuls of wet, sandy shells that they dump right onto Jo's blanket. She's growing accustomed to the sensation of sand infiltrating every corner of her life, so rather than complain about the mess, she just smiles at them. "Found some treasures, boys?"

Jimmy puts his hands on his narrow hips and stares at the pile of shells. "Maybe. Gotta see what else is out there." The boys run off again, dashing for the waves that break right there on the white sand beaches.

"Any word on Jude?" Carrie asks Jo with a concerned look as she pops the lid off her bottle of Tab. She turns the soda around and reads the name on it. "And what is this?"

"A new Coca-Cola soda without sugar. Better for your diet," Barbie says, sipping her own bottle of Tab.

Carrie rolls her eyes at the word "diet" and goes on. "Anyway, do we know how she is?"

Jo shoots a pointed look in the direction of where the little girls are playing together and drops her voice. "Vance was by this morning and said he needed to head back to the hospital, and I told him I'd keep the girls with me. They haven't said a word about it, so I'm not sure if they even know what's going on."

"Strange," Barbie says. She's rocking back and forth with Huck dozing in her arms. As she sits there, four-year-old Heath brings a shovelful of sand over and pours it on her toes. Barbie wiggles her feet and smiles at her oldest son. "I wonder what's going on. Maybe one of us should drop by the hospital this afternoon with a snack for Vance?"

"Or maybe Jo can use her hospital connections to call and find

STEPHANIE TAYLOR

out how she is," Frankie suggests as she pulls a pack of cigarettes from her purse. She looks at everyone else and then tosses the unopened pack back into her bag. "Sometimes I think I should just quit smoking altogether." She grimaces.

"Or maybe do it less," Carrie offers helpfully. "I know it's a habit, but you could replace it with something else."

"Like eating more and getting chubby?" Frankie shoots her a look.

Carrie groans. "You could stand to eat a few cupcakes, girl."

"Don't worry," Barbie teases, still rocking back and forth as she sits. "As soon as she starts popping out babies, she'll thicken right up!"

The women laugh, but Jo catches a glimpse of Frankie's face. There is a flicker of something there. They haven't discussed the fact that Frankie and Ed don't have children yet, but Jo senses that there are things lurking beneath the surface when it comes to that particular topic, and she doesn't want to see Frankie get put on the spot right there during a lovely picnic on the beach.

"Maybe I should run by there," Jo says as a way to change the subject. "The hospital, I mean. I could take Vance some sandwiches and just check in."

"Sure," Carrie says. "You can drop all the kids off with me and I'll watch them while you go over. You're the one who is closest to this situation anyway."

"Drop them all off?" Jo asks in surprise. "Jude's girls and all three of mine? You want to have seven kids running around your house?"

Carrie smiles as she scans the group, counting heads. "Yeah, sure. My two are easy, so what's five more? Besides, my mom raised seven of us while my dad was away during the war. I think I can manage it for an afternoon."

Jo admires her pluck, but isn't sure she'd be as easygoing about seven kids running around her house on a blazing hot afternoon. "Okay," she says. "I'll do it and be quick about it."

In the end, they don't need to do any sort of musical chairs with the kids, as Jo gets back to the house with the station wagon full of hot and sandy children to find Vance waiting in her driveway.

"Hey," he says, lifting a hand. "I just got here. Jude gets to go home this evening, so I thought I'd run the girls back to our place for a quick bath and a change of clothes," he says, laughing as his twins race over to him and wrap themselves around his waist. "And then all three of us will go and pick Mama up."

"Where is Mama?" Hope asks her father.

"She's been resting while a doctor looks after her," Vance says. "And now she gets to come home to us. So let's tell Mrs. Booker thank you for watching you these past couple of days, and you two gather your things so we can go home and get ready for Mama's homecoming."

The twins race off to get their toothbrushes, favorite dolls, and nightgowns, and Jo sends her three kids through the gate and into the backyard to hose themselves off before going into the house. She and Vance are in the driveway alone as she pulls a cooler and the sandy blankets from the back of her station wagon and sets them on the grass.

"How is she?" Jo asks him gently.

"Mild concussion, and she doesn't remember falling into the pool at all. The brain swelling was minor and seems to be diminishing quickly, so I would consider us lucky and in good shape." He blows out a breath and leans against Jo's car. "I have a lot on my plate at the moment, Jo. I don't mean to bend your ear about it and take advantage of your hospitality, but..." Vance digs the heels of his palms into his eye sockets and rubs them. "I want her to get well is all. I'm sure Bill wouldn't understand because he's got you and his life is all squared away, but sometimes things are really messy."

Jo leans against the car right next to him so that they're nearly shoulder to shoulder. She looks out at the street they live on, squinting as a woman two doors down walks to her mailbox, flips open the little door, and slides out a stack of envelopes. The woman raises a hand at Jo and smiles. Jo waves back—this is Marianne, wife of one of the Project Mercury astronauts, and while they don't know one another well yet, she's been nothing but friendly. Marianne stops to pick up a piece of mail that slips from her hands, then disappears back into her house, closing the front door after her.

"Listen. Vance." Jo crosses her feet at the ankles as Hope and Faith come out with their overnight bags in hand. "You're going to be okay. And no one's life is perfect, so please don't think that you're alone in the messiness of marriage and family, okay?"

Vance turns just his head and looks down at Jo, who is about six inches shorter than he is. "You think?"

Jo gives him a nod as she pushes away from the car with her hip. "I don't just think—I know." She gives him a close-lipped smile as the girls bombard their dad, clearly ready to go home and get back to their own routine.

Vance prompts the twins to say thank you to Jo for her hospitality, and she ruffles each of their heads in turn. "Anytime," Jo says, meaning it. She shoots Vance a meaningful look. "And if you need anything at all, you've got my number."

Jo watches as Vance pulls away with his girls in the backseat, wondering how things will go as Jude comes home and recovers. She'd like to spend more time pondering it, but Bill will be home from Arizona tomorrow, and she has her own messy, imperfect family stuff to worry about at the moment.

SEVENTEEN
bill

THE AFTERNOON with Margaret is nothing short of exhausting. As soon as she'd recognized Bill, Margaret had traveled back in time and started imagining that they were still in high school. Rather than correct her, Bill had gone along with the farce, hoping that she'd come around on her own and start living in reality again.

"You're late—again," Margaret fumes now, folding her arms across her chest. She looks at him the same way she had when they were teenagers and he'd shown up at her house later than they'd planned. "It's like you don't even want to see me. Are you here because I'm forcing you to be?"

Yes, Bill thinks. *There is no way I would have left my job and my family and flown halfway across country for any other reason than because you're forcing me to.*

"No," Bill says, holding up both hands defensively so that she can see his palms. "I'm here because I wanted to see how you are."

"See how I am? I'm hurt, Bill Booker," she says, turning back to the window. "You said you'd be here to meet my grandparents, and you missed the whole thing."

Bill knows instantly that she's skipped back in the timeline to a day when he'd promised to come over to her house while her grandparents were visiting, but he'd been unable to make it, and Margaret was furious when he finally did show up. It looks like they're about to relive that moment.

"You have my most sincere apologies, Margaret," he says. This is not how their original argument had gone, but Bill wants to diffuse the tension as quickly as possible. "I did not mean to miss them."

"And yet," she says, spinning around wildly, her hair catching on the stiff white fabric of her pressed and starched hospital gown. "Here you are, showing up without flowers, without any real excuse, and now I'm just embarrassed in front of my family. Is that how you want me to feel? Embarrassed?"

Bill shakes his head sadly. The day this had actually happened, he'd been the one who was embarrassed. Ashamed of where he came from. "No," he says. "I don't want that."

"What happened?" Margaret's eyes soften and she rushes across the room towards him. Instantly, one of the men against the wall steps forward to intervene, but Bill shakes his head to stop him. He's not afraid of Margaret physically. "Why didn't you come?"

Bill swallows hard as she stands so close to him that her breath is on his neck. She looks up into his face. Margaret is still tiny—barely five feet tall and weighing no more than a hundred pounds. Her eyes and hair have a wildness to them that they didn't have when she was younger, but she is still the same woman Bill married all those years ago. At least somewhere deep down she is.

"I didn't come because my dad got drunk again and he hit my mother. I couldn't leave her there until he took off to find some place to cool down." This was the absolute truth of the situation, but it was something he had not shared with Margaret the day it had happened. He'd been seventeen and proud. He'd also been fearful that Margaret and her family would see him as some kind of no-good bum from a bad family. He'd stayed with his mother, holding her as she cried in his arms, and waited for the sound of his father's truck roaring down the dirt driveway. When the coast was clear, he'd left, driving straight to Margaret's to try and smooth things over.

Margaret takes a step back, blinking at him now. "Your dad was... drunk?"

Bill nods. He'd never shared with her that his father was an alcoholic, nor that he hit Bill's mother. They'd grown up in a time when family business was family business, and you kept your problems inside the four walls of your own home.

"He was drunk," Bill says now, holding Margaret's disbelieving gaze.

"So you still want to marry me?"

It's Bill's turn to just stand there wordlessly. He isn't sure whether carrying on this façade is a good idea anymore. "Margaret," he says, putting both hands in his pockets as he takes one almost imperceptible step back from her. "I just—"

In a rage, Margaret flies at him, hands pounding his chest as she wails. Instantly, the two guards have her by both arms and Bill is being shown out of the room and into the hallway. The door closes behind him, but through a tiny rectangular window, he can see Margaret flailing savagely against the grips of the two large men. Her screams are still audible even through the thick door.

"So," May Ogilvy says kindly, standing at Bill's side as he watches through the window. "You've gotten a sample of what we're working with. I think it's much more impactful for you to see it in person."

Bill's hands are in his pockets again. He tears his gaze from the image of his ex-wife being subdued in a hospital bed that he can see through the tiny window. His heart is racing. "Sure. Yes. I can see that she's got some issues."

Mrs. Ogilvy leads him to a small office on that floor, waving a hand at an empty chair for him to sit in. Bill sinks into it gratefully.

"Is this the highest level of care? Are there any options for medication? Will she ever get better?" His questions aren't meant to sound like an interrogation, but they come out that way.

Mrs. Ogilvy sits and folds her hands together on top of the desk.

"Well," she says. "Let me address each issue individually. First of all, this is the second-tier level of restrictive care. The top tier is one that is essentially entirely restrictive. If there is any attempt to actually self-harm, or if real bodily harm is visited upon an employee by a patient, then we relocate them to the top tier immediately." Bill nods silently. "Next, medication is an option. There are all kinds of psychotropic pharmaceuticals that we can use, Mr. Booker, but some will require your permission as her next-of-kin."

"I see," Bill says. He wants Margaret to get the best care she possibly can, but he also has concerns about her quality of life. "If we try one of these medications, will it mean that she's...a vegetable?"

Mrs. Ogilvy smiles with understanding. "That's a harsh term and one that we like to avoid," she explains. "But it's possible that the medications can put a patient into a state whereby they lose the ability or the interest in interacting with the world around them. However, if a patient is a danger to themselves or to others...that might be the best option."

Bill inhales deeply, taking this in. "Right. Okay."

"Now, as to whether or not she'll ever 'get better,' I have to say that her particular type of psychosis is one that generally plagues a patient for the rest of their lives." She stops and watches Bill as this sinks in. "Mr. Booker, once a person loses touch with reality, they often fall into a place that feels real to them. Margaret is doing her very best to get by in a world that she does not understand. She lives on a plane of reality that you and I cannot visit. Our goal is to make her safe, and to keep all of us—herself included—from coming to any harm. Is that clear?"

"It is."

"Okay. Then to that end, I think our best options are to pursue a heavier dose of lithium, and to consider implementing Thorazine and possibly shock therapy."

Bill rears back in his chair. "Shock therapy? Isn't that dangerous—and painful?"

Mrs. Ogilvy holds up a hand. "At Desert Sage, we fully adhere to the standards for pain management during any treatment, Mr. Booker. Shock therapy is used to stimulate the frontal lobe and to incite a seizure that will, under the best circumstances, treat a patient's depression and mental illness. Now, the risks and the cost will go up for these treatments and this level of care, but it's what we feel is necessary."

Bill is momentarily overcome by the crushing feelings of disappointment and responsibility. Mrs. Ogilvy seems to pick up on this as she watches him with sympathy.

"Are there any other close family members with whom you can consult?" she asks gently. "Perhaps any living relatives who might be willing to work with you on the cost of care?"

Bill shakes his head. Margaret's mother had died of cancer shortly after they'd agreed to put Margaret into a care home, and her father had died of a heart attack three years later. There's truly no one but him, and his pride won't even let him consider reaching out to distant relatives or searching for someone who can help him. Bill had married Margaret, he'd chosen to leave her at Desert Sage, and she is—and will forever be—his obligation.

"No," Bill says, looking at May Ogilvy squarely. "It's just me."

"I would imagine you'll want to speak to Mrs. Booker about the situation, so I'll just give you a write up to take home with you, and then you can get back to me about what you'd like to do. How does that sound?"

It sounds exhausting to Bill. It sounds overwhelming. It sounds like something he has to do.

He nods.

"Okay, then let me take you back to Margaret's room. She should be calmed and under control at this point, and you can spend a bit more time talking to her or just sitting with her." Mrs. Ogilvy looks at him from across the desk. "It might be hard for you," she says softly. "But it will be good for her."

Bill is accustomed to doing hard things, and so he slaps his hands against his knees and stands. "Then take me to her," he says. "I want to do what's best for Margaret."

* * *

Bill sets his bags down inside the front door of his own house, tiredly accepting the hugs and squeals of his daughters, as well as a humorously manly handshake from his eleven-year-old son.

"Dad," Jimmy says, holding out his hand.

"James," Bill says, fighting to keep a smile off his face.

"We missed you." Jo is waiting until the children have scattered to wrap her arms around his waist and give him a side-hug. She looks up at him. "A lot happened while you were gone."

"For me too," he says, and this is an understatement. The manila folder that May Ogilvy had given him at the end of an afternoon spent spoon-feeding his sedated ex-wife as she stared out the window had felt like a contract that he'd need to review and sign. He has no energy to look at it now, and therefore he doesn't mention anything about it to Jo. "What did I miss?" he asks instead.

Jo has wrapped up a plate of dinner for him. The children have already eaten, so Bill and Jo sit at the kitchen table together and watch through the glass of the sliding door as the kids take turns jumping into the pool in the duskiness of late evening. They are illuminated under the porch lights and the half moon, and their shouts are filled with joy.

"Oh," Jo says with a world-weary sigh. "I had my hands full."

Bill forks a bite of roast beef into his mouth and chews while Jo sits in her chair with a glass of water.

She proceeds to tell him the entire story of Jude Majors and the fall that resulted in her being submerged in the pool. Jo tells him about the way Jude and Vance's girls stayed with her while Vance was at the hospital with his wife, and about the trip to the beach with all of the wives and kids. She bites her lip before telling Bill how forlorn Vance had seemed when picking up his daughters. "I think he's feeling alone in his problems at the moment," she says, turning the water glass in circles on the tabletop as she watches her own hand. "And truthfully, he's not alone—is he?"

Bill shakes his head as he hunches over his plate, eating hungrily. All he's ingested in the past three days is airplane food, diner meals, and coffee. Jo's roast beef and mashed potatoes are like a warm blanket, and he wants to wrap himself in it. The comfort of home is almost overwhelming.

"I would say that he's definitely not alone," Bill agrees. "I don't think anyone has it totally easy, do they?"

Jo sips her water and then clears Bill's dishes while he goes to change into a t-shirt and sweat pants. They meet in front of the television after the kids are tucked into bed, and Jo turns off the lights in the living room.

"Come. Sit." Bill pats the spot on the couch next to him. Jo curls up at his side like a cat, pressing her body against his and then scooting down even more so that she can lay her head in his lap as she faces the television.

In the darkness, the flickering images from the TV screen are the only sources of light, and they fall over Jo's pale arm and splash across Bill's white t-shirt. He puts his hand in Jo's hair gently and rubs her scalp as they sit there together, watching the end of *Dr. Kildare* on NBC.

When the show ends, Jo finally speaks. "Bill?"

"Mmm?" he says, not really forming a word; rubbing Jo's head rhythmically has made him tired and relaxed.

"Are you okay?"

Bill's hand stills and he rests it on the side of Jo's neck softly. "I'm okay," he says after a beat. "Are you?"

He can see the length of Jo's eyelashes fanned out as she faces the television. "I think so. It's been hard," she admits with a sigh. "I wanted so badly to hate it here that I think it was even harder to admit to myself that it's kind of growing on me."

"Really? So you don't hate it after all?" Bill smiles triumphantly in the darkened room.

Jo shrugs her shoulder and Bill moves his hand down, cupping her smooth upper arm with reverence; his wife—his lovely, sweet wife. It thrills him to hear that she doesn't hate it anymore.

"I *do* still hate how hot it is," Jo says. "But the pool is nice. And the beach is pretty."

"That's something," Bill says cautiously.

"I like that we have air-conditioning," Jo goes on, searching for more positives. "And the other girls are wonderful. Making friends has been so helpful."

"Of course it has. You and Frankie seem exceptionally close. And, Jojo—I want to apologize. I shouldn't have doubted her or said anything about her watching the kids. She's a fine woman, and I totally respect your choice of friends. If you like her, then I'm sure she's wonderful."

Jo is quiet for a long moment. Bill can feel her breathing as she lays against him. Her warm head is still in his lap. "I just want you to know that I'm doing okay. It's been a long summer of growing pains for me—and of being homesick—but I'm good at the moment. The kids are doing great, and I love the time I spend at the hospital. I really want to be supportive. I want to be here for you."

Bill feels a rush of pleasure at these words—not just the bit about Jo supporting him, but also at her admission that she's finding her own happiness—and he smiles as a new program comes on the television, though he pays no attention to what it is. "I'm glad to hear it," he says.

"I'm doing my best, Bill. I'm always doing my best—I just need you to know that."

Bill runs his fingers lightly over Jo's bare arm as he looks down at her. There's so much love in his heart for his wife, but he can't help thinking of Margaret as they sit there, sharing a rare moment of complete marital peace and harmony. In the span of twenty-four hours, he's spent time with both of the women who have been his wives. He's put his arms around both of them—around Margaret in apology, and around Jo because he finds comfort in her embrace—and he's thought of their various attributes. He looks at Jo now and tries to imagine how she must feel: he's just been to Arizona to see another woman with whom he exchanged sacred vows; another woman who has carried his child in her womb; another woman he's held in the dark of night in the most intimate ways that a man can hold a woman. And now Jo is expected to welcome him back without rancor or ill-will, and, so far as he can tell, she has. She's a remarkable woman.

"I do know that you're doing your best, Jojo," he whispers now, his words mingling with the canned laughter of the variety show on the television. "We all are. I think that's the best part of marriage frankly: that we get up every morning, and we try our best every single day. We show up for each other, and we support each other's dreams. Don't ever forget that I support your dreams too, Jo. I really do."

The wetness of her tears seeps through the leg of his sweatpants as she cries. "Thank you," Jo says, reaching up to wipe her eyes. "That means a lot to me."

Bill moves his hand back to Jo's head and runs his fingers through her soft hair. He means it, absolutely—he *does* support her hopes and dreams. He supports her volunteering at the hospital, even though he'd been skeptical at first. He loves the way she raises their children, and her smile still makes him feel the same way it did the day he'd seen her behind the desk at the dentist's office. But Jo—like any other woman—is a bit of a mystery. Bill goes about his life and his work and just assumes that she'll be there, steadfastly cooking and cleaning and welcoming him home every day. But is that fair to a woman whose heart beats and pumps blood to her brain just like his heart does for him? Is it fair to just automatically assume that her wants and wishes might differ so greatly from his own? That she could be completely content with housework and idle gossip with other women and never want anything more for herself? It almost seems wrong to believe that.

Jo is a smart, capable woman. A good mother. An impeccable wife. He looks at her delicate profile there in the flickering light of the television as she stares at the screen. She's complex and complicated. She's knowable and yet still unknown. He wants more than anything to believe in her and to push her towards her heart's greatest desires.

Because of *course* he believes in her hopes and dreams...he just has no idea what they are.

EIGHTEEN

Jo

THE KIDS ARE BACK in school, and Jo is spending more time at the hospital than she had in the summer, heading over there after she sees the children off, and coming home in time for a late lunch. She and Bill have felt increasingly like two ships passing in the night, and if it weren't for Jo's insistence that they all sit down to dinner together each evening, she sometimes worries that she and Bill might end up sharing a bed during the dark hours of night and nothing more.

"So your husband is going into space?" Nurse Edwina asks one day as Jo helps her put away boxes of Dixie cups, packages of paper towels, and sterile syringes still in their plastic wrapping.

"Well, that's the goal." Jo smiles and hands Edwina a stack of Dixie cups. "He was an Air Force pilot, so flying is in his blood. More than anything, I know Bill wants to lead a mission to space."

Edwina whistles as she carefully stocks the cabinet with paper goods. "Lofty goals. All I want is for my husband to get off the couch after six o'clock in the evening."

Jo laughs good-naturedly. "Bill has a lot of energy, I'll give him that."

"And how do you feel about him being an astronaut?"

Jo tips her head and raises one shoulder. "Umm. I support it. I mean, I'm scared sometimes, but I believe in him."

"I'd be scared too, honey. Space is really something else."

"What does your husband do?" Jo asks.

"Dwight is a detective."

"Oh!" The way Edwina has talked about her husband over the months Jo has known her has led her to believe that he does something slightly less exciting for a job. "Does he investigate crimes?"

"He does." Edwina looks thoroughly unimpressed. "But from where I sit, that pretty much means he cuts out of work around four, stops for a few beers, and comes home looking as tired and beat down as a Saint Bernard."

"Being a detective has to be a tough job."

"He makes it tougher on himself," Edwina says wryly. "He likes watching the sports all evening and drinking his beer, which means he ends up huffing and puffing his way through the workday." She gives a dismissive roll of her eyes. "You'd think a man married to a nurse might listen to her when she tells him to watch his blood pressure and lay off the beers, but then you'd be wrong, wouldn't you?"

Jo hands her a box of sterile bandages and Edwina shelves them in the proper place. "Hey," Jo says, changing the subject. "How is Mr. Dandridge doing? I've never asked him what he's here for, but he's been in the hospital for a while now, so I was hoping maybe there was good news. Is he getting better?"

Edwina sets a box on the shelf, pushes it to the back, and then turns to look Jo squarely in the eye. "Oh, honey," she says, her face and voice full of pity. "No."

"No?" Jo frowns. In her mind—despite seeing plenty of evidence to the contrary during her time as a volunteer—Jo still believes that people come to the hospital to be fixed. The doctors work their magic, and the patient goes home. In fact, she's already envisioned herself visiting Mr. D in his little house, wherever that may be, bringing him a home-cooked meal, or letting her kids come by to say hello. They could be kind of like a surrogate family for Mr. D.

Edwina shakes her head. "No." Her eyes are wide and a little watery. "I know you love Douglas as much as the rest of us do—maybe more—so there's no easy way to say this, but he's got terminal cancer, sweetheart."

Jo's heart falls directly from its place behind her rib cage and lands at her feet. The world around her makes a *whooshing* sound and then goes quiet. "Cancer? Terminal? Are they sure?"

Edwina nods and reaches out a hand, taking Jo's in her own and holding onto it. "They're sure. He's been getting treatment, but it's not working anymore, honey. I think you need to be prepared, because there's a strong chance that he won't make it until Christmas."

"Oh." Jo swallows around the lump that's growing in her throat. "Okay. I guess I should have realized there was something serious going on, given that he's been here all summer."

Edwina looks at her softly. "Hey, we all engage in a little magical thinking sometimes. It's the reason I don't work in pediatrics anymore: I found myself bargaining and thinking that if I just did something better in my own life, the universe might give those beautiful little children a better chance at survival." She smiles, but it's a sad one. "Never worked."

Jo nods and squeezes Edwina's hand. "Thank you for just telling me flat-out. I would have asked Dr. Chavez, but I wasn't sure if he'd give me personal information about a patient like that."

Edwina's sad face turns impish. "Oh, I think Dr. Chavez would give *you* anything you asked for."

Jo is puzzled by this; she's never asked him for anything. "Come again?"

"Oh, come on, Josephine. That man is a handsome devil, and a world class flirt, to boot. I even caught him flirting with me one time. I was flattered, but I have enough sense to know that it was just an automatic reflex on his part. You know, that man will flirt with anything in a skirt, but somehow it's not the least bit creepy." She pauses, considering this. "Come to think of it, I spent the rest of the day feeling like a million bucks after he told me he liked my brooch." She glances down at the pearl and rhinestone pin that she always has clipped to the collar of her nurse's uniform. Edwina shakes her head like she's mystified. "He just has a way."

"Ladies," Dr. Chavez says, poking his head into the storage room and making both Edwina and Jo jump guiltily. Jo can't stifle her nervous giggle in time. "Catch you with your hands in the cookie jar?" Dr. Chavez teases, looking confused at their response.

"No," Jo says with a wide, dopey grin. "We were just having some girl talk."

"Well, if you're done chewing the fat, ladies, then maybe I can borrow Nurse Edwina for my rounds this morning? I have some things I need assistance with," he says, glancing at the watch on his wrist.

"I'll see you both later," Jo says, giving them a quick nod as she hurries off to find her cart of goodies and start making the rounds. She's been taking on more of an assisting role with general duties like inventory, arranging for linens to be sent to the laundry and delivered back to the ward, and even making phone calls to families to arrange for them to come in and meet with their loved ones' doctors. But although these things make her feel important, Jo's favorite task is still popping into each room and seeing the patients smile when she offers them cookies and reading materials.

"Hey, kid," Mr. Dandridge says brightly as she enters the room. It's like he knows that Jo has heard the truth about his diagnosis and he's intentionally rallied to impress her, because Douglas Dandridge is sitting up in bed, his wispy white hair combed neatly, hands folded in his lap. "Come on in and tell me everything you've got going on."

Jo leaves her cart on the side of the room, as she usually does. She sits in the chair next to Mr. D's bed, forcing herself to look cheerful. "Well," she says, patting her knees with both hands as she crosses her feet at the ankles under the chair. "All three of my kids are back in school, and it's going well. Jimmy is in the sixth grade, Nancy is in fifth grade, and Kate is in second grade."

"That is wonderful." Mr. D's eyes dance merrily. "Children at the beginning of their educational journey." He shakes his head as he looks at a spot on the wall above Jo's head. "It's all still ahead of them, isn't it? All the learning, the joy, the mistakes, the failures…all of it." He looks wistful for a moment.

"That's true enough," Jo agrees neutrally. "And my oldest, Jimmy, has the opportunity of a lifetime coming up."

"Oh? What's that?" Mr. D snaps out of his melancholy reflection and refocuses on Jo.

"Well, along with Jimmy, in his sixth grade class are the children of three other astronauts from Port Canaveral, and they've all been invited—the whole class—to take an 800-mile bus ride to Washington D.C. to meet the president."

Mr. Dandridge gives a hoot so loud that Jo startles.

"It's amazing, isn't it?"

"You're letting him go, of course?"

"Oh, of course. Bill is completely on board with it. It's an honor for our son to get to meet the Commander in Chief, and I think Bill is going to volunteer as a chaperone."

"Sounds like a photo op in the making," Mr. Dandridge says. "The astronaut fathers accompanying their kids to the White House is newsworthy for sure."

They sit there smiling for a long moment, and between them there is a palpable, unspoken mountain of words.

"So," Mr. Dandridge finally says, "I would imagine that you've been updated at this point on my prognosis."

"Oh, Mr. D." Jo's eyes immediately fill with tears. She slides forward on her chair and reaches out for the guardrail next to his bed, gripping it tightly. "I'm so sorry. I had no idea."

Mr. Dandridge's eyes are glassy with unshed tears. "I preferred it that way, to be honest, my dear Josephine. Every other person who comes into my room is here to draw blood, give me a dose of something that makes me sick, or to tell me bad news, but when you show up, it's with books like *The Heart is a Lonely Traveler* or *Her White Gloves*." They smile at each other knowingly. "I enjoy talking about your children and the weather and books far more than I like hearing about a disease that's slowly killing me from the inside."

Hearing these words makes the tears spill over Jo's cheeks and she cries openly. "I'm so sorry," she apologizes. "It's not my place to be crying like this."

"The hell it isn't," Mr. Dandridge says indignantly. "We're friends, Josephine. I'd be offended if you weren't at least a tiny bit sad to see me go."

Jo's been holding onto his bed so tightly that her knuckles have gone white, and she releases it now, flexing her fingers. "Please don't say you're going," she begs him, wiping at her cheeks with the back of her hands. Mr. Dandridge reaches for a box of Kleenex on the stand next to his bed and hands it to Jo.

"Darling girl, I have to say it like it is. I can use all the poetic devices, all the euphemisms I want, but in the end, the simple fact is that I'm an old widower who is dying. And when I'm gone, the sun will still rise, the palm trees will still wave against a blue sky, and astronauts will still go into space to see what else is out there. Your children will grow, books will be written, and perhaps—just maybe—our friendship will linger in your heart."

Jo pulls a tissue from the box and blows her nose as she nods emphatically. "It will!" she promises. "Forever."

"Okay," Mr. Dandridge says decisively. "Then let's knock off this nonsense for today, and you give me some books that will keep me entertained. What do you say?"

Jo wipes her eyes and stands, tucking the Kleenex into the pocket of her cardigan. She composes herself. "Absolutely," she says with a determination she doesn't quite feel. Given the chance, she'd like to cry a bit more over the fact that she'll—most likely—lose her friend in the near future, but she knows this isn't what's best for him. Instead, Jo takes three paperbacks from the cart that she's borrowed from Frankie and sets them on the nightstand. "Here you go. Plenty of stolen kisses," she says, dropping her voice as if they're being spied on. "Lots of forbidden romance, and a few broken hearts."

"Just the way I like it," Mr. D says with a wink.

Before the tears start up again, Jo gathers her cart and moves to the door. "See you in two days?" she asks hopefully.

"You better believe it." Mr. Dandridge smiles at her, holding her gaze for an extra beat. "Now you get on out of here, finish your duties, and go home to help your young man pack to meet the president."

Jo smiles gamely. "Will do," she says, hanging onto her cart with both hands.

"And you tell him that if he can get a picture with that gorgeous First Lady, then that's the real ticket. I'd like a copy of *that* photo."

Jo laughs at this uncharacteristic display of boyishness from the old man. "You got it, Mr. D," she says. Her eyes linger on him for an extra moment as he turns to the window and stares out at the bright, sunny afternoon. His smile fades just slightly, and Jo leaves him like that, taking the pain in her heart with her.

NINETEEN
bill

BY THE TIME Bill and Jimmy are set to leave for Washington D.C. in mid-September, there is a distinctive pattern to their lives. At home, the kids have favorite playmates. Jo has her work at Stardust General, and she has her increasingly close group of friends in the neighborhood—especially Frankie. And Bill has sporadic updates from Desert Sage (Margaret has days and weeks of silent disassociation, followed by bouts of rage and confusion; treatments are having mixed results), and a predictable routine at work.

Jeanie Florence has become his favorite workmate to chat with over afternoon coffee, though he hasn't quite dared to suggest that the small group of female engineers integrate themselves into the mens' lunch hour or join them regularly at the Black Hole. Her combination of down-to-earth wit, scientific and astronomic knowledge, and youthful innocence have made Jeanie a bright spot in even the most tiring days at NASA.

"So you're going to the White House, I hear," Jeanie says one afternoon as Bill pours a packet of sugar into his black coffee, stirring it with a stick. "Sounds important."

Bill tosses the flimsy stick into a trash can and sips his coffee in the empty cafeteria as Jeanie buys a coffee from the vending machine. "It's mostly a chance to be with my son," he says. "And of course it's kind of a big deal to get invited to the Oval Office."

"The president must love children," Jeanie gushes. "I bet he loves seeing their little faces as they ask questions about our government. Twelve-year-old me is really jealous of those kids who get to go on this trip!"

"I'm pretty sure the whole thing is just about good optics," Bill says. "I would bet that NASA actually arranged the whole thing. From the way it was presented to me, I think they wanted the children of astronauts on this trip—it feels very intentional."

Jeanie looks disappointed at this less magical view of events. "Huh," she says, pouring cream into her coffee and stirring it.

"I mean, Arvin North told me flat-out that we were getting a few days off to chaperone the trip, so now it's me, Young, Trager, and Jameson taking our kids on a bus ride with a bunch of other sweaty sixth graders. It felt more like an assignment than an option, so obviously I got on board. Should be interesting." He raises his cup in a mock toast and sips the coffee.

"Well, your son will never forget it," Jeanie says. "Both meeting the president *and* going on this trip with his dad. I think it's special."

"Without question," Bill agrees. "Hey, how are things going for you so far? You settled in here?"

Jeanie tips her head from one side to the other as she weighs the question. "For the most part. I'm sure it's no shock to you that there are men here who are less than charitable about having women on staff. Not everyone is forward-thinking enough to realize that we have just as much education, just as much knowledge, and certainly, just as much right to be here as you all do."

Bill blows out a long breath and rocks back on his heels. "That's a mouthful," he says, which is his way of agreeing. "But I think you'll wear them down eventually. Just keep doing good work, and don't let them boss you around too much."

Jeanie cocks her head and looks at Bill inquisitively. "Question," she says.

"Shoot." Bill sips his coffee while anticipating what she might say.

"Who wears the pants at your house?"

Bill blinks a few times. "Uhhh," he says, flustered.

"I just mean, when you tell me not to let them boss me around, do you think most women live lives outside the workplace where men *don't* boss them around? Do you think your wife would say that she never feels as though she's there to do your bidding?" Bill remains silent. "Hypothetically," Jeanie adds quickly. "I'm asking you to consider it hypothetically. I'm twenty-six years old. That means until eight years ago, when I went to college, I lived under my father's roof. I answered to male professors in college. I was hired to work at NASA by a panel made up entirely of men. And society tells me to obey a mostly male government, to stop my car when a male police officer pulls me over, to let a male doctor have full access to my body. And—if I choose to marry—I'm supposed to agree to 'love, honor, and obey' my husband."

Jeanie stares at him pointedly for a moment that stretches on so long it actually makes Bill squirm. "So, I can assure you that while I do not *like* being bossed around by men, every fiber of my being has been raised and groomed to do just that."

"Point taken," Bill says, appropriately chagrined. He clears his throat. "Then how about this: if anyone gives you grief—any of the guys I work with closely in particular—you let me know. I'm not a perfect man, nor do I fully understand this whole women's liberation movement that seems to be forming right under our noses, but I don't subscribe to the notion that women are inferior to men. I just don't. I'm on your team."

Jeanie smiles at him politely—almost with pity—and wraps both hands around her paper coffee cup. "Thank you, Bill," she says. Her reaction nearly makes Bill blush with shame; has he explained his feelings incorrectly? Why does she look like his words have offended her? Jeanie backs away, grabbing a napkin from a dispenser as she does. "Have a good time on the trip to D.C., okay? Bring back lots of stories!"

Bill watches her go, wondering whether he came across as patronizing and not supportive. He can't change the world, and he can't change the way that society functions, but he knows that he can use his rational mind and apply it to the way he treats his daughters, his wife, and his female coworkers. Bill tops off his coffee with a shake of his head, forgetting it all for the time being as he thinks about the bus ride to D.C. that he's about to take. Thirty twelve-year-olds packed onto a bus without air-conditioning will be an adventure. Or torture—it could also be very much like torture.

Bill laughs to himself, remembering the places he's been deployed to and the situations he's been in that truly *were* torturous, and he realizes that a few days of hormonal pre-teens on a bus is actually going to be a walk in the park.

* * *

"Now, we are going to take this very special, very important tour of the White House," Miss Black says to the class, holding her index finger to her lips to shush them as they stand in the long, windowed hallway with its polished brick floors.

Jimmy stands at attention next to Bill, hands behind his back like he's being graded on his stance. Bill smiles at his son as a small knot of kids on his other side fuss and shuffle with impatience.

"I want to see the First Lady," a girl named Susan says, poking Bill and looking up at him. "Can we see where they sleep?"

It's Bill's turn to put a finger to his lips, but he does it with a smile. "We'll go wherever they take us," he whispers back, turning his attention to Miss Black as an example of what he wants the kids to do.

"Our tour guide will be here shortly," Miss Black says in a voice tinged with the sizzle of excitement. Her cheeks are flushed pink, and her tight bun has come loose on one side. She looks delirious with anticipation. "When we follow our guide, I expect you all to keep your hands to yourselves, your voices very, very quiet, and to raise your hand if you have a question."

A boy puts his hand up in the crowd. "Miss Black?" he says.

"Yes, Sean?"

"Can we shake hands with President Kennedy?"

Miss Black looks nearly apoplectic at the mere mention of possibly meeting Kennedy. "We will do exactly what our tour guide tells us to," Miss Black says, enunciating each word precisely. "It's entirely possible that President Kennedy is in an important meeting, and that maybe we won't get to meet him at all, but if we do, we will wait for instructions on what to do and what not to do. Am I being clear?" Her eyes skim the group of kids, landing on each one of them as she seeks confirmation. Heads nod all around.

Bill catches the eye of Trager, one of the astronauts whose son is also in the class. The four men are scattered amongst the group, each wearing their NASA-issued shirts tucked into dress pants. Bill is more aware than ever that this is a publicity opportunity for NASA, and that the kids are all benefiting from this event in ways they can't possibly comprehend at the tender age of twelve. Sure, several of the kids took turns on the long bus ride asking Bill, Trager, Young, and Jameson what it would be like to go to space, whether they can eat in a rocket ship, and if they really, *really* want to go to the moon. But as adults, they'll look back on this trip where they had astronauts as chaperones, to meet one of the most popular presidents in history, as a seminal event in their lives. There is no way they won't realize the hugeness of this trip with the wisdom that the years will bring.

Their tour guide, a bespectacled young man named Philip Powers, greets them and gives a long list of easily digestible instructions—most of which are along the lines of what Miss Black has already told them: keep their hands to themselves; stay in a group; voices low; and save up their questions for a moment when they can stop in a quiet spot to talk.

THE LAUNCH

"Ready?" Philip Powers asks, clutching his clipboard to his chest as he pushes his thick, black frames up his nose.

Bill brings up the rear as they wind their way through the West Wing. The children whisper to one another in hushed awe. Bill looks at the oil paintings that line the walls: portraits of George Washington, Abraham Lincoln, Andrew Jackson, Thomas Jefferson, Alexander Hamilton, and Benjamin Franklin. He feels appropriately reverent walking through these halls of greatness, and as the kids follow Philip Powers down a hallway, Bill lingers. He stands beneath a painting of Lincoln, looking up at the proud tilt of the former president's chin.

"That one is my favorite," a woman's voice whispers from behind Bill. He turns, assuming that Miss Black has stayed behind with him. Only it isn't Miss Black, and the look on the woman's face is one of amusement.

It's Jackie Kennedy. She winks at him. "Lincoln just had a way about him, didn't he?"

Bill nods, pulling his jaw off the floor. "Yes, ma'am," he agrees, because who would argue with the First Lady? "He most certainly did have a way."

"It's lovely of you to join the children," she says, glancing down the hallway at the backs of the kids as they turn a corner, listening to Philip Powers droning on about the Executive Branch of the government and the checks and balances provided by having three branches. "I heard we were having special guests today." She looks at his name, which is embroidered right over his heart, beneath the NASA insignia. "Mr. Booker," she adds with a smile. "Or is it Cosmonaut Booker?" She frowns prettily as she laughs. "I'm sorry I don't have that down—it's unlike me not to know a detail like that."

Bill stands up straighter. "Actually, it's Lieutenant Colonel William Booker, United States Air Force, ma'am," he says proudly. "And currently of NASA. I'm not assigned to a mission yet, so just Bill is fine." His face cracks into a goofy smile as the realization that he's standing in a hallway trading banter with the First Lady really hits him.

"Okay, Just Bill," she says cheekily. "I should probably let you get back to the tour before they lose you entirely. It was lovely to meet you." Jackie offers a hand for him to shake, and Bill takes it in his. He will surely forget the finer details of this entire moment once it's over. It's almost too much for the mind to process and retain. "Thank you for your service to our country," Mrs. Kennedy says, "and also for your willingness to explore the universe."

It seems so grand, so outrageous, that Jackie Kennedy has just thanked him for wanting to explore the universe, but Bill grins widely. His cheeks are already starting to hurt. "It was an honor to meet you, ma'am," he says.

When Bill rejoins the group, he can't stop smiling. Weirdly, being in the Oval Office seems almost anticlimactic after having a one-on-one with the First Lady. He stands to the side, hands clasped behind his back as he watches the kids trying not to burst at the seams with their own bottled-up excitement. Within minutes, an advisor ushers President Kennedy into the room, and the kids go dead silent. Their faces fall into the serious masks of young adults. Even Trager, Young, and Jameson are silent, standing at attention like the military men they all are. This is their Commander in Chief, and they treat this moment with all the respect that it deserves.

"Hello there," President Kennedy says to the young girl standing closest to him. He holds out a hand for her, and she looks at it nervously before shaking it. "Who are you?"

"Emily," she says in a near whisper.

"Would you like to sit in my chair, Emily? See what it's like to be in charge of the country?"

As Bill watches, he sees a familiar look cross Emily's face—it was the one that he remembers seeing on his own kids after waiting in line to meet Santa Claus as small children: unmitigated excitement mixed with sheer terror.

Miss Black steps in and walks Emily over to the desk, pointing at the chair. Once the seal is broken and Emily has had her turn sitting there, her hands folded on the desk blotter as a White House photographer snaps a photo of her smiling shyly, every other kid wants a turn. President Kennedy laughs and smiles, asking each child for their name, and adding something charming as they sit at his desk, from "What do you think about that fancy pen?" to "If you were sitting at that desk, would you invite the New York Yankees or the Beatles to visit you at the White House?"—a question which he aims at Jimmy Booker.

"I'd invite Joe DiMaggio," Jimmy says definitively as he sits squarely in President Kennedy's chair. The American flag hangs just so on a stand behind him, and he clasps his hands on the desk, looking right into the lens of the camera for his photo. The shutter snaps, and Jimmy turns back to the President. "I'd invite him to play catch out there on the lawn."

President Kennedy throws his head back, laughing heartily at this and showing all of his square, white teeth. "Oh, that's beautiful, son," he says, reaching over and placing a hand on Jimmy's shoulder. "We're on eighteen acres here, so you'd find a spot to toss a ball around with Joe for sure." He looks right at the photographer, holding up the hand that's not resting on Jimmy's shoulder and snapping his fingers lightly. "Mind getting a photo of me with this young guy?" he asks with a half-smile, putting his free hand into the pocket of his pants and posing with Jimmy.

The shutter snaps again, and Bill feels a thrill of pride: President Kennedy has singled out his son for a photo. Without moving, Kennedy looks over at Bill and motions to him. "Join us for a photo?" he asks Bill, who crosses the office without hesitation and stands behind Jimmy, putting his hand on his son's other shoulder.

He can't wait to call Jo that night from the hotel and tell her everything—every single detail. Even if this is all entirely orchestrated and planned out for maximum positive exposure for NASA, or for the White House, or both, Bill can't think of another time he's felt so happy and excited. So proud to be an American.

"Thank you, sir," he says, turning to Kennedy.

Kennedy holds out a hand to him. "Thank you to you, Lieutenant Colonel Booker," Kennedy says with a nod. He's clearly been briefed on who everyone is, and Bill is flattered and surprised to hear his own name pass through the President's lips.

Bill trails the group through the rest of the White House tour and then all around D.C., making sure everyone crosses the busy streets safely and gets their photo taken in front of the major landmarks. But there's a soundtrack playing in his mind the entire time as they move through the city. As they gather around the Washington Monument, looking up at the tall, narrow obelisk, Bill hears "Save the Last Dance for Me" by The Drifters. When they visit The Smithsonian, all he can hear in his head is "Sleepwalk" by Santo & Johnny. And as the early fall sun dances on the Potomac and he leans against the side of the boat that's bobbing along, allowing the kids to see the sights from the water, Bill hears "It's Now or Never" by Elvis Presley. It's not unpleasant to have his own personal jukebox in his head as they move around the city, and it allows Bill to smile and to watch his son enjoying the trip, while still letting him entertain his own thoughts.

It's only as they board the buses late on the third day to turn around and head south again that Bill realizes how much of the movie that's been playing in his head has been about his past life with Margaret and all of the "what ifs" that surround his truncated first marriage. Some of it is sad, and some is bittersweet, but it's all there nonetheless. Of course he imagines telling Jo about everything and sharing the stories about the President and First Lady, but an amazing amount of his daydreaming on this trip has involved him sharing all the details with Jeanie Florence, or simply of sitting with her in the sunlit break room at Port Canaveral, sharing an afternoon cup of coffee. A few of his mental scenarios involve bumping into Jeanie at the Black Hole with "My Boyfriend's Back" by The Angels spinning on the jukebox as they drink cold beer and trade stories, though this daydream leaves a stain of guilt behind every time it comes up.

The inappropriateness of this train of thought is not lost on Bill. He chooses a seat in the center of the bus, intentionally taking up the whole seat so that no one sits next to him, and then he spends part of the trip back to Florida trying to convince himself that imagining a coffee date with a coworker is possibly the tamest thing a man has ever daydreamed about. The rest of the trip is spent forcing himself to drag his mind back to that night on the roof of the house in Stardust Beach with Jo. He watches the highway whizzing past his window, the miles piling up behind them while he pushes Jeanie from his mind, instead picturing what it was like to kiss his wife under the stars.

And it isn't that he didn't love that night on the roof with Jo, but for some reason, he just can't keep his brain there. For some reason, no matter how hard he tries, his mind keeps traveling back to Jeanie Florence and her long hair, her glasses, her freckles. He can't get her face out of his head.

Bill does not like this.

TWENTY

jo

IT'S the weekend before Halloween, and the women of the neighborhood have gathered to put on a tag sale that will hopefully raise enough money to pay the medical bills of a family Jo has come to know at the hospital. Little Adam Shepherd had been admitted to Stardust General at the end of September with a heart defect. The toddler has struggled to make it through the fall, and he might not make it much further without the surgery that he so desperately needs.

"Should I put this here?" Carrie asks, placing a big, lacquered box covered in orchids on a long table. "Jay brought this back from a trip to Japan, and it *is* lovely, but it doesn't really suit my style at all." She leans in to Jo and drops her voice to a whisper. "Please don't tell him. It's been in the back of my closet for years, so I'm assuming he won't even miss it. I figured it might bring in some money for the Shepherds."

Jo brushes her hair off her forehead and assesses the box. They can probably sell the piece for close to twenty dollars if they hold firm. It's large and really quite beautiful. "Thanks, Carrie," she says. "Your secret is safe with me."

The sale runs the length of the street that leads into the neighborhood, and everyone who lives on a cul-de-sac has gamely brought their donations out and found places along the tables and driveways on the main drag to display their items. Because all the money is going to the Shepherds, no one minds their belongings mingling with other people's things for sale, and there's no need to track who sells what.

"This is a fabulous idea, Josephine," Maxine Trager says, pulling a red Radio Flyer wagon full of dishes along behind her. "I'm donating my wedding china because my mother-in-law picked it out, and frankly, I hate it."

Jo stifles a laugh as she bends over to peer into the boxes. The china, patterned with birds and a lacy design of ivy leaves, looks exactly like something that a meddling mother-in-law would choose. "This will sell. No question." Jo takes a tag off her clipboard, writes a figure on it, and sticks it to the biggest box. "Thank you for your donation!"

The sun is high in the sky and the weather has cooled noticeably since summer. Late October on the Space Coast is pleasant: the high is about eighty degrees, and the breezes occasionally blow things around. The women are dressed comfortably in skirts and capri pants and blouses, relieved to finally not be sweating through their clothing all day long.

Adam Shepherd has quickly become a huge part of Jo's life at the hospital, and she probably spends as much time visiting him and his family as she does visiting Mr. Dandridge. Watching Adam struggle to survive and seeing the poor little boy look so confused by his confinement to a bed and a tangle of tubes and wires is terrible. It breaks Jo's heart every time she walks into the room, and her days at the hospital are now tinged with a palpable sense of loss, and a dwindling of hope on all fronts. But if anything she can do will get Adam closer to the surgery he so desperately needs, then she'll do it; hence her idea to put together a giant neighborhood tag sale and to donate all the profits to the Shepherds' surgery fund.

"This is really impressive, Joey-girl," Frankie says from the lawn chair she's sitting in next to Jo. Frankie is holding a parasol over her head with one hand and smoking a cigarette with the other. She turns her face up to Jo and smiles from behind her cat-eye sunglasses. "You really brought this neighborhood together for a cause, sister."

Jo feels a rush of pride at the compliment, but to her, she's only doing what needs to be done. Back home, if anyone in her community needed something, she was the first person to roll up her sleeves and quietly help. In her mind, it's just what you do.

"It's a worthy cause," Jo says, as if anyone is questioning the veracity of Adam's need for the surgery. "And the Shepherds are truly wonderful people. Did I mention that Adam's mother is pregnant again? She just told me yesterday."

Frankie looks down the street and puts her cigarette to her lips again. "You did not mention that, no. But I completely understand your desire to help." Frankie gets to her feet so quickly that it startles Jo. "Oh," she says, handing her parasol to Jo. "Hold this, will you? I'm going to go and help Jude with her boxes."

Jo takes the flowered parasol and presses the button to close it so that she can lay it across the lawn chair and get back to tagging items with her price stickers. From the corner of her eye, she watches Frankie reach for the big box that Jude is carrying, and the women walk side by side over to a table, where Frankie sets it down carefully. Hope and Faith are trailing the women, wearing matching yellow sundresses. Jo waves at the girls and they wave back.

Ever since Jude's fall into the pool, everyone has been solicitous and worried about her health. Jo hasn't recounted her conversation with Vance in her driveway to any of the other women, so it's still just her private guess that Jude might have a drinking problem, and she worries about it every time she sees the woman, wondering how it affects her family and—most importantly—her children.

"Are you taking art work?" A blonde woman with a baby in a stroller asks Jo, handing her three small, framed paintings. "I've had these on my wall for years, and you know what?" she says, cocking her head and putting one fist on her narrow hip. "I don't even like them."

Jo inspects the paintings: they're of three different varieties of flowers, bold in color, and decent in execution. The frames are nice.

"We'd love to take them," Jo says with a smile, already writing out a sticker to put on the back of one of the frames. "I'll sell them as a trio. Thank you very much for your donation."

The woman smiles, satisfied that she's contributed, and pushes the baby on down the road.

Jo turns back to Jude and Frankie. Frankie is doing a lot of talking, while Jude just appears to be listening. *Has Jude been more vacant since the accident, or is she pretty much the way she's always been?* Jo wonders, trying to compare the pre-fall Jude to the one who is standing before her now. *Sure, there have been times when Jude appeared to drift off mid-stitch in her knitting, and there have been other times when she's gotten her own twins confused, but come on! They're identical, for crying out loud*! Jo runs through the list of things she's observed, playing devil's advocate as she goes. *But then there was that time when she actually seemed drunk at noon, which was so preposterous that none of the other women seemed to even consider the possibility. It's just as likely to them that she's still suffering from the after-effects of the fall and the time she'd spent in the water.*

Jo certainly has her hands full with her own children, her home, her marriage, Margaret, the work she's doing at the hospital, and everything else in life, but Jude is not entirely off her radar; she'll keep her eye on her friend and make sure that anything worth noting gets tucked away for further investigation. The idea that a woman she spends time with might need someone to help her and that her own busy life might obscure that need just doesn't sit right with Jo. She vows to do better and to check in on Jude more.

"How much for this?" A woman who has parked her blue car down the street is clutching a handbag as she bends over, admiring a necklace made of thick amber beads that Carrie has donated to the tag sale.

Jo lifts the necklace and holds it up for the woman to inspect. "This is four dollars," she says with a pleased smile. The necklace is lovely, and she can imagine the older woman standing before her wearing it against a nice dress in brown or yellow.

The woman glances up at Jo. "This is the fundraiser for the sweet little baby in the hospital, right? I saw an advertisement for this sale posted in the window at Publix."

"Yes, you found the right sale," Jo confirms.

The woman unsnaps her handbag and takes out her wallet. "Then I'll tell you what," the woman says, "I'll give you five dollars."

Jo trades the necklace for the cash, which she puts into a metal box on the table, and watches the woman move down the table, admiring the other goods.

Jo looks up at the sky as an airplane passes overhead, leaving a long contrail across the infinite blue backdrop. A breeze picks up, blowing the palm fronds around and lifting a lock of Jo's hair. A pack of kids on bikes ride by, shouting cheerfully as a mother tells them to stay out of the road and to watch for cars.

Jo closes her eyes, and for a moment she can't tell whether she's in Minnesota or Florida.

It's a really good feeling.

* * *

"Mom! Is my costume done?" Jimmy is standing over Jo, looking down at her worriedly. "All the guys are going to meet at six-thirty on the corner to trick-or-treat."

Jo wipes her forehead but doesn't speak, as she has a mouthful of straight pins. She looks up at her son, her beautiful boy, who is growing so fast. He's shot up so much in height over the past six months that he's now almost at eye-level with his mother when they're both standing. Jo spits the pins into her hand.

"Almost done, sweetheart. How are your sisters?"

Jo has made two different dresses for her girls: Nancy wants to go trick-or-treating dressed as Cleopatra (which earned a lifted eyebrow from Bill, who still has misgivings about Frankie having taken the kids to see the movie), and Kate wants to be a fairy princess. Jimmy, however, has proven somewhat easier, as he just wants to go as a cowboy, which allowed Jo to leave the sewing of his Western shirt for last.

"They're fine. Kate wants to wear lipstick." Jimmy is still looking down at his mom as she kneels on the floor of the front room, sewing on the individual snap buttons down the front of his shirt.

"Well that's not going to happen. I'm almost done here, Jimmy. Go and put your jeans on and get your cowboy hat, okay?" As Jo goes back to sewing buttons, their doorbell chimes for the first time that evening. "Bill?" she calls out. "Can you answer that? The bowl of candy for the kids is right there by the door."

Jo finishes the shirt as Jimmy waits impatiently, and a steady stream of police officers, princesses, hobos, ghosts, and firemen all take turns knocking on the door and opening their pillowcases to be filled with candy at each house along the street.

"Here we are, my little pumpkins," Jo says once she has all three kids lined up and waiting for her to snap a photo of them standing by the front door.

"Mommmm," Jimmy says, barely containing his displeasure at being referred to as a *little pumpkin*. "Can we go now?"

Jo takes one shot of the three kids standing in a line, then lowers her Instamatic and shoos them away. "Okay. Go and get the candy, goblins. Have fun," she calls, standing in the open front door with her camera still in hand. Jimmy hits the end of the driveway and starts to run. "Don't forget about your sisters, James!" Jo says, cupping her mouth with one hand.

"Trick or treat!" A little girl dressed like a cat is standing in front of Jo, and she pulls her attention back to her own front porch.

"Well, Happy Halloween to you," Jo says, stepping inside and trading her camera for the bowl of treats. She tosses one piece of candy into the pillowcase of each child who walks up her driveway.

As she does, the sun sinks lower in the sky, and a crescent moon ascends, looking down on the neighborhood with its bright porch lights, its plethora of witches and pirates hauling sugary treats, and its carved, candle-lit pumpkins sitting on nearly every front porch.

"Hiya, Jo," Barbie says, holding baby Huck to her chest as she waits for Heath and Henry, who are both dressed like tiny ghosts in white sheets with cutout eye holes. "How are things going here?"

Jo tosses candy in each boy's bag and reaches over to squeeze Huck's bare foot. The baby is now five months old and getting chunkier every day. He turns his head and gives Jo a gummy smile. "Things are good," Jo says. "I got my three out the door, and Bill is inside with a glass of whiskey." She inhales deeply, hugging the bowl of candy to her stomach. "Ah, I love fall so much. Halloween is the start of the best time of the year."

Barbie nods as Heath and Henry dance around in the driveway, spinning in their bedsheets and nearly spilling candy everywhere. "Oh, I know. Don't you just love the cooler weather? I get so excited for shorter days, and the start of the holiday season." Barbie reaches out and grabs Jo's hand. "Maybe this year we can start a new tradition of doing Thanksgiving with everyone." Her face quickly falls. "Except I bet some of us will have family come to town, and others might leave Stardust Beach for the holiday." Barbie's smile comes back slowly as she thinks. "Or maybe we can do a big Christmas party in the middle of December—or maybe a New Year's Eve party!"

Jo can't help but smile at her friend's enthusiasm. "Sure, Barb. I bet we can make that happen."

"Okay," Barbie says, eyeing her boys, who have taken their sheets off, tossed them onto the driveway, and are now wrestling in Jo's front yard. "I better get these guys moving. Come on, boys," she says to them, pointing at the sheets. "Turn yourselves back into ghosts so we can go scare up a little more candy."

Jo waves them off as she laughs at the sight of petite Barbie holding an already hefty Huck while racing after the older boys.

"Jojo?" Bill calls through the open front door. She's standing in the puddle of light on the porch and she turns to see him there on the couch. He's got one leg crossed over the other as he reads the paper, whiskey in hand. Bill folds the newspaper and sets it aside as he locks eyes on his wife. "You got any Tootsie Rolls in that candy dish?"

Jo walks inside and closes the door. She shakes her head. "You want Tootsie Rolls with your whiskey?" she asks, amused.

Bill reaches for her hip as she comes closer. She digs through her bowl of candy for the telltale brown wrapper. Bill grabs her by the waist and pulls her down next to him as she yelps.

"I definitely want something sweet with my whiskey," he says playfully, nuzzling his face into Jo's neck.

She's caught off guard by this unexpected display of affection, but she definitely likes it. "Bill," Jo says knowingly, letting him kiss her under her jawline as she closes her eyes in pleasure.

Just then, the doorbell chimes. Jo groans. She pushes herself up from the couch, taking the bowl with her.

"Saved by the bell, Mrs. Booker," Bill says as he reaches out and swats her behind. "You better go and give those little monsters what they want. I'll get what I want later."

TWENTY-ONE

bill

THERE IS big talk of Gemini 3 around Port Canaveral for all of November, and Bill is up to his eyebrows in trainings, tests, and design meetings that will allow the first two-man spacecraft to test long-duration missions. Gemini's purpose is to perfect re-entry and landing methods, as well as to rendezvous and dock with another space vehicle. There is also excited chatter about "spacewalking," and the engineers spend nearly every waking moment hypothesizing and strategizing plans and tests that will help them to further understand how longer space flights will affect humans.

In particular, Jeanie Florence is fascinated by the ways that this kind of space travel might alter the men of Gemini.

"But," she says to Bill one afternoon as they walk at a fast clip down a long hallway, "what about the way it affects human organs? I have questions about that. I also think that cosmic radiation is a big issue that we're not worried about enough."

Bill has a sharpened pencil behind one ear, and a stopwatch on a cord tucked into the breast pocket of his short-sleeved dress shirt. He frowns down at Jeanie as they walk. "Sure," he says. "As well as the way long-term travel might change our spatial memory. I've heard that's a potential issue."

Jeanie is carrying a stack of thick technical books, and her heeled shoes click against the floor as she walks. She pushes her glasses up her nose and flings her long, straight hair over one shoulder as if it's merely in her way. "Bone loss is another issue. But you're right—spatial memory, visual motor performance, and what about the ramifications of living in cramped quarters? We could end up dealing with something as pedestrian as claustrophobia that leads to deep psychological distress. I think about all of it."

"We all do," Bill agrees, pointing at the long conference room on their right. "Looks like the meeting is in here."

Bill and Jeanie take seats together at the long table as other astronauts and engineers file in, some carrying clipboards, some notebooks. Everyone is ready to hear the speaker for the afternoon, a doctor who has flown in from San Antonio, where the United States Air Force School of Aerospace Medicine is located.

"Greetings," the man says, smoothing the remaining strands of hair over his rapidly-balding pate. "Thank you for having me here today. I'm Dr. Sullivan, and I'm here to discuss the field of space medicine with you. We have several topics to cover, and we will be together for approximately three days. I'd like to discuss what I think are some of our biggest issues, as well as some that you might not give much thought to. We've done tests on exposure to G-forces, emergency ejection injuries, and even what occurs in situations of low-oxygen and microgravity." Dr. Sullivan walks to the board along the wall and picks up a piece of chalk, where he scrawls his name and credentials.

"See?" Jeanie says, leaning in to Bill as she points at the board. "We need to think about *all* of these issues. Very important."

Bill nods and suppresses a smile; although he does take Jeanie seriously as a scientist—very seriously, as she's one of the brightest people he knows—he also still finds himself charmed by the things that come out of her mouth. Her brilliance only enhances her smooth, freckled face, wide eyes, and at the way she absentmindedly tugs on a strand of her long hair when she's thinking.

Dr. Sullivan spends the next two hours presenting data, test results, and running a Q&A session that is more than interesting enough to keep everyone awake until the coffee break at three-thirty. By the time Bill steps up to the giant silver urn and pours his coffee into a paper cup, Vance and Ed have made their way over.

"I'm ready for space," Vance says, dumping two packets of sugar into his coffee cup. "Earth is kind of getting to me."

"Yeah?" Bill cocks an eyebrow at him. "You're ready to get assigned to Gemini?"

"Hell yeah," Vance says as he elbows Ed. "I'd sell my soul to get word right now that I'm going to be on that mission. How about you, Maxwell?"

Ed nods in agreement, but he looks almost hesitant. Certainly they're all equally sure about their desire to venture into space on the Gemini 3, aren't they? The thought that some of them might be holding out for something else has never really occurred to Bill.

"I'm in," Ed finally says, nodding more firmly and with determination. "I came here for this."

There's a weird tension running through all of them lately that Bill can't quite put his finger on, but if he had to guess, he'd say that perhaps they're all under some kind of stress at home as well as at work. It's not outrageous to think that the other wives feel the same way that Jo does, which is supportive, but occasionally reticent to upend their own lives. And it's possible that they've got family problems from elsewhere: aging parents, siblings asking for money, kids who aren't behaving right. He isn't entirely sure what's going on in each of their homes, but there's a raggedness in each man's eyes that is clearly visible.

Sometimes Bill sees it and it makes him feel less alone. Surely no one else has an ex-wife in a mental facility where she's getting lithium mixed into her oatmeal, but people have stuff—everyone does. If there's one thing Bill has realized in his thirty-five years, it's that everybody's got their own dramas.

In spite of whatever Bill and his fellow astronauts have going on

THE LAUNCH

in their own lives, they put aside their personal troubles on the day that President Kennedy arrives at the cape. It's a Saturday, and everyone is ready for it. They've been prepped up, down, and sideways for his arrival, and every military man in attendance is dressed in uniform. The astronauts are standing at attention when Air Force One lands on the Cape Skid Strip. At the sight of the plane that carries President Kennedy around the world, a feeling of patriotism floods through Bill, and he salutes the Commander in Chief.

Kennedy takes the steps down from the plane, one hand in the air as he waves, the other holding the rail next to him. Everyone squints against the bright sun and the blue morning sky as they watch him descend onto the tarmac. The President is wearing a dark suit with a lighter blue tie, and his shoes are polished to a high shine. This is a day none of them will ever forget.

"Lucky bastards," Vance Majors says from his spot next to Bill as Kennedy shakes hands with the commander of the Air Force Missile Test Center and then with the NASA Launch Operations Director. "After I go to the moon, I'm landing a cushy job as an Operations Director." Vance is talking quietly once they're all at ease. "What about you, Booker? Got your eye on a fat government position someday?"

Bill's eyes are starry as he looks at Air Force One, a majestic aircraft with an impeccable safety record. At that moment, he'd like nothing more than to fly that plane—or any plane, for that matter. It's been a while since he's been in a cockpit, and he's starting to itch for the feeling of being far above the earth, looking down at the vast stretches of land and sea. He shrugs. "Dunno," Bill says. "I like to keep my eye on one goal at a time, accomplish it, and then set a new one."

Vance makes a face like he's impressed. "I hear you."

As the men stand in the sea of blue uniforms, Kennedy is led away with Florida Senator George Smathers. Everyone looks on as they're briefed out of earshot by astronauts Gordon Cooper and Gus Grissom on the current status of Project Gemini.

"I'd like to be a fly on the wall for this conversation," Bill says, lifting his chin in the direction of the President and the astronauts who are filling him in on Gemini. The knot of men stand there in the late autumn sun as the wind combs through their hair and flips their neckties around. "I bet they're going to see Saturn next."

Sure enough, a big, open-topped Jeep pulls up and the group climbs into it for the drive over to the launch pad, where Kennedy will get an up-close look at the Saturn shuttle. The gathered NASA employees and astronauts watch as the Jeep whips away, and then the group relaxes. People start to chatter, and there are hoots and hollers as everyone recounts how close they were standing to Kennedy.

"Wish I'd been chosen to take the helicopter ride to get an aerial view of the space launch area with JFK," Vance says wistfully. "I haven't been in a chopper since Korea."

"Right," Bill says, keeping his eyes on the horizon in the distance as he thinks of the helicopter that will take Kennedy out to watch Polaris launch from a submerged submarine. It will be the President's first time seeing a missile launch, and there's been much talk of this event, given that Kennedy is such a big supporter of NASA's space program.

Vance's mention of Korea is the one blemish on an otherwise exciting and historical day for Bill. He pushes down the feelings that come up any time he's reminded of being in combat. It always comes out of nowhere and hits him sideways, remembering the smells and sounds and the things he saw. And no matter what, there is a moment each time he thinks of Korea when he wonders whether he'll ever be able to close his eyes again and not see flashes of blood, of war-torn villages, of loss.

But instead of dwelling on the images in his mind, Bill waits along with the other men for the helicopter's return. He makes small talk with Ed and Todd, and they joke around, boasting about the planes they've flown, the feats they've accomplished in the air, and how close they are to being chosen for a space mission. It's a small window of time that they stand there in the shadow of Air Force One, shooting the breeze and riding the high that comes from seeing JFK in person, but it's the most relaxed and easy the men have been with one another in months. It feels good to put aside the stress they're under at NASA and just be a group of guys, laughing and talking under the endless blue sky of a Florida morning in the middle of November.

When he gets home that evening, Bill is whistling the last song that he heard on the radio in the car, which was Bob Dylan's "Blowin' in the Wind." He sets his hat down on the table by the door and accepts hugs from his daughters. His house is fragrant with the smell of a warm pot roast, and Jo has a jazz record playing in the front room.

It's only about a week and a half until Thanksgiving, and the holidays are everywhere, including in his kitchen, where Kate has placed a long chain made of paper rings. She's planning to tear off one ring each day between Thanksgiving and Christmas, marking the days until Santa comes. The paper chain blows in the breeze that comes in through the open sliding door, and Jo turns from where she stands at the stove. She smiles at him.

"Hi, honey," she says. "How was it?"

"Incredible." Bill unbuttons the top button of his uniform for the first time all day, and he runs a hand through his hair. "Seeing Kennedy at the White House, and then seeing him again today...it's indescribable, Jojo. It's monumental, you know?"

Jo stops what she's doing in the kitchen and looks at her husband. "Of course it is. You've worked hard to get here, and you've served your country well, Bill." Her eyes search his face and she reaches out to him, putting both hands on his waist and then sliding them around him as she hugs him close. "You deserve this," Jo adds softly, pressing her cheek to his chest.

On his drive home, Bill had been thinking about how remarkable his life is and has always been. He marveled at the very fact that he *gets* to work for NASA after a long and successful career in the Air

Force. This career he's chosen has afforded his family the chance to move to sunny Florida (fraught though it's been with homesickness and growing pains), and it also allowed him to take a trip to Washington D.C. with his son to meet the president. Does any man have as much as he has? Is it right for any one person to be as fortunate as Bill Booker is? It feels impossible.

Bill gives Jo a quick kiss on the cheek and lets her go so that she can finish putting dinner on the table. "It was a really good day."

"We have your parents coming in just over a week." Jo changes the subject as she puts dishes on the table. "Do you think they'll want to go to the beach or maybe take a drive and go south? We could take them to Miami."

Bill pours himself a glass of water and stands over the sink, drinking it slowly as he looks out at the pool. "Sure," he says mildly, "they might."

Bill's dad had stopped drinking more than a decade ago, and since then, he's been the affable, energetic father that Bill had always wanted him to be. Giving up alcohol had had the secondary effect of saving Arnold and Stella Booker's marriage, so naturally Bill is happy to have them come to visit for Thanksgiving.

"The kids will be thrilled to have them here," Jo says as she sets silverware on the table.

"I think this is going to be a really good holiday, Jojo."

Bill's parents will come down and see their new home, and he'll continue working with Desert Sage to make sure everything is good with Margaret. His kids will keep thriving, Jo will keep finding her way, and everything will be good. It has to be good. Life is *so good*.

* * *

On the Friday morning before Thanksgiving week, Bill's stomach is in knots. The sensation that something monumental is about to happen is palpable, though he isn't sure whether it has anything to do with him, his family, his job, or something else entirely. It's just an imbalance; a sense that Earth has tilted ever so slightly on its axis. Bill hasn't admitted to anyone that he woke up with an urgent need to run to the bathroom, and he's gone easy on food and coffee all morning in an effort to avoid a repeat performance of that morning's stomach catastrophe.

"You okay, bud?" Vance Majors claps Bill's shoulder heartily. The jolt actually makes Bill momentarily seasick. He recovers quickly.

"Right as rain," Bill says, glancing at his watch. Eleven o'clock. He's nearly made it to lunch without anything bad happening. Maybe he'd had a bad dream earlier in the week and not realized that it had wormed its way into his psyche. There has to be something— some kind of negative energy—that's tacked itself onto Bill, but for the life of him, he can't figure out what it might be.

At lunch, Bill stands at the counter of the cafeteria, eating his triangle of white bread and bologna with Miracle Whip. He's got a shiny red apple in the other hand, and Ed Maxwell is standing with him and Jeanie Florence. They're laughing about an off-color joke that Ed heard from a guy in a different department, and Bill is relieved that the punchline is still tame enough that Jeanie appears unbothered. You never know with a group of men whether things will quickly venture off into territory that isn't particularly welcoming for the fairer sex, and Bill takes a big bite of his sandwich, relieved and smiling as Jeanie laughs at the dumb joke.

At one-thirty, the astronauts sit down in a board room, ready to receive a briefing from Arvin North on Gemini 3. But as the clock ticks away the minutes, he doesn't show. North is never late, and Bill glances at his watch, noting that they've been waiting for over twenty minutes now.

Finally, Arvin North walks into the room, eyes downcast, face as serious as Bill has ever seen it. The casual conversation halts instantly, and the men sit at attention.

They are former military men, all of them, and they can discern without warning when something has shifted in the atmosphere around them. Their senses have been honed to sense, assess, and avert danger. When a superior appears to be rattled, that information immediately gets fed into the machine, and everything goes into high alert mode as they try to figure out what moves need to be made.

Arvin North clears his throat as he stands before them. He is still looking at the ground with his hands on his hips.

"Gentlemen," he says, as the room is entirely populated by men for this afternoon meeting. "I regret to inform you that at approximately twelve-thirty Central Standard Time, our Commander in Chief was gunned down in Dallas. John F. Kennedy is dead."

Silence. Stunned silence.

"The President was riding in a motor cavalcade with the First Lady when gunfire rang out, and he was struck in the head. The country is in shock, and will undoubtedly remain so for some time to come." North stops speaking and clears his throat, holding his fist in front of his mouth and taking a moment to compose himself. "There's a lot we don't know right now, but what I do know is that we need to be with our families. Please go home now, and hold your wives and children tight."

Arvin North turns and walks out of the room, leaving a table full of men in shock in his wake. No one speaks for what feels like ten minutes, and then finally, Bill stands.

"North has instructed us to go home," he says in the firmest voice he can conjure, though nothing about this moment feels firm to him at all. Rather, he feels as though his voice, his heart, his very being, is suspended in Jello and that the world won't stop shaking. "Let's go."

Port Canaveral is as eerily silent as it must be in the middle of the night when everyone has gone home. Bill walks through the halls, barely making eye contact with people as he passes. They are all walking ghosts, their shock so tangible that it almost hurts. Little do they know, but the rest of the country is stumbling around in the same nearly catatonic state, eyes glazed as they watch and listen to the news, trying to understand what evil force has infiltrated their lives, changing everything forever.

When he pulls into his driveway, Bill turns off the engine and sits there, staring at the sun reflecting off the windows of the house. Jo and the kids must be inside. Perhaps no one has called her yet to tell her the news. Maybe the children are unaware that a gunman has taken the life of their president, inadvertently snatching away a sense of innocence that the country will never get back. Bill hopes they're in the pool, or perhaps playing cards under the palm tree in the grass in the backyard. He hopes Nancy is sprawled out on the ground, holding her book in the air as she flips the pages. He prays that Jimmy is thinking about the Yankees and not about an unseen gunman with his crosshairs trained on the President. Bill wants to walk in and see Kate dressing her Barbies as she chatters to herself in high-pitched doll voices, unaware that the world has changed in an instant.

Bill grips his steering wheel and closes his eyes. He can picture Jackie Kennedy in the hallway of the White House, smiling at him and thanking him for serving their country. He remembers standing behind Jimmy at the desk in the Oval Office, with JFK standing behind his son on the other side. It feels surreal that their president had been alive and well—a breathing, walking, joking man full of hope and ideas—and now he's gone. And for what reason? To what end?

Bill wants to turn back the hands of time and save the president who has promised the United States that they'd put a man on the moon before the decade is out. A president with a vision for the future of their planet, and a vision of how they'll explore space.

Lieutenant Colonel William Booker gets out of his car and stands in the driveway, facing his house.

His family is in there.

A cloud passes over the sun, and the glare on the front window of his house disappears, revealing Jo's stony face and unseeing eyes. She's standing in the front room, arms folded across her chest, staring back at him in a way that makes Bill feel as though she can't see him, though he knows in his heart that she can.

Bill and Jo hold steady for one more moment this way, looking at one another from opposite sides of the glass. It's almost like they're holding onto this one brief slice of silence before they exchange words about what's happened—before they say it out loud and make it real.

The moment passes and Jo bolts from her spot in the window. She throws the front door open and runs to him, a sob escaping her as Bill folds his collapsing wife into his arms. He covers her, wrapping his body around hers, as if he's protecting her from radioactive fallout.

But it's too late—the damage has been done. History has been made, the future changed. All Bill can do now is hold her while she cries.

And if Bill can't turn back time and undo this tragedy, then he wants to *be* one of the men who sets foot on the moon before 1970. He wants to honor their fallen president's wishes.

If he can't do anything else, he can at least do that.

As he rocks his wife back and forth in his arms, he knows that he can at *least* do that.

stardust beach book two...

Frankie Maxwell is a woman with a past...and that past is haunting her present and upsetting her marriage. Can her new best friend Jo help her to untangle her messy past so that she and her husband Ed have a future? Come back to Stardust Beach for more friendship, drama, and romance. Supernova is available here.

also by stephanie taylor

Stephanie also writes a long-running romantic comedy series set on a fictional key off the coast of Florida. Christmas Key is a magical place that's decorated for the holidays all year round, and you'll instantly fall in love with the island and its locals.

To see a complete list of the Christmas Key series along with all of Stephanie's other books, please visit:

Stephanie Taylor's Books

To hear about any new releases, sign up here and you'll be the first to know!

about the author

Stephanie Taylor is a high-school teacher who loves sushi, "The Golden Girls," Depeche Mode, orchids, and coffee. She is the author of the Christmas Key books, a romantic comedy series about a fictional island off the coast of Florida, as well as The Holiday Adventure Club series, and the Shipwreck Key series.

https://redbirdsandrabbits.com
redbirdsandrabbits@gmail.com

Printed in Great Britain
by Amazon